T0157027

The Messenger Trilogy

Don't Kill the Messenger
The Messenger Adrift
Messenger in a Battle

INSTANT MESSENGER

a prequel to The Messenger Trilogy

Joel Pierson

iUniverse, Inc.
Bloomington

Instant Messenger
a prequel to The Messenger Trilogy

iUniverse books may be ordered through booksellers or by contacting:

iUniverse
1663 Liberty Drive
Bloomington, IN 47403
www.iuniverse.com
1-800-Authors (1-800-288-4677)

ISBN: 978-1-4620-3749-0 (sc)
ISBN: 978-1-4620-3750-6 (e)

Printed in the United States of America

iUniverse rev. date: 7/18/2011

Acknowledgments

Thanks to Dana, for helping me create this new endeavor. Sitting with you in the hotel lobby in Galesburg will always be a high point for me. Thank you, Melissa, for being an early reader and being so excited about a new adventure for Tristan. And my sincere gratitude to Juliet, for her unflinching honesty in giving me notes as I went along—all the while enjoying the ride, too.

Hear, O Israel, for unto you this day comes a messenger.

—Found in a cave outside of Jerusalem, 1763
Author unknown

Chapter 1

Esteban Padgett is going to die on Thursday.

Powerful stomach cramps. A wave of nausea, from out of nowhere.

This Thursday, at 6:28 p.m., his wife, Annalisa, will kill him with the handgun they keep in the house for protection.

The stomach cramps travel up my chest, gripping my lungs with a pain like nothing I've ever experienced before. And still the strange thoughts continue.

She's having an affair, and she needs him out of the picture. When he comes home from work, she's going to kill him.

I struggle to breathe. This must be what an asthma attack feels like, though in all my thirty-four years, I've never had the slightest sign of asthma. I put my hand to my chest and will myself to breathe in and out.

Annalisa will try to make it look like Esteban surprised a burglar, but she will pull the trigger. She will kill him—unless you stop her.

In an instant, the pain and tightness are gone. I realize that I have clenched my eyes tightly shut, and I open them slowly, silently marveling at how intense the pain was and how swiftly it has passed.

"What the shit was *that?*" I say aloud, to no one in particular. Of course, I am alone, in my own bathroom, in my own home, but the sensations I have just experienced are so disorienting that it actually takes several seconds to remind myself where I am, and more disturbingly, *who* I am.

"You're Tristan Shays, and you're safe in your home." I say the words aloud, as if needing the sound of my own voice to reassure me. "You must've had a nightmare and sleepwalked into the bathroom. But it's over, and you're

1

awake now, and the pain is gone, and Esteban is fine and is going to be fine."

I allow myself to absorb the reality of this explanation, but in the back of my mind is a single troubling detail: I wasn't asleep. The alarm had gone off at 6:45, as it does every day, and I had gotten out of bed, used the toilet, and even brushed my teeth before the strange thoughts and the unbearable pain came over me. All of which leads to my original question—what the shit was *that?*

Absent an answer, I am left with two choices: believe the strange information or don't. It makes more sense not to believe it, as I've been friends with both parties for several years and never had any reason to suspect that there was even disharmony between them. Besides, it's a big day; there's a shareholders meeting this morning, and I've got to focus on what I'm going to say to them. I'll see Esteban afterward, and I can ask him then if everything's all right.

So I shake off the odd physical and mental feelings and proceed to get ready, the way I do on any workday. I'll dress a little nicer today, out of respect for the meeting, but I'm certainly not going to let this fluster me. There's probably a very reasonable explanation.

At 10:00 a.m., Esteban Padgett stands at a podium in front of a crowd of more than three hundred people, gathered in an auditorium in the company's headquarters. I'm seated on stage behind him in a row of chairs, waiting to be introduced. Esteban tells the crowd, "In 1961, when Shays Diode Corporation was founded, Leland Shays had a vision of a new kind of illumination device: the light-emitting diode. Through this simple yet groundbreaking innovation in semiconductors, he built a brighter world for us all, literally and figuratively. In the beginning, there weren't many prospective uses for the new technology. Primarily, the LED was used as a power indicator in electronic devices. The little red light would tell you if the device was on or off.

"Leland continued to explore and expand on the LED's potential, first with different colors, then with brightnesses, sizes, and delivery methods. Last month, Shays Diode manufactured 400 million LED lights." This earns applause. Shareholders love big numbers, especially ones that help line their pockets. Of course, I can't complain too much. Thanks to my late father's money sense, anytime an LED is manufactured by anyone, anywhere in the world, I get a fraction of a cent. I'd be applauding too, a little, if it weren't gauche.

Esteban continues, "When Leland died four years ago, many people thought it was the end of an era. Our founder, the inventor of the light-emitting diode, had passed on. Surely that meant the sun would finally set on this venerable corporation. But those people didn't count on Leland Shays' *other* greatest creation." Again the audience applauds. *Other greatest creation? Man, that's hokey. I have to start approving these speeches before events like this.* "His son, Tristan, my boss and my good friend, stepped up to take the reins of Shays Diode, knowing that in this world of burgeoning technology, LED applications were destined to skyrocket. He was right, and through his management, we remain the industry leader in illumination science today. Here to present his report to the shareholders, I'm proud to introduce the president and CEO of Shays Diode Corporation, Mr. Tristan Shays."

I step up to the microphone as the crowd applauds and rises. Esteban turns to shake my hand, and—covered by the crowd's adulation—I quietly say in his ear, "These introductions get cornier every year."

"That's the goal," he replies quietly. "Go greet your public."

I turn to the crowd as the applause starts to taper. "Esteban Padgett, senior vice president," I tell them. "Brightest bulb in the place." I get a hearty laugh and some more applause for that one. *Ha, now who's corny?*

"Ladies and gentlemen, thank you for joining us for our annual shareholder meeting. In the past twenty-four hours, we've shown you some of the many ways that this corporation is advancing the lighting and semiconductor industry. Today, I want to tell you just a bit more about how we're using this technology in new, and I think pretty fascinating ways."

The speech goes on for a while. It's business-speak, a language for which I'm gently ashamed of my fluency; occupational hazard. But it gets them excited about the future, an excitement I share. Clever sayings about "lighting the way" aside, the company really has made giant strides in the past ten years with what LEDs can do, and I feel partially responsible for that success. I think Dad would be proud.

Needing some time away from the crowd, I invite Esteban to join me for lunch at a Thai restaurant a mile or so from headquarters. Salisbury, Maryland, is a very pleasant place to work. It's large enough to support a corporation of our size but small enough that it doesn't feel oppressive, the way big cities so often do. Plus, it's only about a forty-minute drive from my home in Ocean City, which to me is the most beautiful place on Earth.

We sit at the table with a plate of basil rolls in between us; magnificent things, crisp and chilled, full of far more flavor than their diminutive size should hold. He has a glass of water, and I'm nursing a Thai iced tea, a personal favorite of mine. There's a conversation pending, and I have to be the one to begin it, but I just don't have a good entry point. *So, Esteban, has the wife talked about shooting you lately?*

"How are things?" I hear myself say these words and realize that I didn't authorize the start of this dialogue.

"Fine," he says. "Busy, of course, but that's nothing new. How about you?"

"Oh, good. Woke up with some pain this morning. That was unexpected."

"Could be your mattress. When my last one wore out, I started waking up with back pain. Annalisa did too."

"Ah, Annalisa," I reply, not quite sure why I chose those words and that inflection. After all, it's not like he said *bowling ball* or *triceratops*. "How, uh ... how's she been?"

"Well enough."

"Good."

"At least I think so," he adds. "Truth is, I haven't seen much of her lately. She's been working a lot of extra hours these past few months."

All of a sudden, I feel cold. *"Extra hours?"*

"Yeah, putting in a lot of overtime." His response makes me realize, to my dismay, that I have said those two words, rather than merely thinking them.

"I don't want to pry, but if you guys are having money issues, I could do a salary review and adjustment for you."

"Thanks, but that's not it. We're doing fine. Plenty of bills, sure, but we're not hurting. It's not about the money. Her employer is just leaning on people in her department to increase productivity, and unfortunately, part of the deal is some extra hours for Annalisa for a while."

I pause briefly to take this in, as the waitress brings our entrees, *tom kha gai* soup for him and duck in red curry sauce for me. I don't want to press matters, but the discussion feels incomplete. "But you two are doing all right when you're together?"

He looks up at me, with a little smile on his face that seems to hide some confusion. "We're fine. Why the sudden interest? Do you know something I don't know?"

I offer a small laugh to dismiss the idea. "No, no. Course not. It's just—you're my friend. My *friends,* both of you. You know me. If my friends are happy, then I'm happy."

There, everything's fine, and I'm being paranoid and crazy, and nothing is wrong. I'm going to eat my curry and enjoy my time with my friend, and not think about messages of death and destruction.

Sleep doesn't come easily on Monday night, as far too many thoughts race through my mind. I feel like I have let Esteban down somehow, like I should have come out and told him the truth, no matter how strange and implausible it sounded. But I did my best to determine if there were any warning signs, any red flags that would suggest that his life could be in danger. I mean, people don't just go from happily married to shooting their spouse. *Do they?*

The news of Annalisa's recent overtime did strike me as suspicious, but it obviously didn't for Esteban—at least not that he let on. And then, of course, there's the very real possibility that the whole thing is a product of my imagination, in which case, all this worry is for nothing.

For the sake of my own peace of mind, I allow myself to accept that explanation as I finally close my eyes at 2:23 in the morning. Whatever happens, it won't be helped by my being exhausted.

The pain in my head awakens me. It is beyond agony. I sit up, clutching my head with both hands. A low scream escapes my lips, making the pain that much worse.

Two days left. Esteban dies on Thursday. You must stop this. You are the only chance he has.

From a seated position, I shift to hands and knees as a wave of dizziness washes over me. Even this position is not sustainable, and I fall over on my side, legs and arms tucked in, in a strange mockery of a fetal position. How can this be real? How can this be happening?

Tell him what you know. Let the decision to believe rest with him. You cannot stand in the light of knowledge and not speak. Tell him!

Mercifully, the pain recedes quickly. This was a warning, a reminder; like Hamlet's father coming his tardy son to chide. But this is no ghost in armor standing and speaking. Whoever or whatever is acting through me has access to every nerve in my body and can fill me with unparalleled suffering.

I look at the clock. It is a few minutes after 5:00 in the morning. In less than two hours, I have to get up and go to work. I could try to lie down and get a little more sleep, but I'm too distracted and more than a little afraid that the pain will return. So I get up and put on a pair of jogging shorts and a T-shirt. I call them jogging shorts, though I never actually jog. I will run if chased or if I happen to see the ice-cream truck a block or less away. My exercise comes in the form of swimming, racquetball, and the occasional foray on the treadmill, if I feel particularly motivated.

Now dressed, I open the french doors that lead from my bedroom to the wraparound balcony that encircles the entire second floor. The early morning air feels good, but I need to be closer to the ocean—my ocean.

I leave the house and walk down the wooden ramp through my backyard to the four hundred feet of private beach that came with my property. This is my haven, my sanctuary, the place where I can restore my soul's peace, and mercifully, it is right outside my back door. Daylight has not yet begun to peek over the horizon as I step onto the cool sand in my bare feet. Overhead, the stars still radiate faintly, as a half moon illuminates a stretch of ocean water. The silence is blissful. Apart from the occasional wavelet brushing the shore, there is almost no sound. As I look up, I realize that this would be a good time to ask God for answers. If only I were religious. I'm not an atheist—though I know several, and I respect their ideas and ideals. I do believe in God, but I also believe that he's not listening. Everybody talks about "God the Father." Okay, maybe he is our father, and in the days of the Bible, the human race was young, childlike. So it made perfect sense for our father to be very present, very involved. Warning, cursing, smiting. He grounded us on many occasions. Well, we were young, and we needed that tough love. But we've grown up in those past six thousand years, and like all fathers, God knew we couldn't stay with him forever. We had to move out of the house, figure things out for ourselves. He still calls us from time to time, sends us his love on our birthday. Slips us a miracle every now and then, when we're running short.

But in my mind, God the doting capital-F Father of the Old Testament is no more. He's sitting by the phone, waiting for his children to call, but they're too busy updating their MySpace pages.

So if it's not God sending me agony-laced messages about my friend in imminent peril, then who's pulling the switch? I don't *feel* insane, which is good, I guess. I almost wish I were. It beats the alternative—that the message is real and Esteban Padgett's life will end in two days if I don't save him.

The fundamental problem, as I see it, is that this sort of message is traditionally delivered to a hero, and I'm *really* not heroic. Sure, I'll donate money to various charities and worthy causes, but I've got more money than I'll ever need, and I'm not addicted to drugs or fancy cars or high-end electronics. The house was my only indulgence, and I paid cash for it three years ago. So, yeah—heroics? Not really the type. Rushing into burning theaters, saving cats from trees, getting people to safety before a building collapses—that's not really me.

I walk down to the water's edge, feeling the cool, compressed wet sand with every step. It's not really me, but maybe it has to be me. Maybe I was chosen by someone, for some unknown reason, because I'm the only one who can convince Esteban that his life is in danger. Granted, it's not an easy thing to tell someone: your wife is going to kill you. But I think if I had a wife and she wanted to kill me, I'd like a little advance warning, so we could have an awkward but much-needed conversation.

Then there's the very practical consideration that *not* telling him seems to be linked to the continuation of the worst pain I've ever felt in my life. Heroics and nobility aside, it fucking hurts, and I never want to go through that again. But before I go and make a decision I might regret, I need to rule out the reasonable explanations first.

"Tristan, you're the healthiest man I've ever met." These words come three hours later from Doctor Norton Mitchell, my personal physician for the past eleven years.

I sit up from the exam table where I've been reclining. "Are you sure there's nothing on the MRI?"

"Nothing. And nothing on the head X-ray either. Your temperature's fine, your blood pressure's fine, you have the heart of a teenager. Apart from this unexplained pain of the past two nights, you don't have a single complaint. I'll give you a prescription for a narcotic, and a second one for a single dose of a drug called M Contin—it's morphine, so I only want you to take it if the pain is absolutely unbearable. You promise?"

"Yes, I promise. Thank you."

I deliberately avoid telling Dr. Mitchell about the message I'm supposed to deliver. I don't like withholding things from my physician, but I don't want him prescribing a psych consult. Not yet, anyway. If this whole thing persists, I might end up getting one on my own. I thank him for his time and effort, pick up my prescriptions from the clinic's pharmacy, and head to the office, very aware of the hours of work I've lost this morning.

Absent a medical explanation for what's bedeviling me, everything reasonable is now telling me that the right thing to do is to tell Esteban what I've experienced and let him decide for himself. It has to be today. But where? Not at work; that'd be uncomfortable. Not in public; we'd need to be able to discuss this privately. Certainly not at his house; I couldn't risk Annalisa walking in during the conversation. It will have to be at my house. Dinner, tonight. No special reason; I just felt like it. Then, when he gets there, I can tell him what I know, and we can talk about it.

With the shareholders gone from headquarters, it's a less eventful day than the past two. Of course, their presence has put me behind schedule, not to mention my adventures in Western medicine this morning, so I have some catching up to do. Very much on my mind is the need to invite Esteban over tonight, but as fate would have it, he's in meetings all morning, and I don't see him. Finally, around 3:00 in the afternoon, I'm able to pull him aside in the eighth-floor hallway.

"Esteban, can I see you for a second?"

"Just for a second," he replies. "I'm late for a meeting. What's up?"

"I ... was wondering if you were free for dinner tonight."

He looks surprised at the invitation. "I, uh, I guess so. Gee, lunch yesterday and dinner tonight? People will start to talk."

"Ah, let 'em," I reply. "How about 7:00?"

"That'll work. Annalisa's working overtime again tonight anyway." *Yeah, I bet she is.* "Where would you like to meet?"

"Actually, I was thinking you could come over to the house."

"To the house? To *your* house?" he asks.

"It's where I keep my kitchen, yes."

"So the CEO is going to invite me to his home and cook for me. Oh God, I'm fired, aren't I?"

"What?" I reply in complete surprise.

"I'm fired, and this is how you're breaking it to me gently."

"You're not fired. Now stop being paranoid," I tell the man whose wife is planning to kill him, "and accept my invitation."

"Okay, okay," he says, "you win. I accept. I'll see you at seven."

I am not a chef; let's get that detail out of the way early, so there's no confusion later. I am not in the TV dinner and canned soup crowd either, I should point out. Living alone for as long as I have, I've cultivated a certain skill level in the kitchenly arts, to the point where I can create a couple dozen easy dishes that taste good enough for me but won't win me any awards. I decide that spaghetti is a good choice for dinner tonight—something reasonably dignified but easy enough to make in a limited amount of time.

I cheat on the sauce and use something out of a jar, adding some exotic mushrooms and imported sausage to it, to make it distinctive. The good part about cooking is that it occupies just enough of my brain to allow me to figure out what I'm going to say to Esteban tonight without letting me dwell on the difficulty of saying it. *When* is important, too. Not before dinner, and probably not during dinner either. It's more of a dessert conversation, and I've picked up a blackberry pie. I'm hoping it's difficult to be angry while eating blackberry pie.

Esteban rings the doorbell at the stroke of 7:00. Punctuality and reliability are two of his best traits. I welcome him in, and—as he always does when he visits—he marvels at how beautiful the house is.

"You have a lovely home too," I remind him.

"Yes, but not like this. I want to have oceanfront property one day. I love the water."

"Can I get you a drink?" I ask.

"Not just yet," he says, taking a seat at the island in the kitchen. He looks a little nervous, and I guess that's my fault. Even after our years of friendship, the CEO/VP gap still exists between us. He's eight years my senior, so I imagine it must be challenging for him, reporting to a younger man who inherited the business. But he never shows me anything but the deepest respect and friendship, and that means a lot to me.

"Something smells good," he chimes in. "What are we having?"

"Caesar salad, spaghetti with sausage and wild mushrooms, garlic bread, and blackberry pie with french vanilla ice cream at the end."

"Sounds great. Thank you for having me over."

"Well, we're always working, and I don't get to see you socially much anymore. I just wanted you to know you're appreciated."

"Thank you. It's good to know. It's been a challenging year at work. You've been great to work with. It's just, with the economy the way it is, I feel like we have to work twice as hard to get half as much. But I've been keeping on top of my departments, making sure—"

"Esteban," I interrupt, "it's fine. Really. I appreciate everything you're doing, but I didn't bring you over here to talk about work. I'll get the salads out, and I'll open up a bottle of bonarda."

"Bonarda?" he says. "From Argentina, like my mother. It's one of my favorites."

I open the wine and let it breathe while I put the salad into wooden serving bowls. The wine goes into crystal glasses, and I hand one to my associate.

"What should we drink to?" he asks.

"To friends who should spend more time together as friends, not just as colleagues."

"I'll drink to that." Glasses clink delicately, and he tastes. "Fantastic. I haven't had this in years."

"Enjoy it."

The wine flows freely as we start with our salads and then move on to the spaghetti. Esteban loosens up as we talk about favorite pastimes—sailing, photography, the occasional Orioles game at Camden Yards. I have to admit that it feels good to be talking openly and honestly this way. Yes, it's a pretext to get to a much more serious subject, but his presence makes me remember that too much of my life is spent in isolation. I'm the boss, and the boss (it says somewhere) shouldn't be friends with the employees. Outside of work, I don't have much of a social circle either, since most people get on my nerves. My money frees me from the financial worries that most Americans face, but at the same time, it exiles me from that same society of Americans. I'm the rich loner in the big house on the beach, and if I allow myself to think about it too much, it kind of sucks.

As I clear away the dinner dishes, I chirp, "Hope you saved room for dessert."

"Ay, Tristan, you're trying to fatten me up."

"Just a little. Come on … blackberry pie and french vanilla ice cream. You know you want it."

He thinks a moment. "Can you warm the pie up in the microwave?"

"Can I warm the pie up? Of course! This is the world of tomorrow, filled with light-emitting diodes, warm pie, and cold, delicious ice cream."

"Okay, okay, you've convinced me," he answers with a laugh.

As I'm warming two slices of pie, I know very well that I have run out of small talk. It's time. Shit or git, as Dad used to say. I bring the pie a la mode to the table and sit down with him. "It's good to see you," I tell him.

"Good to see you too, my friend."

"I'm sorry things at home have been rough for you." The first toe enters the proverbial waters.

"Oh, it's not so bad. I mean, yeah, she's working more than I'd like. And maybe when she's home, she's a little …"

He hesitates. I prompt. "A little …?"

"Distant, I guess. But it's understandable. I mean, we're in our forties now. The relationship doesn't have to be all about sex. There are other things that are just as important. I just … I feel like I haven't been there for her, the way I should be, and I don't know what to do about it."

It's enough of an opening that I can say what needs to be said. "Esteban, I did bring you over here tonight for a reason. I'm sorry I couldn't say anything to you at work, but it had to be in private. It's not easy for me to say, but it's important that I tell you. It's about Annalisa."

"Tristan, wait. I think I know what you're going to say."

"You do?"

"Yes, and you don't have to say it. I think I know you pretty well after all these years, and the message is clear."

"It is?"

"The nice private dinner, the wine; pie and ice cream. Your questions about trouble with my marriage. Tristan, you're a very good man and a dear friend, but … there can never be anything romantic between us."

"What?"

"I didn't know for sure that you were gay, but I've suspected. Please don't feel embarrassed."

"Esteban …"

"I'm flattered, really I am. And if *I* were gay, I think you'd be an amazing catch."

"*Esteban …*"

"But I think it's best if we just stay friends. I promise I won't say anything about this to anyone."

"Esteban, I'm not gay."

A moment of indescribably awkward silence passes between us.

"You're not?"

"No."

"So ... you didn't bring me over here to tell me you're in love with me?"

"No."

"I'm fired, aren't I?"

"You're not fired, so stop asking. I really do have something important to talk to you about, and like I said, it concerns Annalisa. Are you in a frame of mind to hear it?"

"I ... yeah, I suppose so."

"You haven't had too much wine?" I ask.

"No, I'm all right. I'm a little embarrassed over what I just—you know. But otherwise okay."

"Shake it off, because this is important. Maybe the most important thing I'll ever tell you."

"Okay, now I'm a little anxious. What's going on? What do you have to tell me that's this important?"

"Esteban ... I have reason to believe that you might be in danger."

"Danger? What kind of danger?"

"I think Annalisa may want to kill you. I'm sorry."

He looks at me intently for a moment with a strange expression on his face, a half-smile, as if he's waiting for the punch line. When none comes, the half-smile falls. "What ... why would you think that?"

I have to tell him. "This is going to be very difficult to believe, but for the past two nights, I've been stricken with terrible pain, like nothing I've ever felt before. Both times, with that pain came a message, a very clear, distinct message that told me that your life is in danger. It said that Annalisa is planning to kill you on Thursday night when you come home from work."

"That's crazy. She loves me, and I love her. Why would she want to kill me?"

I sigh audibly. *In for a penny ...* "Again, this is just what the message said. Apparently, she's having an affair ..." He reacts with a shrug, throwing his hands up, but does not interrupt. "And she wants you out of the way. Do you keep a handgun in the house?"

After a moment, he replies, "Yes, but neither one of us has touched it for years. It sits in a closet. I don't even think she knows how to use it."

"The message I received says that's what she's going to use to kill you. She's going to make it look like you interrupted a robbery. I'm sorry to tell you this, and I hope like hell I'm wrong, but I couldn't let another day go by without telling you. Not if there's even the slightest chance that I'm right."

His answer betrays resentment in his voice. "Well, there isn't. Jesus,

Tristan. I'm starting to wish you *did* bring me over here to tell me you loved me. *That* I could at least deal with. But this? Where do I start to tell you how many kinds of wrong this is?"

"Please know that it was my sincere friendship for you that motivated me to tell you this. I really hope this doesn't compromise that friendship."

Now it's his turn to sigh. "It doesn't. But I really think you should talk to someone about this. Maybe see a doctor. That level of pain, coupled with unexplainable thoughts in your head? I mean, maybe something's medically wrong. Maybe I'm here to warn *you*."

"Maybe so," I reply quietly. "And I did see a doctor. He couldn't find anything medically wrong with me."

"Well, that's good news, I guess." He rises from his seat. "I should probably get home. Thank you for dinner."

As he makes his way toward the door, I follow behind. "I'm ... I'm sorry. I really didn't mean to upset you with this."

Rather than replying, he simply says, "I'll see you at work tomorrow. Good night, Tristan."

"Good night."

Well, I've made a complete balls of that. He's too polite to say so, but I could see the anger and resentment beneath the surface when I made that outrageous claim. But what did I expect? Did I really think he was going to look at me and say, "You know, come to think of it, she *has* been shooting things in my direction lately"? No, he's going to say what any reasonable man would say: "My wife loves me, and she doesn't want to kill me."

Fine. It's done, I've told him, and I never need to think about it again. The celestial voices can officially go fuck themselves. Now that I've delivered the message I'm supposed to deliver, that should be the end of it.

Chapter 2

THE NIGHT IS PEACEFUL, free of pain and free of messages. When I awaken at 6:30 Wednesday morning, I am pleased to discover that I've slept through the whole night. This could mean one of two things: either the whole thing was a product of my imagination and now I'm over it, or I was legitimately supposed to tell Esteban what I told him. In either case, it's over, and I can get back to the business of living my own life.

Just before 10:00, I'm in my office, going over some figures—which seems to occupy an inordinate amount of my professional life. That and meetings. I would like to find the person who invented meetings and commit grievous bodily harm upon him. Meetings, to me, are an alternative to actually doing things. I try to tell my employees that they don't have to include me in every meeting; I only need to be there for executive-level business. But they constantly include me anyway—probably concerned about not telling me things.

So at 10:00, in between one meeting and another, and in the midst of the endless act of going over figures, I hear a knock at my office door. "Come in," I offer.

Esteban pokes his head in. "Is this a bad time?"

I give an awkward half-smile. "Of course not. Please, come in."

He enters and closes the door behind him. This is unusual, except in cases where he's discussing personnel issues. But the door is closed, and he approaches my desk. "It's about last night," he says, to no surprise.

"I'm sorry about that. Chalk it up to bad judgment on my part. I wouldn't give it another thought."

"I've done some digging," he says. Exactly what I was afraid he'd say.

"When you told me what you told me, I thought, no way. Not possible. Then I started thinking about the past several weeks, and about things that didn't add up, but I just disregarded it at the time. But then, you made me think maybe I shouldn't disregard it. Maybe something is happening."

"What did you do?"

"Her timecard from work is online, and I know her logon. So I checked her hours for the past month. She's worked a few extra hours, but nowhere near the number she says she worked. I looked at her personal e-mail account, but I didn't find anything suspicious in there, either sent or received. I'm thinking she might have a different account that I don't know about. I checked her cell phone for calls or texts to numbers I didn't recognize, but I didn't see anything there either. But I found a cell phone bill that doesn't match her number, so I think she has two phones, two numbers."

"Esteban, I'm so sorry. I wish it wasn't the case, but that sounds like pretty damning evidence."

"Yeah," he replies, "it does. And not just for her. Tristan, tell me again how you know this about Annalisa."

"I wish I could explain it. Like I said, a few nights ago, I got this message in my head, a warning to give to you. It was accompanied by terrible pain, worse than anything I'd ever experienced. It wouldn't go away until I gave you this message. Last night, after I did tell you, the pain was gone, and there was no more message to deliver. Things are back to normal again. And based on what you're telling me, it sounds like the message could very well be right."

"Yeah, I'm starting to believe that it is. The only part that's hard to believe is your story about how you know all this."

"I understand. I can't really explain it myself. It's possible that there are forces at work in the world that defy what we can understand and explain."

"Or maybe there's a simpler explanation. Maybe you know all of this because the person Annalisa is seeing in secret is you."

Stunned silence falls over me. In all the scenarios I played out in my head regarding the sharing of this information with Esteban, I never expected this possibility. "Me? Esteban, think about what you're saying."

"It makes sense to me. She's been seeing you, and then she took it too far. She talked about wanting to kill me, and you couldn't let her do it."

"Esteban, please. If this were some kind of mystery movie, then yes, it would be a plot twist. But I don't even like Annalisa."

"What?!"

"I mean, I like her, but I don't *like her*. I'm certainly not involved with her romantically. I don't know who she's seeing; I wasn't privy to that information. But everything that's happened so far is telling me that your life may really be in danger tomorrow. You've got to get the gun out of the house."

He pauses a moment, and a troubled look visits his face. "I looked for it last night ... and it wasn't where we usually keep it."

"What? It's gone?"

"Gone. Or moved."

"Esteban, please. After all you've seen and heard, you have to at least entertain the possibility that Annalisa could be dangerous."

"I know," he answers quietly.

"If you want to go to the police, I'll go with you."

"No, not until I have proof."

"By the time you get that proof, it could be too late. Come and stay at my place until you know you're safe."

"I have to be there at the time and place when you said this was going to happen. I have to know."

"And what will you do if she kills you?"

He gives a humorless laugh. "Not much, I suspect."

"You still have a full day before this is supposed to happen. Couldn't you talk to her tonight? Don't even accuse her of anything. Just ... ask her about the overtime or the cell phone. Tell her you're ready to do anything it takes to make the marriage work. This doesn't have to end badly."

"Doesn't it? You saw the future. You know what she's going to do."

"I know what she's *planning* to do. But I have to believe that I received that warning because it's not supposed to happen. That's why I was sent to warn you. Maybe God or ... somebody believes that you're supposed to live."

He stands there for many long seconds, alternately looking at me and looking out the office windows. I see what I think is acceptance on his face. We've been friends long enough that I sincerely hope he trusts me. But he spent last night believing that I was his wife's secret lover, and that's gotta mess with a man's head.

When at last he speaks, his voice is small, defeated. "Why would she want to kill me, Tristan? I've never raised a hand to her, never hurt her in any way. I mean, there's counseling, separation, divorce. If she was unhappy, we could have explored any of those possibilities. Why murder?"

"I just don't know. That's the one detail the message didn't give me." A thought occurs to me. "What if it isn't her idea? If there is another man, this might be his doing."

"Then why have Annalisa do it? Why not do it himself?"

"I don't know. I'm trying to work that part out. Are you willing to believe in me enough to fight for your life?"

"Yes. This isn't my time. I don't know what's got into Annalisa's head, but I'm not going to sit still and let this happen. May I please have some time off?"

"Of course. Be careful, though, please."

"I will."

For the rest of the day, I do not see Esteban, but he is very much in my thoughts. I'm certainly relieved that he listened to what I told him, but there also remains the very real possibility that, despite all the accuracy of my message, Esteban's life really isn't in danger, or worse, that by telling him this, I've actively put him in danger. But I won't interfere. I've done enough.

I try to tell myself this as the workday ends and I make my way home. I check my cell phone, my e-mail, even my mailbox at the house, for any communication from Esteban, but there is nothing. One day before my vision is supposed to come true, and I haven't heard a word from him. After 9:00 p.m. passes without a word, I pick up the phone and I begin to dial his number, but then I stop.

No, no, not like this. Anything I touch, I could make it worse. If I'm supposed to be a part of this, I would know about it.

Still the hours pass in silence. I watch the local news and CNN, hoping to see—or more precisely, hoping *not* to see—anything about Esteban. Not a word there either. For the fiftieth time today, I contemplate calling the police. Let the professionals handle it. But even this I can't do. Instead, I let the hours pass, slowly, quietly, agonizingly, as I wander the rooms of my home, handcuffed by my own hesitance.

Despite the knowledge that sleep is a futile effort, I go through the motions of getting ready for bed. My bedroom is dark and exactly the right temperature for sleeping, and yet I lie awake, staring at the ceiling, the walls, anything to try to keep my mind off of what matters. Though I am certain that sleep does not come, at 2:15 in the morning, the pain returns. It starts as a numbness in my hands and feet, and as it works its way through the rest of my body, it manifests as a burning sensation. Not a gentle "it hurts when I pee" sort of burning, but more of a "holy shit, did someone light me on fire?" kind of burning.

I am pinned to the bed by this sensation, hurting so badly that I just want to pass out and make it stop. But I am not granted that luxury. Instead, I am quite awake as words fill my mind. *You have done well, but there is more to do. Esteban needs you. The time is upon him, and the peril is real. You must be there, in order to stop what may come to pass. His enemy is your enemy.*

"Who are you?" I ask the question aloud, and—I realize—loudly. My voice echoes in the emptiness of the room. "Why do you talk like that?" The verbiage I hear sounds archaic, even ancient, and I want to know who's doing this to me.

Find him, and prevent this.

In an instant, the words and the pain are gone. I am alone with partial knowledge of what I must do. Granted, the absence of full understanding is annoying, as is the new little detail that I must actually prevent my friend's horrible death. It's settled, then—the time for indecision is probably over. The time to stand up and do the right thing—unless it turns out I really don't have to—is here.

I decide to make Esteban's presence or absence from work the deciding factor in whether I intervene. Somehow, I make it through the remaining hours of the night, after which I proceed to work as normally as I can, given the circumstances. I leave the online in/out board open on my computer throughout the morning, and the line for Padgett, E. does not change from OUT. *Well, of course he's not here. He asked for the day off.*

The day—Thursday the twenty-sixth—the day I was warned Esteban would die. And where is he? Is he safe? Is he even alive? If so, why wouldn't he contact me to tell me? *Because today is about him, not you.*

Still, his absence would be the deciding factor, and he's not here. It's time to act. I pick up the phone, dial 9, and dial three more numbers. After one ring, a woman answers. "911, what is your emergency?"

"My name is Tristan Shays. I'm calling because I believe my friend Esteban Padgett is in danger."

"Is that E-s-t-e-b-a-n P-a-d-g-e-t?"

"Two t's at the end, but yes."

"Thank you. Can you please tell me what happened to make you believe this?"

Okay, the tricky part. How to tell this without sounding insane.

"He confided in me recently that he's been having marital problems, and the handgun he keeps in the house has gone missing. Esteban didn't come in to work today, and I'm concerned that something may have happened to him."

"When was the last time you spoke to Mr. Padgett, sir?"

"It must have been ... yesterday morning. He told me about the problems he's been having, and he said he was going to talk to his wife. That's the last time I heard from him."

"Have you made any attempt to contact him since then?"

"No, I didn't want to interfere, in case he was able to work things out."

"We can do a welfare check, but I would encourage you to try to contact him as well."

"I would, but today's the day when ..."

"Yes, sir? The day when—?"

Now I've said too much. I can't finish the sentence honestly. "The day when I'm in meetings most of the day. I'd be grateful if you could do a welfare check."

"What's Mr. Padgett's address?"

"It's 2186 Kestrel, in Salisbury."

"We'll send a unit to that address. Please let us know what phone number you'd like us to use to contact you."

I give them my cell phone number and thank them for their help. I'll give them a couple of hours to report back, but if they can't find Esteban, then I know I have to. The prospect isn't terribly appealing. Again, not the heroic type. If I truly have to step up and make this happen, I don't have the first idea how to begin.

Forty-five minutes later, my cell phone rings. Startled at first, I quickly recover and answer it within just a few seconds. "Yes, hello? Tristan Shays."

"Mr. Shays, this is Sergeant Burkholder of the Salisbury Police Department. We were performing a welfare check on a Mr. Esteban Padgett at your request."

"Yes, thank you. What did you find?"

"We went to the residence, and we found that neither Mr. or Mrs. Padgett was at home. We walked the perimeter and found no evidence of suspicious activity or foul play."

"What about inside the house?" I ask. "Did you find anything?"

"Well, sir, we're not authorized to enter the residence on a welfare check unless there's reasonable cause to do so—someone screaming, blood visible, shots fired, the interior of the home in disarray. None of those things were evident at the Padgett house, so we did as thorough a search as we could from the outside. From what I saw, there was no indication of any danger."

"So, is that the end of it? Case closed?"

"If circumstances change, we can do another welfare check later, if you'd like."

"I'd appreciate that. I'll let you know if I learn anything more."

"That'd be fine."

"Thank you, Sergeant."

"You're welcome, sir. You have a good day."

As I disconnect the call, it is inescapably apparent that I am not going to have a good day.

During the noon hour, I visit Esteban's favorite lunchtime haunts, all the restaurants in town he enjoys. I realize I must look like a stalker, but I don't care. I call his cell phone several times but get his voicemail every time. Just before 1:00, I decide to go to his house. As I pull up in front, I see the same state of nothingness that the cops saw this morning. No cars in the driveway, no signs of life, and no signs of trouble.

Unlike the police, I am unconstrained by proper behavior, so I go to the ceramic pelican to the right of the front door—the one where they keep the spare key. I brought their mail in for them last year when they were on vacation, and I know the pelican is their hiding place. I open the door a bit, poking my head in. "Esteban? Annalisa?" No answer. *No one is here. I should go, but this is my chance to look around.* Cautiously I move from room to room, looking for anything that might give me some answers. I consider it a slight handicap that I have no idea what I'm looking for. Still, I find nothing at all of interest, nothing out of place.

Where are the voices when I really need them? I stand there in the living room, utterly clueless how to proceed. "Think, Tristan, think." Okay, this is supposed to happen tonight, when Esteban would normally come home from work. That's 6:30 or so. I'll come back then, and I'll find some way of stopping this.

I return to their house at 6:15 in the evening, with a growing feeling of dread rising within me. This time, I see Annalisa's car in the driveway but no sign of Esteban's. This is it. I've never wished so hard in my life to be wrong. I park at the curb and slowly make my way up the driveway. My mind races, searching for the best course of action. Finding none, I simply knock on the front door. There's no reply, so I wait a bit and then knock again. Still no answer. Against my better judgment, I slowly open the front door. To my surprise, Annalisa is standing right in front of me.

"Tristan," she says, sounding surprised to see me.

"I knocked," I answer apologetically. "No one answered."

"I was just coming to get the door. I didn't expect to see you here. Are you here to see Esteban?"

Say yes, say yes, say yes. "No." *Schmuck.* "I'm here to see you."

"Okay. Well ... can I offer you anything?"

"No. I have to say something, and I have to say it now. Annalisa, I know everything. Every bit of it. The affair, your plan to kill Esteban. Everything."

"I don't know what you're talking about."

"I think you do. I think if you really didn't, your voice would sound different."

Immediately, she drops the façade. "This is very awkward, Tristan. It was difficult enough, making the decision to do this when nobody else knew. Now that you know, it changes things. Who else have you told?"

"Everyone," I reply. "The police, the FBI."

"Now *you're* lying," she says calmly. "If that were true, they'd be here instead of you. Let me try another explanation on you. Somehow, you found out about this plan, and you warned Esteban. That's why he spent the last two days asking me difficult questions. I'm not sure how you found out, but I'm guessing it was unusual, so you couldn't go to the police. So instead, you decided to come here yourself and try to stop me. Just like I was warned in a dream I had last night."

"How can you be so calm about this?" I ask her, standing there in disbelief as she tells me all of this.

She pulls a handgun out of her purse, which is sitting on a shelf next to her. "Because you're not going to stop me, so I have every reason to be calm. I didn't count on killing you too, but if I have to change my plans, I will."

"At least tell me why you want to do this. Why would you want to kill Esteban after everything you've shared?"

She thinks a moment and then decides to tell me. "He would never divorce me, no matter what I do. So this is the only way I can be with Claudio."

"Wait a minute. Claudio? Esteban's brother? *That's* the person you're having an affair with?"

"You didn't know?"

"Holy shit," I muse to myself. "Esteban's brother. It really is *Hamlet.*"

"What?" she asks, apparently even more confused.

"Inside joke. Why would you choose him over your own husband?"

"I don't owe you an explanation," she snaps.

"Well, how about me then?" The voice comes from behind me, as Esteban lingers in the front doorway. "I'd kind of like to know."

"Esteban, this ..." She hesitates, taking a few steps back. "Tristan just showed up here, spouting wild accusations."

"Stop it, Annalisa. I heard what you just said. Claudio? *Mi hermano?* How could you?"

I can see her fighting back tears. "It was Claudio's idea. All of it. The affair, the plan to kill you, the plot against the company ..."

"What plot?" Esteban asks.

"Which company?" I add.

"Your company. After Esteban was gone, he was going to offer his services to you, Tristan, to get established in your company. He had plans of taking over everything."

I remember the words of last night: *His enemy is your enemy.* "So he was trying to get into bed with both of us."

"But now you've ruined everything," she says, pointing the gun at me. "What am I supposed to do now?"

"Give me the gun," Esteban tells her.

"You can still walk away from this," I remind her. "Nobody has to die tonight. If this really was Claudio's idea, you can help us get him out of all of our lives."

I take a step in her direction, gently and non-threateningly, but it isn't non-threatening enough. She points the gun at me, and my hands go up like they were on strings.

"You don't know what he's like!" she says, sobbing openly. "I have to do this."

"I've already notified the police," I inform her calmly. "They know about all of this, and they're on their way here right now."

"Then this is on your hands," she says.

What happens next happens fast, faster than I could have thought possible. I watch as she turns the gun away from me and places it under her chin. In the movies, moments like this are shown in slow motion, making them feel like you've got lots of time to react. But the truth is, there isn't time for rational thought or decision-making, only instinct. Instinct tells me to throw myself forward, to try to knock the gun out of her hand, and I feel myself propelled in her direction, awkwardly, off-balance, lumbering and almost falling in a desperate attempt to reach her in time. My hand touches steel, and the next thing I know, the loudest sound I've ever heard overwhelms my ears, leaving me dizzy and unable to hear anything but ringing.

Disorientation replaces memory in the minutes that follow. The next thing I recall clearly is lying down on the couch in Esteban's living room with something cold covering my forehead and my eyes. As clarity slowly returns, I realize it is a frozen gel pack, and I realize further that it is on me to try to conquer the unbearable pain in my head that has put me on the couch in the first place.

My eyes focus, and details start to creep back in. There are uniformed police officers in the house, several of them. The front door is standing open, and men come and go. I look over at the place where we were standing, and I see blood on the floor—quite a bit of it. Glancing down at myself, I see more of it on my shirt. *But I don't feel injured.* I'm puzzled at not knowing what took place. *You were starting to go into shock. That's why they put you here. The pain in your head is from the noise of the gunshot and your own frayed nerves.*

With all the people entering and exiting the house, no one is paying attention to me at the moment. I make the mistake of trying to sit up, which only serves to send a wave of pain and nausea through me. But it does catch Esteban's attention, and he rushes over to me.

"Not so fast, not so fast," he says gently, easing me back down onto the couch. "You shouldn't get up just yet."

"This is gonna sound stupid," I reply weakly, "but what happened?"

"What happened is you saved Annalisa's life."

"But ... there's blood, and I remember a shot—"

"The blood is hers. She put the gun under her chin, and she was going to use it, but then you rushed her and knocked her hand away. The gun went off, but it was at such an angle that it only grazed the side of her head. She lost some blood, but they took her to the hospital, and they think she's going to be all right."

"How long have I been here?" I ask, not remembering any of this.

"A little more than an hour. You were close enough when the gun went off that it gave you a minor concussion, but you'll be all right. You were right about what you told me. All of it. And because you were here, you saved her life ... and mine."

"What's going to happen to her?" I ask.

"Well, the police want to talk to her once she's doing better. I'm more interested in finding Claudio. Maybe they'll let her make a deal if she helps them."

"And you? What will you do?"

He shakes his head a little. "I think we're beyond the couples' therapy stage. Right now, I don't know what I'm going to do."

"If you need some time off from work, you've got it. As much time as you need."

"Thank you. And thank you for all of this. I still don't understand it, but I can't deny that you're the reason I'm still alive tonight."

Alone with my thoughts that night, the full impact of what has happened begins to sink in. The warning was correct, and my actions may well have saved Esteban's life. The biggest question of the hour is why warn me? Why not just warn Esteban directly? That would make more sense. He was the one in danger. If he were warned ahead of time, he could have defended himself. Sure, this involved me too, but much less directly. Why use me as some sort of message service?

It's almost midnight, and I'm not tired, so I go to my computer, pull up a Web browser, and open up a search engine. But what am I searching for? Predictions? Warnings? Messages from beyond? I enter "warnings" and get millions of options. I amend it to "advance warnings" and still have hundreds of thousands to choose from. I then add "+ pain," and that narrows the field to about two thousand entries. Finally, I hit upon "advance warnings + unbearable pain," and that is the winning combination. One single match.

The page is entitled, "Screaming into the Abyss." *Cheerful thought.* It appears to be someone's online diary. I click on the link, and a page opens, with a simple background and plain text. No photos, no decoration. It is a diary, from all indications, but it has only a single entry, dated December 31, 2006. About seven months ago. And this is what it says.

My name was Devin Larimer. I say "was" because who I am and everything I understand about my life is no longer relevant. Four months ago, I started getting what I thought were bad dreams. In them, I received messages, advance warnings about people who were in danger. At first, I didn't think anything about it. I've had strange dreams for much of my life, and they never meant anything. But the dreams didn't stop. They got more vivid, more detailed. And there was more to it. I started feeling unbearable pain. Not just in one place, but it seemed to strike wherever it would hurt the most. Nothing I did would make the pain go away. I tried ice, heat, pressure, pain relievers, even acupuncture, but nothing made a difference. Until one day.

The warning I got that day was about someone who lived about twenty miles from me. So I decided I would find this person and tell her what I saw in my dream. I don't know if she believed me, and honestly, I don't care. All I know is that as soon as I told her, the pain stopped. It was like a miracle, like a gift from above. For the next three nights, I slept soundly, with no dreams, no messages, and no pain. I thought I was finally free. But then, I got another message. Another person in danger, and instructions on where to find them and what to tell them. And with it came more pain. Worse than anything I'd known before. It kept me up the rest of that night, wondering what I should do. I didn't want to believe that I had to find this person to make the pain stop, but I was desperate. I had to know if the first time was a coincidence. So I went, the next day. I drove two hundred miles to talk to someone I'd never met. And with each mile I drove, the pain got a little better. As relieved as I was to be rid of the pain, I secretly wished that it wasn't the answer. Because that means it wasn't a coincidence. It wasn't a fluke. Every dream I had ignored was a warning for someone who never received it. Worse yet, they would keep coming, maybe for the rest of my life.

So I finished that two hundred-mile drive, and I met a seventy-six-year-old man, and I told him that if he tried to drive himself to the grocery store that day, he would crash into a minivan, killing himself and four other people. How do you tell somebody that? How do you tell a stranger that his life will end and he's going to kill a family of four? All I could do was deliver my message and leave there. I couldn't even wait to see if he would listen. I had to get out of there.

But before I could even get to my car, I saw a man standing there, waiting for me. I'd never met him before, but he talked to me like he knew me. Only he didn't call me by name. He called me Shalosh. To this day, I still don't know what it means. He said that I was given a great gift, an opportunity to save lives, and all I had to do was accept it. He wanted me to join him, to meet others "like me," who had the same gift. He told me the name of the group, but I don't even remember it. Because I didn't want it. And I don't want it. This man wanted to give me answers, but I turned him away and went back home.

Day after day, week after week, these messages kept coming, and whenever I could, I kept going to warn people. I lost my job, and soon I'm going to lose my home. I can't maintain a relationship, and my own family thinks I'm crazy, because I made the mistake of telling them what I've been going through. They want me to get psychiatric help, but I'm beyond that. I'm beyond the pain and beyond the constant demands on my time. I'm beyond all of it. That's why I'm writing this entry. My last. If this isn't meant to be, then someone will send me a person very much like myself, who feels terrible pain unless they deliver their message.

If someone comes to my door tonight and tells me that I'm meant to live, I'll listen, and I'll choose to live. And I'll find a way to deliver these messages and have a life of my own. But if there's no knock on my door tonight, I know what I have to do. I don't know if I believe in God, but if he's there, I hope he forgives me for what I'm going to do.

My blood chills at reading the final paragraph, as I realize that what I am reading is a published suicide note. I scroll back up to the top to reread the name, which I quickly enter into a search engine. There are several dozen hits, so I add the word *obituary* and search again. My heart sinks when I see one result.

You don't want to see this.

But I have to know. I open the page and find a reprint from a small-town newspaper in Colorado.

DEVIN LARIMER, 35 (August 22, 1971–December 31, 2006). Devin Larimer, 35, of Loveland, passed away at 11:30 p.m. on December 31, 2006, at his residence, of a fatal injury.

Born August 22, 1971, in Fort Collins, he was the son of Michael and Elaine (McCarty) Larimer. Until recently, he was an employee of Allied Information Systems and a volunteer with Big Brothers, Big Sisters.

Survivors include his parents, grandparents, and a sister Clia, age 29. Funeral services will be conducted at 1 p.m. on January 3 at the Kensington Mortuary in Loveland. Burial will follow at Garden of Peace Cemetery. In lieu of flowers, please send donations to Project SAVE.

I'm numb with this discovery. Devin Larimer, a man roughly my own age, blessed or cursed with the same situation I've just gone through. Only his situation didn't stop. It continued time and time again, until he didn't want to live anymore. A volunteer with Big Brothers, Big Sisters; this wasn't a selfish, uncaring man. This was a man accustomed to giving of himself, of his time. What was so horrible about his situation that he would choose not to live anymore? And what about me? Am I next? Will these messages and the pain continue until I can't take it either?

I turn off the computer, not wanting to see anything more of Devin Larimer and his sad ending. I need a shower, and I need sleep. Most of all, I need to believe that my life as I know it hasn't come to an abrupt end.

Chapter 3

THOUGH I CANNOT SAY for certain when sleep came to me during the night, I am aware of waking up on Friday morning, feeling as close to refreshed as I've felt in a week. The night contained no messages, no physical pain. The only pain I felt was for Devin Larimer, who I never met and never will. Reading his story felt like being a newly diagnosed cancer patient who has just met a stranger dying of the same disease.

I try to be reasonable about it. What I went through could have been a one-time situation; I got a premonition about someone I know. It happens. Until it happens again, the safest, sanest way to proceed is to believe that it was a fluke and not believe that I'm doomed to the same fate as Devin Larimer.

When I arrive at work, I find Esteban waiting for me in my office. "I let myself in," he says. "I hope you don't mind."

"Of course not."

"I brought coffee. The good stuff." He hands me one and takes one for himself.

"So, are you all right, or should I ask another time?"

"I've had easier weeks," he says, "but I'm alive. And I suspect I have you to thank for that."

"Any news with Annalisa and Claudio?"

"Claudio's been arrested. Annalisa's cooperating with the police in exchange for immunity for her part in this."

"What happens next for the two of you?" I ask.

"That part's not so clear yet. I'll have to decide if I want to stay with her. I won't lie; this hit me hard. It'll be hard for me to ever trust her again."

"I'm the last guy to ask about relationships, but whatever you decide, I'll back you. And if you need a place to stay for a while, you're welcome at my place. Now that you know I'm not in love with you, and all."

He gives a little laugh at this. "I'll let you know, thanks." He hesitates a moment before saying, "I'd really like to know how you knew to warn me about this."

"I wish I could tell you, Esteban. Now that it's done, I don't know much more than I did before. But I did find something last night." I call up the online diary page of Devin Larimer and let him read it.

"Jesus, Tristan. That sounds like what you went through."

"Yeah. A little too close for my comfort."

"He's dead? He killed himself?"

"Yeah."

"What are you going to do?"

"Wish I knew. So far, I've only had the one message and no other pain. So I'm really *really* hoping that it won't happen again."

"And if it does? If you get another warning to deliver, will you deliver it?"

"I'll have to decide that if and when it happens."

"I don't want to see you end up like this Larimer guy, where delivering these warnings takes over your life."

"Believe me, Esteban, neither do I."

The workday is uneventful, and I even manage to put my anxieties out of my mind for the time being. On Saturday morning, after the second decent night's sleep in a row, I decide to reward myself for the week's adventures by driving to Virginia Beach. Yes, it could be argued that someone living in a beachfront resort community wouldn't need to drive three hours to another beachfront resort community for recreation. But I've always had a fondness for Virginia Beach. It has the crowds and the amenities and attractions that Ocean City lacks. And nobody knows me here, which is precisely what I need right now.

I arrive just before noon and stake out a patch of sand where I can lay down my towel. It's a hot day, well over ninety degrees, and I'm grateful to slip out of my clothing and into a swimsuit. After the requisite sunscreen, I lie down on my towel and close my eyes. Seconds later, I open them again, but to my amazement, I am somewhere else, only I'm not sure where. It looks like a small office building, but one that has been converted into a chapel or a sanctuary. It's night, and the light inside the building is dim. The strangest feeling washes over me, a sense that I am an intruder here but welcome at the same time.

"Where am I?" I am aware of asking the question aloud.

"Where you belong," a voice replies from behind me.

I turn to see the gentle face of an old man. He stands there in the dim light, looking at me with kindness in his eyes. "You have questions," he says.

"How did I get here?" I ask him.

"You haven't yet. When you're ready, you will."

"I don't understand. What is this place, and who are you?"

"Before you learn that, you first have to learn who *you* are."

"Wait a second—you're not going to tell me I have to go help someone, are you?"

"Tristan, the only person you have to help right now is yourself. You're feeling great confusion now, and that's understandable. You've just completed your first assignment, haven't you?"

"First assignment? You know what's happening to me, don't you?"

"Your mind is in some disarray. You've come here before you're ready. You have to believe me that you have important work to do. Work that will change your life, change the lives of others. Change the world."

"Is that what you told Devin Larimer?"

He looks at me silently for several seconds before saying, "I can't talk about that."

"You don't have to. I know all about it. He got 'assignments.' He got to change lives, and it cost him his own."

"We all have choices, Tristan. Decisions that only we can make. You'll make them too."

"I can't do this. I didn't ask for this!"

"Few do. We didn't."

At this statement, seven other older men enter the room and stand with him. The first man continues, "But we have known blessings beyond what ordinary men will ever know in their lives. When your time has come, Tristan, when you have an understanding of yourself and your path, find us and join us. Complete us."

"Complete you?"

"Without you, she will die."

One of his friends interrupts, "No, it's too soon."

"Who?" I ask. "Who will die?"

"Someone you love. And she will be the first of many."

I open my eyes and sit up with a start, taking a moment to realize that what I've just been through was actually a dream.

"That must have been some nightmare," a voice chimes in from beside me.

I turn to see a woman of about thirty with dark hair and a tanned complexion. She's by herself on a blanket not far from me.

"Huh? I … uh— Yeah, I guess it was."

She sits up, orienting herself more toward me. "You want to talk about it?"

"I … um, no. No, thank you. I'm fine. I've just had a hard week. Thank you."

I close my eyes again, but she persists. "Does my gesture of compassion earn me the right to know your name?"

The eyes open again, and I look at her. She's attractive enough, but this is *not* why I came here. I consider giving her a fake name but decide to go the honesty route instead. "I'm Tristan."

"Genevieve," she says. "Nice to meet you." I don't return the greeting, so she continues. "Not much of a talker, are you?"

"I guess not. I haven't thought about it."

"I'd rather not give up on you just yet," she says. "But I will if I have to. If you're truly going to stonewall me, I could read a book or something. I'd rather talk with you, though."

"Why?" I ask, trying to make the question sound curious and not suspicious.

"I see people, and I get a feeling about them. I guess I got a feeling about you."

Now I'm intrigued. I sit up and face her. "What kind of a feeling?"

"I'm not sure yet. That's why I want to talk with you some more. Maybe see if you'll buy me a drink."

"From where?"

At that moment, a male voice behind me asks, "Something from the bar, sir?"

"Beach waiter," Genevieve says. "And yes, he'd like to get an amaretto sour for me …"

"And one for me as well," I tell the waiter.

"Very good, sir. I'll be right back with those."

She smiles at me with what looks like victory on her face. "Is this how you generally meet people?" I ask her.

"I resent the implication," she says playfully. "And no, to answer your question. Generally speaking, I'm a bit on the shy side."

"You hide it well."

"I'm on a campaign of self-improvement, and the shyness is part of it. How am I doing so far?"

Damn it, she's winning me over. "Not too bad. So, what brings you to Virginia Beach?"

"I'm an ornithologist," she replies, "studying deviant migratory patterns of emperor penguins." I meet her with a blank stare. "It's a beach, Tristan. I'm here to lie on it."

"In every sense of the word," I counter. "And for the record, sarcasm is not an effective remedy for shyness."

"Sorry. I overcompensate sometimes."

The waiter brings our drinks, and I pause long enough to pay him. I raise my glass in Genevieve's direction. "To the penguins."

"To the penguins," she says, taking a sip. "This is good. Lots of places don't make them right."

I taste mine. "You're right. Not my usual drink, but it sounded good. Thanks for the recommendation."

"So," she says, "I'll skip the part about what brings you here and ask the cliché pick-up line, come here often?"

"Not nearly often enough. I live only about three hours away, and I'm lucky to get here even once a year."

"Too busy?" she asks. "You one of those workaholic types?"

"I can stop using workahol anytime I like. But yes, there are days … lots of days … when I feel like my job owns me."

"And what is that job, if I may pry?"

You may, but not too deeply. "Middle management at a company that makes pretty, pretty lights."

"Sounds festive."

"And you, Miss Genevieve? I'm guessing ornithologist is a cover story. What's the real occupation?"

"If I tell you, you're not allowed to laugh at me. Okay?"

"I don't know. Is it an occupation that's worthy of laughter?"

"Some people think so. You can understand, then, why I'm asking for your indulgence."

"How bad can it be?" I ask. "Underwater basket-weaver? Sports gynecologist? Horse whisperer?"

"I do psychic readings," she says in all earnest.

I do not laugh at this announcement. It is, I will admit, not what I expected her to say, but there are worse occupations, I suppose. What I do manage to say is, "Huh."

"Huh," she repeats. "I guess that's better than laughter, so there's that."

"I've just never met a psychic-reading … person before. Are you the storefront twenty-dollar readings type of psychic or the help-the-police type of psychic?"

"A little of both," she answers. "It's a respectable profession."

"I have no doubt," I tell her. "And I've seen some things recently that have opened my mind a bit."

"Yeah," she says, looking at my face intently, "you look like you've seen some things."

"So tell me how an intelligent, attractive woman decides to become a psychic reader."

"Okay, style points for the smooth delivery of flattery—which I accept, by the way. And because I believe your inquiry is sincere, you will get the actual story. I was nineteen and in college. I needed a little extra money, so I took a job as a scheduler at a psychic fair that was being held in town. They paid me to schedule people for psychic readings, channelings, that sort of thing. Well, it wasn't a huge psychic fair, so there was some down time, and I got to talking with one of the psychic readers. She asked me if I'd ever been hypnotized, and I said no, I hadn't. So she asked me if I'd be willing to, and I thought, 'yeah, right, that'll never work.' But I tried it, and she recorded the session. The things I saw ... Tristan, it changed my life forever."

She's got me hooked now. "Tell me."

"The reader invited me to go back into my past and revisit my childhood. And I did, I suppose. I relived things I had forgotten about. Then it got weird. She invited me to step outside of myself, to open up to voices that wanted to speak through me. Now, bear in mind as I tell you this that I don't actually remember what happened next. All I have to go on is the tape of the session, but I know that it's real, and it wasn't doctored in any way. I heard my voice change. It got deeper, kind of distant. She asked who she was speaking to, and I identified myself as Quetzalcoatl."

"As who?"

"That was my question too, after it was all over. Quetzalcoatl was the central deity of the ancient Aztec religion."

I absorb this with as much credulity as I can muster. "Uh-huh. And you were, what, him in a past life?"

"No," she corrects, "I was a conduit for him to speak. Like a radio that picks up signals from other times and places. I picked up this ancient voice—one whose actual earthly existence was debated by scholars for centuries. And there I was, talking as if I was him. They called a professor in from the university who specialized in the Aztec culture, and he sat there and had a conversation with me—with Quetzalcoatl—asking me minute details about religious customs and rituals, about historical events, about the downfall of the society at the hands of Cortez. And every single time, I gave him answers that were completely accurate in every detail."

"Is it possible that you learned these details somewhere? In a class or on the History Channel or something?"

"No, I had never heard of this deity, and at the time, I couldn't have even told you where the Aztec culture was located. But there I was, answering these questions, taking this professor to school for forty-five minutes. A crowd had gathered around, and everybody there said it was the most fascinating thing they'd ever seen. That was the day I decided to change my life and make this my calling. I trained and developed my skills for the next year, and then I went out on my own."

For several seconds, all I can do is stare at her in wonder. This clearly reads as disbelief, and she says to me, "Oh my God, you totally think I'm crazy right now."

"No ..."

"You're sitting there thinking, 'How do I get away from this crazy woman?'"

"Genevieve, I'm not. Believe me, of all the people on this beach here today, you're talking to the one person who is least likely to think you're crazy."

She smiles a bit at this. "Well, that's good. Is there a story that goes with that announcement?"

"There is, but it's not something I can talk about here. Are you staying at a hotel in town?"

"Yeah, the Royale." She hesitates a moment. "Wait a second, is this just a tactic to get me to take you back to my hotel room?"

"No. Well, by the strictest definition of those words, yes. But I really do have something important to share with you."

"All right," she says, getting up. "Follow me."

I walk with her down the beach to the Royale Hotel, a block and a half away. The place is pleasant enough; not terribly fancy. Of course, I've been spoiled by years of top-end hotels for business travel and meetings. This is what she can afford, and I like it.

She takes me to her room on the fourth floor, which is clean and well-kept. She seems to have been here a couple of days, with enough of her belongings for a couple more. "Well," she says, "this is the place."

"I like it. Looks like a great room."

"Can I get you anything from the mini-bar?"

"No, I know how much that stuff costs. I'm fine, really."

"Okay. So what is it you wanted to tell me that you couldn't tell me on the beach?"

"Genevieve, in the past week, things have been happening to me that I can't begin to explain. I don't expect you to have all the answers or even any of the answers, but I want to tell you, to see what you think."

"Well, you certainly have my interest. What's been happening to you?"

I tell her all of it, from the first moment of pain through to the finding of the online diary and even the dream I had on the beach just before we met. As I talk, I watch her face to gauge her reaction. She listens intently, and I see no sign of disbelief in her. Neither do I see a spark of explanation.

When I finish, she sits quietly for several seconds, taking everything in. "That's quite a story. You say nothing like this has ever happened to you before?"

"Never."

"And you've never had flashes of psychic ability, little gifts you didn't understand?"

"Nothing that I'm aware of."

"Well, I've heard of late-onset psychic development, but usually in teenagers. Sometimes people will get flashes of premonition if someone they care about is in danger, but I've never heard of one being accompanied by that amount of pain. You said that the pain came back every day until you told your friend what you knew?"

"That's right."

"That seems to suggest real importance in sharing the information; the pain was an external motivator, making sure you told him. And once you did, it stopped?"

"Yes, it did."

"And you haven't had any pain or any new information since then?"

"No, but it's only been a couple of days. That's the part that really scares me. If this was a one-time thing, that's fine. I did what I had to, I endured the pain, and it's done. But if I find out that this is my life now, I'm not sure what to do about it. And I sure don't want to end up like that other guy."

"Tristan, I think it's significant that we met. Of all the people on that beach I could have talked to, I chose you. That has to mean something. With my background and your recent experiences, I believe you were meant to meet me. Will you let me read your tarot?"

"Umm ... I guess so. I've never done anything like this before. What does it involve?"

She leads me to a table in the corner of the hotel room and turns on a light. "We sit, and you watch as I deal some cards and tell you what they mean."

"Uhh—sure. Why not?"

It's not the most enthusiastic response, but it's what I can muster. She goes to her suitcase and pulls out a deck of cards, slightly larger and thicker than a traditional deck. I don't know much about tarot, so this will be a learning experience for me.

We sit, and she puts the deck on the table. "Shuffle the cards, please," she says.

I pick up the cards and try to shuffle them like a standard deck, but because of the size of the pack and the stiffness of the cards, they resist, so I manually re-arrange cards to approximate a full shuffle, putting them down on the table.

"Thank you," she says. "Now take the deck in your left hand and separate it into three piles, placing them side by side on the table between us." I do so, and she takes the middle stack and places it on top of the one to my left, placing those two on top of the remaining pile.

"Now I need you to ask me a question," she says.

Without thinking about it, I ask, "What is the capital of Pakistan?"

She gives me a look that gently suggests I'm the biggest dork she's ever met. "Islamabad," she replies, "but that's not what I meant. To make the reading meaningful, the cards have to know something you want the answer to. So I want you to ask a question aloud, preferably one that starts with the word 'what,' rather than 'why,' for example."

"Okay ... what ... is going to happen to me in the near future?"

She nods a little, seeming to accept the question. "Let's begin then," she says. With that, she pulls the first card off the top of the deck and sets it down in front of me. "The Hermit," she says. "It signifies wisdom, peace, and tranquility of spirit. But also a life of solitude." She pulls a second card and places it on the table, next to the first. "The Fool."

"Charming," I reply.

"Shhh. I'll explain. The fool doesn't have to represent *you*. He represents travel to places unclear and uncertain. You see how he carries his possessions with him? That means he has everything he needs right there. But you see the cliff? He could very easily fall over that cliff, so the Fool is a warning to be careful."

She pulls a third card and places it next to the others. On it is a figure in a long, dark cloak. "Death?" I ask, concerned, reading the card's name.

"Don't be alarmed," she says. "This card doesn't mean you're going to die anytime soon. It's about change, about transformation. One period of your life is coming to an end, and another one is about to begin; maybe something powerful and special."

"Yes, but given what I told you, that card *could* be a death sentence. The change you're talking about may be the exact kind I don't want."

"Do you want to see the next card?" she asks.

Though I'm not sure I do, I tell her, "Yes."

I am not heartened to see a figure suspended from a tree, his legs sprawled in an approximation of the number 4. "The Hanged Man," she says. "One of the most famous cards in the deck. His mythology dates back to Odin, who was hanging on the world tree for nine days as a sacrifice. This card's appearance means that your future will include a time of trial, of meditation, of prophecy. And one of sacrifice. That could mean the future you're concerned about will happen. But it could also mean that you'll use what's just happened to you to become more self-sacrificing in your normal daily life. Do you want me to keep going?"

"Yes. Keep going."

She turns over the next card and we both look at it. Her face falls, displaying considerable surprise and concern. The card is The Hanged Man. "Two of a kind," I say, not sharing her expression. "Is that good luck?"

Genevieve doesn't answer, but instead turns over the next card from the pile. It too is The Hanged Man. Now looking fearful, she tosses the rest of the deck down on the table and gets up quickly, taking two steps backward.

"Genevieve, what's wrong? Is three of a kind a bad omen?"

"You don't understand. In a tarot deck, The Hanged Man appears only once."

"But then, how—?"

"I don't know, and it's scaring me a little."

"What about the rest of the cards in the deck?"

"I didn't look," she says. I reach for them, and she says, "No, don't look at them. I'm not quite sure what I'd do if they're all The Hanged Man."

"There's got to be a reasonable explanation. Cards from your other tarot decks got mixed in with this one ..."

"I only have one deck. This has never happened before, and I don't know what it means."

I search for anything resembling an explanation or a way of comforting her. "What about the voices?"

"Voices?"

"The- the channeling that you do. Can you talk to the voices and ask them what's happening, ask them what's going to happen to me?"

"I don't know. I'm not sure it works that way. I can't control which voices speak through me. I just open myself up, and they talk."

"Genevieve, if there's some force at work here that's strong enough to change the cards in your deck, maybe it's strong enough to speak through you. I'll be here the whole time. I won't let anything happen to you."

"Okay. I'll try, I guess."

"Good. Now, what do I do in case things go wrong and you're in trouble?"

"You'll have to wake me."

"Wake you?"

"I'll be in a kind of self-hypnosis; a trancelike state. Call my name, shake me, slap my face, throw cold water on me. Whatever it takes to snap me out of it. Can you do that?"

"Uhhh … probably."

"All right, I'll try this. I'm a little agitated right now, and I'm supposed to be calm."

"Do what you have to. I can wait."

"Oh, and there's one more thing. Usually when I do this, there's somebody else with me, to control the session and speak to the voices, to moderate the whole thing. Nobody else is here, so you'll have to talk to them."

"Talk to who?" I ask.

"Them. The voices. Whoever shows up."

"Well … what do I say?"

"I don't know. Ask them whatever you want to ask them. I have to get ready now."

What am I doing? I mean, really, what am I doing? It's bad enough that I'm in the hotel room of a strange woman I just met, but it's about to become a threesome, and God knows who's going to show up. I could run. Running works. *Nice to meet you, but I've really gotta go.*

She sits on the bed and folds her legs, closing her eyes in what I guess is an attempt to enter the trance she was talking about. I'm trying very hard not to feel stupid as I stand and stare at her face. I'm attracted to her. I realize this now, and I want to believe that it doesn't factor into why I'm staying. But I know me, and as much as I want answers, what I really want is our clothing in a pile on the floor and us in a pile on the bed.

So why not dispense with the tarot cards and the channeling, and just say, "Genevieve, you're attractive, and I want to get to know you better"? Because I really do want answers, and that shit with the cards was just weird enough to make me think that something bigger might be happening here.

After a few minutes of silence, I lean in closer to her. Her eyes are closed, and she's breathing regularly—whatever that means. I pull a chair up next to the bed and sit facing her. I whisper, "Genevieve?" No answer. Again, a little louder, "Genevieve?" Still nothing. I don't think she's asleep. Maybe nobody by that name is home. So I switch tactics. "Hello?"

A voice emerges from her—like hers, but breathy, a little deeper. "Approach."

I look at my position, less than a foot away. "Umm, I'm about as approached as I can get."

The voice asks, "Whom do you seek?"

Whom? The spirits, they use the good grammar. This is serious. "I seek one who can give me answers about my future."

She extends her right hand—or rather, someone extends her right hand. "Place your hand in mine, that I might know you."

And down the rabbit hole we go. I reach out my right hand and place it gently on hers. Suddenly and forcefully, she grasps my wrist, and the sensation I feel is unlike anything I've ever known. It's not painful; that sensation I'm all too familiar with. This is more of a visitation, as if my brain and my soul are having an open house, and I'm home to watch people rifle through the cabinets of my thoughts and feelings.

"You are a mystery," the voice says.

"Uhh—thank you?"

"You possess ancient knowledge, ancient wisdom, and yet you seek answers. You have more answers than you will ever know. What more can we tell you, Ben Hosea?"

Not a name I recognize. Are they sure they have the right person? The next words I hear answer that question.

"The path is laid before you, Tristan Shays. You must choose to walk it."

"And if I choose not to?"

"Many will die."

Great. No pressure.

"What about me? Will this take my life too?"

There is silence for many seconds. I begin to wonder if I've pushed my luck. But then I get an answer, just not the answer I was looking for. "Find the singularity."

"Singularity? What's that?"

"The one that draws all to it. But do not fall—"

In an instant, and apparently in mid-sentence, Genevieve releases her grip on my wrist and returns to the world. She looks disoriented and then realizes that I am next to her, holding on to her hand. "Did it work?" she asks.

"Something did. Someone was here. You don't remember?"

"I never do. While they're here, I'm not. Did it say who it was?"

"No."

"Did it give you any answers?"

I recount what the voice told me and ask, "Does any of that make sense to you?"

"I was kind of hoping it made sense to you, seeing as how it pertains to your life."

I rise in exasperation. "None of it did. Paths and singularities. Ben Hosea? Who's that? And apparently, I have ancient wisdom and knowledge? Hell, that's news to me."

After several seconds, I realize I am pacing around the room like a nervous dog. She rises and walks over to me, putting her hands on my shoulders to calm me. "Tristan, I'm sorry. I didn't mean for this to upset you. Sometimes the voices give good news, and sometimes they don't. I can't control it; I'm just a pathway for them."

My head drops to my chest, and frustration laces my every word. "I can't do this. I don't know how, I don't have time, and this isn't who I am. It's not what I want."

She puts her arms around me, and I unconsciously put mine around her. "What *do* you want?" she asks gently.

Though it sounds like the worst pick-up line in history, I honestly answer, "I want to be held." It's true; more than anything else in the world, I want the warmth of human companionship right now.

Genevieve leads me to the bed and lays me down on it. She then climbs in next to me and holds me. Face to face, we claim this moment as ours. In truth, *she* is the mystery. Not lover, not mother, barely even friend, but forces unknown have utilized her to see into the very essence of my being. And now I offer myself to her at my most vulnerable—scared, confused, utterly unsure what to do and where to go. I ask her to hold me, and she does, caressing my face, sliding her fully clothed body close to mine. Warm against me, she looks into my eyes and I into hers. Strangers in a hotel, clinging to each other. In another context, it would feel needy, unsavory, even desperate. But I sense that there is more at work here, something weightier than this moment, and it lends everything an honesty, a legitimacy. A humanity.

I am so entrenched in the moment that when she inches forward to kiss my lips—as amazing as it feels—I draw back and look at her in surprise.

"I'm sorry," she says, sounding genuinely contrite. "Is it too fast? Too much? I thought …"

"No, it's … it's all right. I'm okay. I just didn't expect. When I asked you to hold me, it wasn't about taking this further. I don't want to lead you on."

"You're not," she replies. "You aren't the only one who wanted to be held. Believe it or not, I don't just meet men on the beach and take them back to my room. I really feel like we were supposed to meet each other."

This time, I take the initiative and kiss her. It feels good; she feels right. But then, in the middle of all this goodness and rightness, I remember the words of the old man from today's dream: *"She will die … someone you love."* Instantly, it is the grandfather of all buzzkills, and it makes me draw back from her. Two in a row; smart girl, she notices.

"Is it my breath or something?" she asks.

"No, nothing like that. Kissing you was … *is* … very pleasant. I'm just a little distracted by everything that's happened to me in the past two days. I'm sorry."

"Put those thoughts out of your mind and just feel this." She kisses me again, and I don't let anything else occupy my thoughts. I just focus on the softness of her mouth against mine, the way her fingers feel as she caresses my hair and my face. Minutes pass exactly this way, and it is precisely what I've been missing. I return the affection, evoking quick, excited breaths and little sounds of arousal from Genevieve.

We allow our hands to explore each other, and the feeling is perfection. She's gentle yet confident, soft but firm in all the right places, and she even smells good. Everything feels so right, and yet, when she reaches down to undo my pants, I give her a look that immediately puts on the emergency brake. Seeing the look, she says to me with a tone of surprise, "You don't want to take this further."

I sit up a little. "Genevieve, it's not like that. You're very attractive, very desirable, and you've already felt what you do to me. There's a side of me that would like nothing more than to tear your clothes off and give in to every passionate urge that's raging inside of me."

"No objections from this side," she says, "but I know there's another shoe about to drop."

"It's going to sound foolish and old-fashioned, but I feel like if I have sex with you now, it will feel like a one-night stand, like something I didn't earn and don't deserve. And it will feel like an excuse never to call you again or see you again. And I *do* want to call you again and see you again."

My words disarm her, and all she can do is smile. "That's the nicest rejection I've ever gotten."

"Believe me, it's not a rejection. I want to see you again. I don't even know where you live, though."

"Richmond, Virginia. What about you?"

"Ocean City, Maryland. It's not exactly next door, but it's not too far. Three or four hours by car."

"So ..." she says, "I just want to be clear. Are—are you asking me to be your girlfriend?"

I give a little laugh at this. "I'm not entirely sure what I'm asking, but I know that I want to spend more time with you this weekend, and when this weekend is over, I don't want you to disappear from my life just yet."

Chapter 4

I SPEND THE REST of Saturday in Genevieve's company, learning more about her as she learns more about me. I am selective in what I tell her; I've found that people tend to react strangely to someone who has a great deal of money. And since I don't let my finances dictate who I am, I omit that part of the story for now. Once we know each other better, I can tell her about that. For now, she gets the usual stuff—my childhood, college, an embarrassing fact or two about me to make me seem sweet and awkward.

I should point out that I didn't come to Virginia Beach looking to start a relationship of any kind, least of all romantic. I am what is commonly called "difficult to love," and I admit that freely. Bearing that knowledge, my internal critic typically screens prospective paramours not with "not good enough for you" but with the more self-deprecating "no way she'd ever go for you." But with Genevieve, no such flags go up, and no alarms blare.

We stay together Saturday night in my hotel room, just up the beach from hers. Though we share a bed, I make good on my promise not to turn this into a one-night stand. If sex is to happen, it will happen later, when the time is right. Maybe that makes me old-fashioned or just plain stupid, given how attracted to her I am, but when I wake up Sunday morning, I can face the person I see in the bathroom mirror, under those horrid fluorescent lights.

She sleeps in for a bit, which is fine. I pass the hour by myself on the balcony to the room, looking out at the ocean. It's a beautiful day, not too hot or too humid. Just the right mix of clouds and sunshine to make the sunlight perfect. I could stay here for weeks and never tire of it. But something reliable and ominous tells me I do not have that luxury.

I hear the sliding glass door to the balcony open behind me, and Genevieve steps out, wearing her sleepwear. She walks up behind me and kisses my face. "Did you get enough sleep?" she asks.

"Enough for me," I answer. "How about you?"

"I did. I feel very rested."

Time to make sure of something. "I hope you're not too disappointed about what did and didn't happen last night."

"Not at all. How can I fault you for respecting me enough not to have sex with me the same day we met? I just hope you don't think less of me for suggesting it in the first place."

"What, you mean for finding me attractive and desirable enough to offer yourself to me sexually?" I ask playfully. "Oh no, how dare you."

She laughs a little. "Okay, point taken. So we still like each other, then?"

"'Fraid so. Question is, what do we do about it?"

"I don't know. I have to go home today."

"So do I," I remind her. "But I've got your contact information, and you've got mine. And I really hope you use it. Because this weekend has been wonderful in your company."

"And in yours. I looked at my tarot deck yesterday, before we came over here. The Hanged Man card only appears once."

"Freaky. Any explanation?"

"None that makes any sense. And none that I want to explore. With my luck, I'd fall hopelessly in love with you, only to find out you're possessed."

"Wouldn't *that* be unfortunate for you?" I ask, feeling quite strange at the choice of scenario.

"Okay, probably not the best example. But you have to admit—from everything you saw and everything that's happened to you—something strange is going on."

"Yeah. Something strange is."

"What if ..." She hesitates, looking uncertain of what to say.

"Go on."

"I was just thinking out loud, and wondering what if ... I ... went with you?"

"Went with me where?"

"The next time you get sent to warn someone. You know, if there *is* a next time."

"Out of the question," I reply quickly and decisively.

"Tristan, it—"

"I'm sorry, Genevieve, it's out of the question. First of all, there isn't going to be a next time, and secondly, even on the nearly impossible chance that there is, whatever it is could be very dangerous, and I wouldn't want to risk your safety." She doesn't reply, so I continue. "Why would you suggest such a thing?"

"I don't know," she says. "That's not true. I *do* know. It's because this is a chance of a lifetime, to observe paranormal activity firsthand. And because … because I just want to spend more time with you."

Now it's my turn to be silenced by her words. For many seconds, I honestly don't know what to say. Finally, all I can manage is a quiet reply of, "Oh, sure. You had to go and say something nice."

"At least let me be your phone-a-friend."

"My what?"

"The person you call when nothing makes sense. When everything feels like it's closing in on you at once. Call me, talk to me. Ask me anything. Let me at least do that for you."

I smile and nod. "I'd like that."

The drive back to Ocean City gives me time to reflect on the past two days. I'm grateful for the hours, because there's so much to go over in my mind. Of course, I'm savoring the memories of every intimate moment Genevieve and I shared, but more than that, I can't get past the confluence of circumstances that led to our meeting. My dream on the beach, her decision to talk to me, my willingness to trust her; it almost feels like someone or something made this happen. But, of course, that's impossible. Just like everything else that's happened in the past week.

I'm not in love with her; I don't believe in love at first sight, and this was most definitely first sight. Yes, I'm attracted to her, and I can remain open to the possibility of a relationship with her, if she can deal with the limitations of my schedule and living several hours away from me. And I'd like very much for her to be my "phone-a-friend"; I like the idea of having someone caring and compassionate to call when life doesn't make sense, when I feel overwhelmed, when I feel alone in the world. It doesn't just have to be in case of supernatural emergency. Because every instinct I have tells me that what happened with Esteban isn't going to happen to me again.

Seven hours later, the pain begins in my right calf. I'm stretched out on the living room sofa, barely paying attention to something on TV. At first, it feels like a cramp, maybe a charley horse from overextending the leg. But when I try to stand on it, the leg gives way under my weight, the pain too extreme to support me. I crumple to one knee, but even that is too painful to sustain, and within seconds, I am face down on the floor, with a fiery pain shooting through my entire right leg and up into my spine.

Pleasant as the taste of the carpet is, my present position lacks dignity and ease of breathing, so with a surprising amount of effort required, I manage to pull myself up to the sofa again, lying down on my back. Sadly, this offers no mitigation of the agony, but it does allow me to close my eyes and try to focus on anything else.

Call 911, stupid. Get an ambulance here, go to a hospital, and get a new battery of tests until you know what the hell is causing this.

I actually begin to embrace this idea, and I am seconds away from reaching for the telephone on the end table, when suddenly the imagery appears. A place name: Demeter, Georgia. A church, the United Assembly of God. It feels like I am watching a movie sped up, one that skips over subtext and character development and goes right for the action. Anything directed by Michael Bay, in other words. I am taken to a basement store room, one with an open electrical junction box near file boxes filled with old paper records. I watch as ancient fuses fail and sparks drop from the junction box, illuminating the little room in a shower of tiny orange points, like malicious fireflies seeking out a place to land. Many of them find the file boxes, and in seconds the room is ablaze.

Terrifyingly enough, I can actually feel the heat of the fire on me. It is not close enough to burn me, but it is making me sweat, and my lungs are aware of the feel of burning paper. Worse is the feeling that the heat and smoke are getting closer—close enough that if it persists, I may be in genuine peril. The pain has me immobilized; I couldn't run away from this if I tried. Just as I genuinely begin to fear for my personal safety, the images and sensations of the fire vanish in an instant, replaced by the minute details of the situation. The fire will happen Tuesday morning, just before 2:00. The church will be empty at the time, but the fire will cause total devastation of the building, a place of worship for almost three hundred people. I am shown the address of the building and the best route to get there. I am given the senior pastor's name and shown what he looks like. And with a final flare-up of pain in my leg, I am reminded that the only thing that can prevent this fire is me.

The room is overwhelmingly silent once this prescient fugue state leaves me. I reach down and touch my calf; my skin is still unnaturally warm. While the pain that immobilized me has left, I am aware of a steady dull ache there, like a latent reminder that a clock is ticking.

"Son of a bitch!"

I am actually startled by my own words, and I realize that exclaiming them was not a conscious act. My tone surprises and disturbs me. It is seething with resentment. A second attack of pain combined with detailed instructions for preventing a tragedy means the first time with Esteban was not a fluke, not a coincidence. It means this is my life now; these are my circumstances until such time as I am released or until I can take it no longer and I choose my own way out—like Devin Larimer did. I have never in my life even contemplated the possibility of suicide. *I wonder if he told himself the same thing in those final days.*

No. I'm calling bullshit on this whole thing. They can show me the fire, they can wrack me with pain, but unless they've got some pretty goddamn impressive levitation powers that can float my ass to Georgia, they can't make me go.

"You hear that?" I shout to my empty living room, in exactly the way a crazy person wouldn't. "You can't make me go! I don't know who you are or why you think I'm your boy, but I'm saying no! I reject your job offer."

Just like that, the pain in my leg gets stronger. I'm not imagining it; my words have resulted in increased sensations.

"Oh, so you're listening, is that it? Well, why don't you show yourself?" It is important to emphasize once again that I vocalize these questions as a fact-finding tactic, rather than in a random insane-person-shouting-at-people-who-aren't-there way. To no great surprise, "they" do not show themselves. I'm actually not even sure there is a "they" to show; I may very well be shouting at a conglomeration of very organized electrons. This does not, however, dissuade me from continuing my very one-sided conversation.

"If you can make me hurt, you can make me understand. You show me pictures of burning churches and my friend being shot. Now show me the picture that explains why you chose me to do this." My volume level is considerably reduced, reasoning that a show of impotent rage did nothing to impress, so maybe a display of polite inquiry is the way to go.

No dice. The pain continues, with no accompanying exposition to serve as an analgesic. Would understanding make it hurt less? Maybe; I don't even know. What I do know is that it's time to draw the line, make my stand right here and now.

"Those are my terms. Do you hear me? If I don't get a full explanation of why this is happening and how long I can expect it to go on, I'm not going to Georgia. That church is on its own."

Minutes turn to hours, and the pain steadily increases in my leg. It hurts enough that I can't even climb the stairs to my bedroom. With great effort and accompanying anguish, I am able to make it to the first-floor bathroom, retaining some small shred of my dignity, but that's as far as I get—there and back to the sofa. Fortunately, it's a comfortable piece of furniture, because I know it's where I'm spending the night. The price I pay for playing chicken with forces that may very well have created the universe. I'm still betting he'll swerve first.

By 4:00 a.m., I am successfully convinced that the pain is unswerving, as is its originator. I vaguely recall something from the book of Job, a passage I read in my childhood, in which Job gets fucked over pretty soundly because God and the devil have some kind of bet. And Job looks up to God, as memory serves, and says words to the effect of, "Dude, WTF? How'd I get on your shit list?" God basically replies, "Oh, I'm sorry. Did I owe you some sort of explanation?" The story eventually has a happy ending for old Job, I seem to recall. Although there was significant collateral damage to pretty much everyone he loved. Lucky me; I get to answer to Old Testament God.

I have to laugh at the image. It's quite a leap of logic, and a little on the arrogant side, to think that little Tristan Shays has become the Almighty's telegram service. Instant messenger, just add pain and stir. But if it's not God, who else would—or for that matter *could*—do this to me? Terrorists aren't big on recruiting their enemies to help *save* other enemies. I'm not being hypnotized into acting against my will. That doesn't leave too many choices. So, implausible as it sounds in twenty-first-century America, I've become a subcontractor for the capital G.

But, oops. First week on the job, and already I've gone on strike. Too bad, so sad. Guess you'll have to fire me, right? Right? Send that pink slip any old time, big guy. "Dear Mr. Shays, we regret to inform you, blah blah blah." Because if you don't, I've got one fucker of a worker's comp claim coming your way.

The rest of the night passes in much the same way, with me simultaneously thinking too much and hurting too much. But I figure that as dawn breaks, the pain will subside, like it did the first time, when I was sent to warn Esteban. As daylight seeps through the windows and illuminates my plight, I find that this is not the case. The pain continues, and if anything, it is getting worse. I try to stand, and I am able—but just barely. Getting to work won't be possible today.

At 8:00, I reach for the phone on the end table and call in to the office. Esteban answers on the first ring. "Tristan, good morning. Is everything all right?"

"Not entirely. I've managed to injure my leg somehow over the weekend, and I won't be able to make it in today."

"I'm so sorry to hear that. Do you need me to take you to a doctor or the hospital?"

"No, but thank you. What I really need is for you to cover for me today. I'll check back with you later this afternoon, and if I'm not feeling better by then, I might just take you up on that. For now, please hold down the fort. You have access to my day's schedule in Outlook. Please represent me at any meetings I had scheduled for the day."

"I'll do that."

"Thank you."

"Any idea how you hurt yourself?"

"Not really. I'm hoping the pain will go away on its own today."

"Well, you do whatever you have to do to make that happen."

Yeah, right, like going to church in the Deep South. "Thank you, Esteban. I'll call you again later."

"Be well, my friend."

I suppose I could have told him the details, but I don't want to upset him; everything with him and his wife is still very fresh and recent. So there's no point going into the potentially supernatural explanations for my pain. Not yet, anyway.

Besides, I'm still determined to win this one. The way I see it, this is a test, to see if I have the strength to withstand the pain. If I give in, they know they can manipulate me, and then I'm theirs to do with as they please for as long as they see fit. If I resist, I'll have a few more hours of pain, and then they'll realize that my resolve is strong and I won't go traipsing all over creation to do their bidding.

With each passing hour, I begin to question the correctness of my assumption. The pain shows no sign of diminishing at all. I reach the point just after 11:00 in the morning where I can no longer walk on the leg. I'm forced to crawl to the bathroom downstairs, contort myself until I can reach a bottle of ibuprofen, and shake three of them into my hand. There is no drinking glass in the bathroom, so I manage to get just enough water out of the faucet to swallow the pills before crawling back to the sofa that is my sanctuary—hopefully not for the rest of my natural life.

For one incoherent instant, I consider cutting off my own leg to relieve the pain, but it is more a thought driven by desperation than an actual plan of action. Yes, there are plenty of expensive knives in the kitchen, but limb self-amputation has never been on my five-year plan, and I figure now's not the right time to try new things. So I quickly ditch that idea and try to focus on my breathing, anything but the current state of my leg.

As the afternoon wears on, I find no relief from the ibuprofen. I didn't expect it to work, but I have to keep hope alive. Then it occurs to me—I have Dr. Mitchell's morphine dose in the kitchen cabinet. All I have to do is get to it.

With a struggle befitting an eighty-year-old stroke victim, I pull myself off of the sofa and belly crawl into the kitchen. Each foot forward I progress is exhausting. I feel every pound of my body weight. You go through life thinking you're in good shape, until the moment when your own mass becomes an anchor dragging you down. The transition from the friction of the carpet to the smoothness of the kitchen linoleum is a godsend. Were I covered in butter at the moment, life would be even better, but absent the desired basting, I continue my best efforts at locomotion until I reach the final hurdle: the cabinet.

Of course, I have placed the pill bottle in an upper cabinet, to the left of the stove. I couldn't put it in a waist-level drawer or a lower cabinet, in anticipation of my present plight. No, I put it way up high, keeping it safe from the pets I don't have and the children I probably never will. And now, desperately in need of that pill bottle, it might as well be at the top of the Matterhorn, surrounded by rabid mountain goats. My kingdom for a reaching stick.

But I've come this far, the 383 miles from the living room to the kitchen, and I'm not leaving this room without the good drugs in me. I will conquer the wood-and-Corian mountain and plant my flag at its peak. Step one: survey the scene. I am approximately six feet below my destination, flat on the floor. My upper body is in relatively good shape, so I decide to start by knocking the first couple of feet of elevation down to size. I turn over and get into a seated position; so far, so good. If I try to stand, my right leg will give out on me, so I have to find a way to support my weight on my left leg.

I look at the stove and see the handle to the oven door. This might just work. Reaching over, I grasp it with my right hand and try to pull myself up. I succeed in opening the oven door on three consecutive occasions before I notice something that will help: the locking lever that I engage when cleaning the oven. With a bit of reaching, I grab hold of it and pull it into the locked position. My next attempt at pulling myself up by the door handle is more successful; the door remains securely latched, and I pull myself up off the floor.

The effort is clumsy, and I end up considerably off balance. As I list to the right, the inclination is to put my weight on my right leg, but the slightest effort to do so results in weakness and the feeling that I'll fall once again. So I fight the momentum and shift all my weight to my left leg, which begrudgingly supports me, while reminding me that I need to do something for its twin brother.

"I'm workin' on that," I say aloud, having now graduated to talking to my body parts.

At least I am standing and at my full height. I'm glad there's no photographer present to capture this moment, but still, I can reach the upper cabinet with no problem. Inside I find the bottle, with just two pills in it, and a glass, which I quickly fill with water. I swallow one of the pills. Just as I'm about to put the bottle back, I take out the second pill and swallow it as well. *To be sure.*

Staying in the kitchen isn't an option, so I have to make my way back to the living room, which leaves two options: hop or crawl. Clearly, in my daily routine, these are not conventional choices for getting from point A to point B, but my current circumstances are anything but normal. Crawling has already proven to be an exercise in degradation coupled with carpet burn, so I opt for hopping. It takes me a moment to ponder the mechanics of it, never having consciously hopped before. The first move forward lands me on the proper foot but leaves me off balance; I compensate with my arms. Two feet closer to the sofa now. Another hop and then another. I may actually be getting the hang of this.

I make it all the way through the kitchen on one leg, like I am playing some bizarre solo playground game. Mother, May Red Rover Hopscotch on a Green Light? This amuses me in the minute and a half I give myself to rest before the home stretch. I reason, if I can conquer the slipperiness of the kitchen floor, the living room carpet should be no problem.

Foolish human. While the kitchen floor was a bit slippery, it was also even terrain. By comparison, the carpet has topography, which positions it perfectly to disrupt my landing. Try as I might to catch myself, I end up doing a face plant on the floor. On the bright side, this new pain makes me forget about my leg pain for a minute or two.

So it's back to the front crawl, all the way to the sofa. What it lacks in respectability, it makes up for in safety, and soon I am back on my gray leather haven. I'm dismayed to discover that the crossing of two rooms has left me winded. What if it doesn't improve? What if it never improves? By refusing to help, have I consigned myself to a lifelong invalid status? I don't know if I could get used to that, particularly knowing that I could have prevented it. I could go to Georgia—catch a flight out of Baltimore and be there in an hour or less, deliver the message, and return home, to be rid of this pain.

No. No, I have to stand my ground. I have to know what will happen if I refuse. Whether I'll be afflicted even after the time this is supposed to happen; whether I'll no longer be called on to do this again. I have to know.

An hour later, I still feel no effect from either of the drugs I've taken. Moreover, I feel very alone, like no one can help me or even understand what I'm going through. But that's not true. One person can understand. I reach into my pants pocket and pull out Genevieve's contact information, still in the clothes I wore home from the beach yesterday. I struggle to get to the cordless phone, but I am able to reach it without too much trouble, and I dial her number.

Her phone rings three times, and I fear I will get the dreaded fourth-ring voicemail message. But just before the fourth ring begins, she answers. "Hello?"

"Genevieve? It's Tristan."

I can hear the smile in her voice right through the phone. "Couldn't bear to be away from me, huh?"

"Something like that." My words can't mask the profound pain I'm feeling, and she hears it.

"Something's wrong, isn't it?" she asks.

"It happened again. I got another ... message. More orders. And with it came a pain in my leg like nothing I've ever felt before. It's kept me trapped in the first floor of my house since yesterday evening."

"That's awful. What is it? What do they want you to do?"

"There's a church in northern Georgia, and there's going to be a fire in the middle of the night tonight, unless I can warn them. It's not arson, it's an accident, and I know how to prevent it."

"This late in the day, are you going to fly there? Will that stop the pain?"

"I'm not going."

"What?" I can hear the disbelief in her voice.

"I'm not going. I have to refuse this, otherwise I'm afraid this will be my life from now on. I'm sorry about what's going to happen to this church, but I have to make a stand and say no to this. If I can stand up to the forces that are compelling me, maybe they'll let me be."

"I—I don't know what to say. To me, the answer seems very easy: go and warn these people and you'll save a building and stop the pain you're feeling."

"Yes, on the surface, you're correct. Both of those things are true. But if I do that, it's like ... it's like I'm signing a contract that says they can use me whenever and however they want me."

She hesitates a moment before speaking again. "Yeah, I see what you mean, but I'm not entirely convinced that that's such a bad thing."

"If this was happening to *you*, could you uproot your life, give up everything you've worked for, just to help strangers because someone or something compels you to?"

"I'm sorry, Tristan. I know this isn't the answer you want to hear, but yes."

"Then you're a better person than I am."

"Don't say that."

"It's true. I'm not ready to hand my life over to a higher power to take control of me."

"Isn't that step one?" she asks, a hint of self-satisfied glibness in her tone.

"Oh, an addiction joke? Very clever, but I'm not an addict."

"Maybe you're just addicted to free will."

"I thought you were my phone-a-friend, someone who would understand what I'm going through."

"I *am* your friend, and while I can't completely understand what you're going through, I understand it well enough to know one thing: you're in agony right now, and you've been given the exact information about how to make it stop—and in doing that, you'll save a church from destruction. To me, that seems like an easy choice. Is it about money? Can you not afford to take a last-minute flight right now? Because I could lend you—"

I suppress a laugh, even through the pain. "No, it's not about money. But thank you. It's a matter of principle."

"Can't you at least call them?" she asks.

"Call who?"

"The church. To warn them by phone. Could you do that and still maintain your principles?" There is a moment of genuinely stunned silence from me. A very protracted moment, long enough that she actually has to say, "Hello?" to make sure I'm still there.

"Holy shit," I reply softly.

"What?"

"You're going to think I'm the biggest idiot in the world. The idea of phoning the church to warn them honestly never occurred to me."

"Really?"

"Really."

"How could it not occur to you?"

"I was so fixated in my mind on the idea of having to go there and warn them in person—with that being the only way to relieve the pain. I never even contemplated the possibility of phoning them."

"I've got an Internet connection open," she says. "What's the name of the church and the city and state?"

"United Assembly of God. Demeter, Georgia."

"Give me a sec." I hear her typing, and then she comes back with the phone number. "Call them, Tristan. Call them right now. See if it ends the pain. And if it does, I think you can live with making helpful phone calls for Jesus every now and then."

"I will. I'll call them. I can do that."

"Good. And call me later, once you know if you're going to be all right again."

"Genevieve, thank you. I ... I hope you don't think I'm completely incompetent mentally."

"Stop. These are extreme circumstances; I get that. Now hang up and call the damn church."

"I'll call you later."

Chapter 5

As SOON AS I hang up the phone, I pick it up again and dial the number Genevieve gave me. Are churches even open when it's not Sunday? Guess I'm about to find out. It takes a full five rings before I hear a woman's voice answer, "United Assembly of God, may I help you?"

"Yes, it's very important that I speak to Reverend Carson," I tell her, using the name of the minister I received in my vision.

"I'm sorry, sir, but he's left for the day. Can this wait until morning, or is there something I can help you with?"

"It's very urgent that I get a message to him today."

"I'd be happy to take that down for you. Who shall I tell him is calling?"

"That's not important. What's important is what I'm about to tell you, so please listen carefully. Your church is going to be consumed by fire tonight if you don't do what I say."

Several seconds of tense silence follow my announcement. I can hear the open line, so I know she hasn't hung up, but I've clearly left her speechless. Good, I suppose, given the importance of my warning. When at last she does speak, the fear in her voice is evident. "Please, there's no need to do this. We're good people; we don't want any trouble from anybody."

At this moment I realize that the combination of physical pain, sleeplessness, and the nature of my information make me sound exactly like a frustrated arsonist making a threat. I try to put her at ease. "No, no, you don't understand. It's not like that."

But by now the poor woman is near tears. "When we did the fundraiser for Christian orphans, we didn't intend to exclude children of other faiths.

There was just only so much money to go around. Please, you don't have to do this!"

This isn't going well. "Listen to me. I'm not going to burn down your church ..." I realize that I don't have too many good ways to follow up that sentence, but if anybody's going to believe the God angle, it's a church. So here goes. "God sent me a warning that there's going to be a fire tonight, but I know how to prevent it. All I need you to do ..."

It's as if she didn't hear me. At this point, short of kissing her on the forehead and telling her a bedtime story, I stand zero chance of appeasing her. "Please, sir, please. We all serve the same God, and I know in my heart that he wouldn't want you to do this."

Damn it, I suck at this. Okay, if she's only getting terrorist out of my message, then I can play terrorist. Maybe she'll listen. "All right. Remain calm and you stand a chance. God has told me there is one path to your salvation." *Am I really saying these words?* "Tonight, before midnight, you must go to your basement storage room and remove all file boxes containing records of your ... your ... sinful dealings. You must bring these upstairs to your ... you know ... main church room place. Where people meet. For church. Offer them up to the Lord and beg his forgiveness! Remember, you have until midnight. Signify to me that you understand."

Now sobbing openly, this unfortunate creature says, "I understand. Bring the files to the sanctuary by midnight."

"Yes!" I reply, feeling like the biggest dick in the world. "The sanctuary. That is the place I have declared. You have done well. Now go and do this thing ... that the Lord commands. And then ... lie down and rest ... and know that you have done good work."

I hang up the phone before she can even reply. What the hell did I just do? Did I really just place a call to a church and pretend to be an arsonist? Well, yes, but she gave me very little choice, didn't she? And at least I got the instructions across in a way that will let her prevent the fire from happening. Since I didn't leave my name, it'll just be treated as an anonymous call from an extremist group of religious fanatics who wanted to give the church a chance to redeem it—

Oh, fuck me—caller ID.

As I look at the phone in my hand, I see the lovely LCD screen with its record of the last three phone numbers to call me. The same sort of record, I now realize, that comes standard with damn near every phone in America these days, and will conveniently tell every law enforcement officer in Georgia where to find the anonymous arsonist who lives at my area code and phone number.

It takes me two full minutes of willing a panic attack not to start before I realize the one little detail that has eluded me since I finished the phone call: *my leg doesn't hurt.* When I embrace the full meaning of that realization, it stops me in my proverbial tracks. I touch my leg; it feels fine, better than fine. I actually start to giggle, a strange, humorless laugh that comes from a place I didn't know existed inside of me. The laughter continues—I don't even know how long. It could possibly have gone on for hours, were it not for the phone ringing in my hand.

That stops my laughing, evokes a brief but loud shriek, and—if I'm not mistaken—releases a little bit of liquid from a place I wish it had stayed. In the time it takes for the phone to ring a second time, a remarkable amount of thought goes through my head.

Holy shit holy shit how did they find me so fast? What do I do what do I do? Deny everything—you didn't make that call. What call? You've been home sick and asleep all day. A call from this number? Somebody must've been using rerouting technology. That sort of thing exists, right? I'm a respected businessman. Why would I want to call a church in Georgia?

"Hello?"

"Tristan, are you all right?"

Esteban. Resume heartbeat. "Yes, thank you, Esteban. I'm feeling much better. I must have over-exerted. But a day on the couch and some pain pills" *and the delivery of a portent of fiery doom* "have got me feeling much better. Thanks for checking in on me."

"I'm glad to hear it. Is there anything I can get you?"

"No, I should be fine. Did I miss anything important at school today?"

He laughs at my question. "Nah, the teacher was out, so we had a sub. That's always a goof-off day. I've got your homework assignments. I'll give them to you in the morning."

"Thanks for covering for me, friend."

"Just don't make a habit of it. I'm not sure I'm ready for the big chair."

Don't make a habit of it. It occurs to me as I end the call that I may have to do just that. If this is to be my new circumstances, will I still be able to remain the active CEO of a major corporation? I don't need the money; that's not an issue. It's a question of time and energy. If I do have to step down, Esteban is a logical successor, even if he doesn't realize it yet.

One step at a time; one step at a time. First to see if I can get off the couch.

I stand and walk without even the ghost of a pain. It's as if the last twenty-four hours never happened. I look up to face the purported whereabouts of my suspected tormentor. "You let me off the hook for a phone call? Why didn't you tell me that part in your big spooky vision? Would've saved us both a lot of grief."

As I place the phone back in its cradle, I think again about my carelessness in not blocking the caller ID. In fairness, I didn't expect to put on the persona of a terrorist. I thought it would be a simple exchange. I've got some helpful information that will save their building. Kind of like a crime-stopping tip. But it didn't work out that way. Who knows if they'll follow my instructions? Who knows if they'll follow up on the desperate stranger who called with such an ominous message? I could be preemptive and call the FBI and let them know what I've done. But no, that could raise too many questions. For now, I'll wait and decide what to do if they come to me.

The hours of the day pass in blissful silence. The phone does not ring, not even once. I call Genevieve back, letting her know what happened and thanking her for her idea. She receives my thanks gracefully, with a minimum of gloating, and wishes me a good night. And, truth be told, it is one. I take a much-needed shower. I make myself a simple but very satisfying dinner. I spend some time on the second floor of my house, primarily because I can. Then I spend some time in my living room, primarily because I want to.

In a quiet moment, I reflect again on my odyssey, especially the last several hours of it. Because I made a phone call, I may have saved a building. Underneath it all is a fundamental question that lacks a good answer: why do these obviously powerful forces need a person to stop these things from happening? If you have the strength to create the world, why not send a rainstorm to stop a fire or a temporary paralysis to stop a dangerous person with a gun? I try not to couch my question is the verbiage of "why me?" but rather in the more general "why *anyone?*" For now, I have to file this under "things I'm not allowed to know."

Is this my life now? My new calling? Two in a week feels like more than a coincidence. And the dream I had on the beach felt like more than just random scenes viewed from sleep. I was hesitant to do this if it meant chasing all over the country to deliver messages in person, but if I can make a phone call and have the same effect, that's not too much of a hassle. In fact, I could even get used to this hero thing.

By 9:30, I am ready for a good night's sleep. The previous night offered almost nothing in terms of useful rest, so I figure I'll make the most of my improved condition tonight. I'm perfectly willing to put this day behind me and face tomorrow refreshed and open-minded.

Tuesday, July 31, 2007

I awaken just after 6:30 in the morning, and I truly feel fine. Recovery from a natural injury to my leg of that intensity would leave me with days of lingering soreness, stiffness, and tingling, but right now, I feel like I could do a 5K.

After the morning ritual, I head downstairs and switch on CNN as I have a bowl of cereal. There's talk about the economy and Iraq. Ingmar Bergman has died, but he had a good life. I'm actually just about to turn the TV off when a segment catches my eye, and it actually makes me drop my spoon.

The correspondent is standing outside of a building that is smoldering. In the background, a few firefighters mill about, packing up their equipment. He reports, "In the small town of Demeter, Georgia, an overnight fire at the United Assembly of God Church caused thousands of dollars of damage." *What the fuck?* "But it is the circumstances surrounding the fire that have arson investigators scratching their heads and church officials searching for an explanation."

We cut to videotape of an interview from earlier this morning, in which the same reporter is talking to an older woman in front of the smoking building. He narrates the lead-in. "Yesterday afternoon, Doris Peterbaugh was in the church office, when she received a very strange phone call." *Her name is Doris. I like that. She sounded like a Doris.* My fuzzy feeling at this thought disappears immediately as the story continues with a grainy playback of the very call I placed—every word of it, complete with the little show-the-words-on-the-screen thing that newscasts do.

"Shit on a bagel, they got it on tape?" I exclaim, now wondering why I am not currently in federal custody.

Doris sheds some light. "Our phone system is hooked up to our computer, so I have a recording of every call. It's supposed to say where the call is coming from, but that part didn't work, so I have no idea."

The correspondent resumes his story. "The mysterious caller never identified himself or who he represented. Also unclear was the reason why the church would be given this warning, if the caller's intention was to burn the building to the ground, as retribution for some unspecified sin or wrongdoing."

We return to Doris, who explains, "He told me to go to the basement and put the file boxes in the sanctuary. I thought that was strange, but I didn't want to take chances, so I did what he said. Then I called our pastor and the police."

News guy again. "Police listened to the tape several times but were unable to identify much of any useful information from the voice. They suspect the caller is a white male, age twenty-five to forty-five, with no identifiable regional accent. But the strange story doesn't end there. Alerted to the possibility of arson, county officials stepped up police patrols at the church, even leaving a squad car parked there overnight. And while the fire did start in the church basement at approximately 1:55 a.m., there was no sign of a break-in or even the presence of a single individual on the premises. Investigators tracked the source of the fire to a faulty electrical box in the church basement, and what's more, they confirm that if the room had not been cleared of all of the file boxes that had been there earlier that day, the fire would likely have spread so quickly, it would have been nearly impossible to extinguish before it consumed the entire building."

So I did make a difference ...

"We may never know who placed the fateful call or what his motivation was to do so, but for the residents of Demeter, Georgia, one thing seems certain: forces beyond what can be explained were at work on this night. Phil Sikeston, CNN, Demeter, Georgia."

They cut back to the newsroom, where the anchor begins, "After the break, we'll take you to the Florida Keys to meet an adorable species of deer that may be facing extinction ..."

I turn off the TV and sit there in stunned silence for several minutes. CNN? I've been the CEO of a major corporation for a few years now, and I've never once been on CNN. But I make one phone call, rant like a crazy person for two minutes, scare the piss out of someone named Doris, and I'm in the morning report? How in the hell does that make anything resembling sense? I search for a handle on the moment, but it is in vain. Nothing I've experienced, nothing I've read, nothing I've ever learned can offer me a shred of understanding of my circumstances. All I know is, it's time to go to work.

An hour later, I am back in the familiar world of my company headquarters, where things by and large make sense. Every walk through the halls is a string of greetings from managers, colleagues, and front-liners who want to be seen greeting the boss. *Morning, sir. Hi, Mr. Shays. Morning, Tristan.* One of my managers even calls me "Admiral." I always get a secret smile out of that. I can't tell if he comes from a navy family or he's just a middle-aged *Star Trek* geek. It doesn't matter; I kinda like it.

Esteban catches up with me just before the door to my office and follows me in. "Welcome back," he says cordially. "You're looking well enough."

"Why, thank you. You too. Anything on fire this morning?"

"Literally, no. Figuratively, also no, I'm pleased to say." He hands me a small stack of papers. "Yesterday's D-16s, PPTs, quarter-to-dates, and perf reports. Everything's so normal, you should be a little nervous that we did so well without you."

"Well, I think I have you to thank for that, Mr. Padgett."

"You're very kind to say so, Mr. Shays."

I remember something. "Do I still have a meeting with Delgado today?"

"No, that's been moved to Thursday. Your schedule looks pretty clear for the day."

"Good to know." I settle in behind my desk and notice a certain look on Esteban's face, like there's something he's not telling me. I leave a nice big pocket of silence into which he can insert that something, but he doesn't take the bait. So it seems a little prodding is in order. "Esteban, is there something else?"

"Hmm? I don't think so."

"It's just that you have a look, and I can't quite place it. I'm no expert, but it resembles something you're eager to say, but you don't know how to start."

"Oh. Uhh, I don't know. Probably nothing."

"Go on," I say to him. "Probably nothing, *but* ..."

"But I was watching CNN this morning." *Oh, shit.* "And there was a story on that was very interesting."

"Was it about deer?" I ask. "Because I heard something about that, but I didn't get to see it."

He knows he's busted now, so he cuts right to it. "That was your voice on that recording."

"Recording?" I repeat, hoping to forestall the awkward conversation.

"From the church in Georgia. You know, the one that got the anonymous phone call warning them of danger before it occurred. On the same day you were bed-ridden ..."

"Couch-ridden, technically," I correct.

"For an entire day with a mysterious pain that seems to have gone away completely today. It happened again, didn't it?"

"Something ... out of the ordinary happened, yes. I don't know if I'm quite ready to classify it."

"Only this time it wasn't a friend you were warning. It was strangers four states away. You called that church."

"The identity of that caller was never revealed," I remind him.

"I don't get why you had to pretend to be a terrorist, though."

Okay, game's over. "I wasn't trying to. I was trying to deliver the message in a normal, friendly, non-scary way, but I was so tired and in so much pain, and so not good at doing this that it came across all ... arson-y. And that poor woman."

"Doris," he says.

"I know," I reply with a little smile. "Didn't she look like a Doris, too?"

"Yeah, kind of."

"Doris just ... freaked out and thought it was a threat. So I went with that. It worked ... kind of."

"So, is this … is this *you* now? Is this what you do? Deliver messages from God?"

"Nobody said anything about God. There's no burning bushes or any of that stuff. This could easily be the work of Satan or the United States government or the Shriners."

"Shriners?"

"Granted, it seems unlikely. But, knowing what you know of me, it could be argued that God seems unlikely too."

"How do you feel about this?" he asks in earnest, with a tone of compassion.

For a few seconds, I'm without an answer. "I don't even know. The one-word answer should be *honored,* and I guess to some extent I am. But mixed in with that are words like *annoyed, inconvenienced, used.* And you could throw in *pissed off,* with a side order of *scared shitless.* This falls on me now. If I don't give these warnings, people could die. *You* could have died."

"But because of you, I didn't."

"I know, and believe me, I'm very thankful that's the case, and more so because I was part of making that happen. But that's a lot of pressure. Send me these warnings and start the clock. Bring bad news to strangers? You know what they used to do to the messenger in ancient times."

"I've heard the saying, yeah. But these aren't ancient times."

"Very true. This is the age of the Internet and downloadable mp3s and online banking. It's not exactly prime time for messages of doom from on high."

He pauses to take it all in and then asks, "Can you refuse the job?"

"I tried that. You saw on the news how that turned out. It seems that I am theirs, as Tolkien put it, until my Lord release me or death take me."

"Let's hope for the former and not the latter."

"I need you to cover for me again today," I tell him quite suddenly, not exactly sure where this new notion comes from or even why. "I need to go back home in a couple of hours."

"But I thought you were feeling all right."

"I am. Never better. But I need to talk to the minister from that church, and I need the privacy of my own home. So I have to impose on you again. Will you do this for me?"

"Of course, whatever you need."

"Esteban, I don't know how this new situation of mine is going to impact my life. It may be a twice-a-year thing or it may be every day. If the time comes when I can't effectively run this company, I need to have someone in place who I know can do it. For my money, that's you." That announcement leaves him with a deer-in-headlights expression. "Don't worry, I'm not handing the reins over to you today. But I want you to know that if it happens, you're at the top of a very short list of people I'd trust."

"Thank you," he says quietly, his voice hollowed by what sounds like a mixture of honor and fear.

"Now, shoo. I've got some stuff I want to accomplish this morning. I'll stay until noon."

"Yes, sir."

"And, Esteban?"

He turns back to me. "Yes, sir?"

"My secret needs to be safe with you."

"It will be."

At midday, I grab a quick sandwich on the drive home and head back to Ocean City. Until the moment I informed Esteban of my intentions this morning, I really didn't intend on calling the United Assembly of God in Demeter, Georgia, and talking with Reverend Samuel Carson. And as I pull up to my home and go inside, I'm still not exactly sure what I hope to gain by doing so. Maybe I want to apologize or explain; maybe I want an explanation of what's happening to me. I just don't know. But something that feels like my own free will is telling me that I should call him.

In the living room, I find the church's number that I had scrawled in the depths of my pain. The number is legible, though barely recognizable as my handwriting. I remember to dial *67 first; I may have gotten lucky with their caller ID the first time, but I can't count on it happening twice. I dread the prospect of talking to Doris again, knowing that I owe her a colossal apology, so I take the coward's way out and decide to pretend to be someone else when she picks up. I even have an English accent standing by, just in case.

After three rings, I am surprised when a male voice answers, "United Assembly of God, may I help you?"

"Umm, yes," I reply, ditching the concept of the accent. "May I speak to Reverend Samuel Carson, please."

"This is Reverend Carson."

"Ah, I see. Good. Reverend Carson, I …" Just like that, the words fail me, reminding me that my motivation for this call is shaky at best. "I'm the …"

He helps me the rest of the way. "You're the man who called yesterday."

"Yes," I tell him quietly. "I am."

"Will you tell me your name?" he asks calmly.

"You can call me Thomas." *Not sure why.*

"You caused quite a stir here yesterday, Thomas. I suppose you know that."

"Yes, sir, I do. How is Doris doing today?"

"I gave her the day off. I think she needed it, given the circumstances. But I think she'll be all right."

"That's good," I answer. "I'm sorry I scared her. That wasn't my intention."

"Thomas, I really hope you called me today to talk about what your intentions were, because it's been a matter of considerable discussion. I've listened to the recording of your call many many times, and I don't have all the pieces to the puzzle."

"Neither do I, but I may be able to shed some light."

"Best I can figure," the minister continues, his gentle Southern drawl seeping into his voice as we talk, "you didn't set that fire. No one did. In fact, the more I listen to that recording, the more I think your intention was to prevent that fire from happening."

"That's correct. What else did you determine by listening to it?"

"I heard desperation in your voice, like a burden you had to relieve that was causing you emotional pain and maybe even some physical pain. And I think you intended to give your warning to us as a good citizen, with no malicious intent, but my office manager misunderstood your words early on, and you felt the best way to make her listen was to pretend to have some sinister purpose. You feel free to stop me if I've missed the mark."

"No, you're right on target. Every bit of it."

"I'm glad to hear that, Thomas. Because I'd hate to think that someone out there would want to burn our church down."

"Does it make things any better," I ask him, "knowing that it was actually God who wanted to burn it down?"

He reacts quickly and corrects me with just a hint of Southern preacher sharpness to his tone. "God didn't want this church to burn. If he had, he wouldn't have sent you to stop it from happening."

"You don't want to know how close I came to ignoring the warning. That was the pain and desperation you heard in my voice."

"And yet you called."

"Yes. Before you go thinking it was out of nobility, understand that it was a matter of self-preservation."

"I understand that," he replies. "The nobility is in making *this* call."

His answer is unexpected. "How do you figure?"

"You could very easily have left things as they stood last night. You made your call, you relieved your burden, and if you turned on the news this morning, you saw that your actions prevented a much worse catastrophe. But something honest and decent in you compelled you to call me again today, to make sure me and mine are all right. I appreciate this. It seems I've done a fairly decent job of discovering why you did this. The part that's still a puzzle to me is *how* you did this. I'd like to spend some time talking with you about that, if you're willing."

And so I open up to this stranger, sharing the details of my weeklong odyssey, changing the names to protect the innocent—or at least me. He listens without judging or interrupting as I go on for minute after minute. I've told this tale several times already, and each time sounds just as strange as the last. Finally, when he is convinced that my story is done, he speaks in a tone of gentleness and caring. "That's quite a tale, Thomas."

"It's all true, Reverend. I can't explain it, but I can assure you of its truth."

"I don't doubt you. I've been a minister for twenty-seven years. In that time, I've seen a lot of strange things. Wondrous things that the Lord has allowed man to do. I feel his hand in this. I feel him at work in what you're doing."

"I wish I could feel that too," I tell him.

"Are you a believer, son? Are you a Christian?"

"Raised that way, although the best I can cop to these days is agnostic."

"Every good Christian is an agnostic sometimes. That's why we call it faith and not knowledge. Can you see God's work in what you're doing?"

"I'm trying to, but all I feel is the pain. I'm afraid that the only reason I'm doing this is to stop that pain. To make myself feel better. That's not very Christian of me, is it?"

"We're allowed to look out for ourselves, Thomas."

"Tristan," I interrupt him. "It's ... Tristan." He can know.

"Tristan. The body is a temple, and we're commanded to care for that temple. In caring for yourself, in relieving that pain, you're given the divine gift of sacrifice for others. You saved your friend's life. You protected my church from harm. When you can turn your eye outward and look upon this as a blessing from God himself, then it will feel like a miracle. And though you have pain, still shall you walk. Though you are blinded by it, still shall you see. Though it weaken your very soul, still shall you be strong. For this is the gift of the Lord bestowed upon you, Tristan. Though you walk through the valley of the shadow of death, you will fear no evil."

I have no words in reply. After giving me a few seconds to try, he continues. "Why did you call me today?"

"I don't know."

"Yes you do. You just don't want to say it. Were you seeking forgiveness? Absolution? Guidance?"

"Yes. All of that, I think."

"Why seek that from me? We've never met. You don't know me."

"Because I've wronged you. And because you're a man of God."

"Then listen carefully, because what I'm about to tell you is everything you need to know. Are you ready?"

"Yes."

"You haven't wronged me; your warning prevented my church from burning to the ground. And yes, I am a man of God, but so are you, Tristan. I preach his Word, but you practice his work. So the next time you feel that pain afflict you, don't hesitate. Deliver your warning. Do whatever it takes to fulfill that divine mission. Go with God, Tristan. Because he certainly goes with you."

Chapter 6

WITH CONSIDERABLE RELIEF, I note that three whole days pass without even a glimmer of anything painful, visionary, or supernatural. My life is blissfully normal—much like it was just a week ago, a time that seems far away now, for some reason. During those days, I do anything I want to do—eat and drink, sleep normally, awaken when I should. I watch mindless things on TV, and I don't dread the broadcast of the news.

Reverend Carson's words did help me. He showed sympathy and understanding, even after the utter awfulness of my call. For that, I owe him, although he thinks he's in my debt. Even though I helped prevent a worse fire, I still consider the church call a failure. Because of my hesitance, combined with my lack of skill, the fire still started, and there was damage to the building.

It was the phone call; I'm sure of that now. I've had three days to mull it over, to relive it again and again in my head. I hear myself start to say all the right things, but then, once things start to veer out of my control, I just begin blathering, and poor Doris, who never asked to be a part of this, panics and assumes the worst. All because my stubborn resistance kept me from going there and telling them in person, so they could see my face, hear my words directly, and know that I was on a mission of care. Well, never again. If I get more visions—and by now, I'm fairly certain I will—I'll go to those places and talk to those people. Maybe they'll think I'm crazy, and maybe they won't listen. But maybe they will. Every person who does listen has another chance, a chance they wouldn't get if I hadn't been there.

Yes, it will impact my ability to do my job, but maybe it's time for me to step back, let someone else take charge of things for a while, until I get this whole thing figured out. That doesn't scare me as much as it should, so maybe it's a good idea.

The drive to work is uneventful this Thursday morning. It's hotter out than I like, close to ninety degrees, so the air conditioning in the car is cranked up. I have an important meeting this morning with a prospective client, so I forgo the usual commute music in favor of being alone with my thoughts to strategize. Phillip Delgado will be in my office, the man behind some of the most successful casinos in Atlantic City, and he wants to talk about using our LEDs to light a new 500 million-dollar resort. And that's just the beginning; if we get this contract, we can probably sign on for every new project he builds and even convince him to retrofit his existing properties with LED lighting to save energy and manpower. It's a very important meeting, so I've got my good suit on—the gray Armani with the white shirt and the royal purple tie, my favorite tie.

Esteban meets me in my office as soon as I arrive. We have an hour and a half to prepare for this meeting, and I absolutely want us on the same page every step of the way. "What've you got?" I ask him.

"My team compiled a complete proposal package for the new resort," he replies, "costing it out and comparing it to conventional lighting alternatives, based on the schematics and blueprints we got from Delgado's people. I have the five-year and ten-year projections for energy savings, the carbon footprint report, durability stats for every instrument we're proposing."

"Good, good."

"I've also worked up a proposal for retrofitting the Park Place Towers with our instruments, including the cost-versus-savings analysis, the tax benefits, and the proposed timelines."

"I like it. Now, little details. What's his wife's name?"

"Sheryl with an S," he answers.

"Children's names?"

"Anthony is fifteen, John is eleven, and little Ellie turns seven in August."

"You're good," I tell him with a little smile. "Favorite cuisine?"

"Spanish. Not Mexican, but authentic Spanish. So I have a reservation for lunch at 1:00 today at Gibraltar."

"Okay, good. Have you run intel on any other companies bidding for the contract?"

"It's in progress. I should have the information before we meet."

"Make sure you do. I want to go into this knowing who our competition is, if there even is any. I want this one, Esteban. Not only for the value of the contract itself, but to show the world that we can be the primary light source for a property this size."

"I think we have him. He's been in frequent communication with us, asking all the right questions. The meeting today should seal it. As long as we say and do all the right things, I really believe this contract will be ours."

We gather the remaining members of the team that will be at the meeting with us—two more vice presidents and two department managers. They report that there are actually two other companies competing for the contract, but neither of them is looking to light the property with LEDs. Through some industrial espionage that I don't know about and I don't want to know about, I learn that we are not the low bidder in initial cost, but the energy savings over five years makes us the most attractive package financially.

My office intercom beeps at 9:25, activating the speakerphone. "Yes, Kayla?" I call from the conference table.

The voice of my executive assistant sounds through the speaker. "Tristan, Mr. Delgado and his associates are in the lobby. Would you like me to send someone down to bring them up?"

"No, I'll get them myself, thanks."

"Very good." She disconnects the call.

I look to Esteban. "This is it."

"Shall we?" he asks.

"Let's do this."

I instruct the others to meet us in the sixth-floor conference room, as Esteban and I head down to reception to meet with the man I hope will be our new best friend. Waiting for us there is the man himself, one of the top power players in the country. Phillip Delgado, whose net holdings make me look like a welfare mother by comparison. With him are a man and two women, all vice presidents in his organization. We make the introductions and escort our guests upstairs, where the other members of our team greet our visitors. I've had the room stocked with water, coffee, and fruit.

The people are in place, the numbers are very solid. What could go wrong?

My answer comes just eleven minutes later, shortly after I start my initial presentation speech. Right about the time I get to the words, "something no other lighting manufacturer can provide," my concentration is shattered. The pain afflicts my head, and I feel as if a thousand needles have been inserted into my face and skull at the same time. *No, no—not now, not here!* But I can't will it away. The anguish continues, intensifying as each second passes.

I am dimly aware of the others in the room. All eyes were already on me, but now, their expressions turn from interest to concern. I can't hide this, and I can't continue speaking. Every word I had practiced and committed to memory is wiped from my conscious mind, clearing the way for the details that are sure to follow.

Esteban alone knows what is happening. "Tristan?" he says softly.

Phillip Delgado rises from his seat, asking, "Mr. Shays, are you all right?"

"Yes, I … I apologize, everyone. I hit my head at home this morning before coming to work, and I'm not feeling my best." *Not quite sure where that story came from, but it'll serve as an explanation without making me sound sickly, dying, or intoxicated.*

"Should we call an ambulance?" Delgado asks, with a tone of genuine sympathy.

"No, no. I'll be all right," I assure him. "If you would all excuse me for just a few minutes, I'll go to my office and lie down until the feeling passes. Fortunately, Mr. Padgett is ready and eager to tell you all the good things I was prepared to tell you. Esteban, would you do the honors?"

"Of course," he says, and from the look on his face, I know that he sees through my story.

I leave the room at a normal pace, but as soon as I am out of sight of them, the pain throws me against a wall of the corridor. I'm lucky no one is in the immediate area, because it looks, I am sure, like I'm being soundly beaten by an invisible assailant. *Got to get to my office. Got to write down whatever instructions I'm sent.*

Mercifully, I make it to the elevator without looking too defeated. I can't let too many employees see me in this condition. Male pride aside, if the admiral looks weak, the troops will either worry or mutiny. Neither benefits the company.

I enter my outer office looking as awful as I feel. Kayla stands up immediately. "Tristan, why aren't you in—"

Before she can even finish the sentence, I burst through the door to my inner office and throw myself down on the leather couch in the corner of the room. "Oh my God," she says, "you're sick. You're hurt! What happened?"

My answer comes through ragged breaths. "Quietly … please … speak quietly. Head hurts. Terrible pain."

"I have Tylenol," she says quickly.

"No. Beyond Tylenol. *Way* beyond Tylenol."

"What can I do? How can I help? Do you want me to get you to a doctor?"

"No, thank you." I struggle to catch my breath. I hate this, hate having my personal assistant see me in this diminished condition. But she's here, and she sees me, so she's in it now. And I realize that my vision is so blurred, I couldn't write if I had to. So I need her. "You can … help me."

"Anything. Just ask."

"I told you ... when you started ... that I'd never ask you to take ... dic—"

The pain stops my speech at this very unfortunate moment, and I see Kayla's face register surprise and alarm. Luckily, the rest of the word follows. "Tation." She looks relieved. "But I need you to write some things down for me now. Would you do that?"

"Of course."

"And Kayla ... you're going to hear some things. They'll ... sound strange ... but I need you to take them down exactly and not question until it's over, okay?"

"It's not your will, is it? You're not dying?"

"No, no. Please hurry ... get pen and paper."

She rushes to her desk to get the needed objects. Already in my mind, images are forming, images I will need if I am to complete the task that will end the pain I'm feeling. Moving faster than I've ever seen her move before, Kayla returns with a steno pad and a pen. She pulls a chair up next to the couch where I lie on my back, one of my hands covering my eyes to block the light that is drilling into my brain. With me on the couch and her in the chair, ready to take notes, I imagine I look like a psychiatric patient.

If the shoe fits, right?

"Okay," she says quietly, "I'm ready."

I close my eyes and prepare to receive the flood of images. The first word comes almost immediately. "Boston. Tomorrow, 11:35 a.m. The Museum of Natural History. Child abduction by a stranger. The child's name is Logan Mansfield, age ten. Lives with a single mother named Eileen Mansfield. Address 12288 Persephone Court, Boston. Go today. Warn the mother. Don't let Logan go on the field trip."

And just like that, the images and the instructions stop. The pain subsides a little, but not much. I close my eyes and maintain only dim consciousness of my surroundings. I hear Kayla get up from her chair and walk to the private bathroom in my office. She turns on the light but doesn't close the door. I hear water running for a few seconds, and then I hear her approach me again.

I'm briefly startled to feel a cold, wet washcloth placed over my forehead and my eyes. I start to sit up, but she holds me down gently with one hand. "Shh, shhhhh," she says softly. "It's okay. I got it all written down."

"You must ... have questions."

"I've been your assistant for three years. In that time, you've trusted me with the company's most sensitive information and materials. Part of the reason I'm good at this job is because I don't feel obligated to ask questions. What this stuff means is for you to understand."

"You're … too good to me."

"Quiet. Talking is bad for your head."

"Thank you."

"Just … be careful in Boston, please."

The last words I remember uttering in a fading whisper before consciousness leaves me are, "I promise."

I awaken disoriented, with the now-tepid washcloth still covering my eyes. I know I've slept, but I have no idea for how long. This concerns me, as my assignment is tomorrow, and out of state too. The pain is still there, but the feeling is dull enough that I remove the washcloth. "Holy shit!" I exclaim upon seeing Esteban in the chair that was formerly occupied by Kayla. This does nothing to subdue the pain, but I don't care. I sit up quickly.

"Sorry," he says. "Kayla had to work, so it was my turn to watch you."

"What time is it?" I ask him, looking outside at the daylight.

"It's 3:15."

"Oh my God—the rest of the meeting! I missed it. I missed lunch with them." I stand up, not quite sure what that will accomplish.

"Relax, relax, it's all right. I covered for you. It went very well. Delgado and his people have left."

"Damn it. I'm so sorry."

"They left with a contract in hand. He needs to show it to his legal team, but if everything clears, he wants to sign. I think we got it. I really do." For the first time, his face betrays a hint of a smile.

Mine follows suit. "You did it. Son of a gun. While I was flat on my back, you closed a multimillion-dollar deal for us."

"I'm not counting chickens yet, but it sure looks positive."

"Esteban, when this deal closes, I will see that you get a bonus deserving of this accomplishment. I can't thank you enough, and I can't apologize enough for having to leave."

He hesitates a moment before asking, "Was it … what I think it was?"

"Another assignment, yes. For tomorrow. In Boston, a child is going to be abducted while on a field trip to a museum, unless I can convince his mother not to let him go."

"*Dios mio,*" he says. "This is getting serious."

"Meaning it wasn't serious when your wife wanted to kill you?"

"Of course it was, but … I mean the rules are changing. You're being sent to different states to warn strangers, people you don't even know. Tristan, what if this takes over your life?"

"I don't know. It might. I just don't know. But I know that I can't run this company effectively while all of this is going on. I need to step down."

He stands up at this announcement. "The timing is all wrong. With the Delgado deal on the table, if you step down now, it'll make the *Journal*. There'll be rampant speculation, our stock will tumble, and Delgado's people will get the wrong impression."

"Or the right one," I offer.

"Either way, it's not a good move."

"I still have to do this. Let people know that I'm out of town on business. I'll check in as often as I can, but I won't be in the office. You run things in my absence."

He looks uncertain. "Are you sure that's a good idea?"

"After what you achieved today, I have no question. You can run this place, Esteban. You've proven that time and time again. Take care of things for me. You can call me anytime you have a question. But I know now that this is something I have to do."

"Please don't get hurt," he says. "A child abduction—there's a lot of things that can go wrong. Just don't get in the middle of it."

"I'll try my best. Besides, I'm supposed to warn the mother, stop her from letting her son go on the field trip tomorrow. If it goes well, I'm in and out before anything happens. How long does it take to drive from here to Boston?"

"About eight hours."

"Shit, that's too long. Even if I leave now, I won't get there until after 11:00, and I need to talk to the mother tonight."

"You could catch a commuter flight out of Wicomico Airport into Boston. Should be able to get you there in about two and a half hours."

"I guess I'll have to. Mind the store while I'm away."

"You got it."

"And thank you again for what I'm sure was a remarkable effort today."

"Go on, you're burning daylight. Get outta my office," he says with a little smile.

"Hey hey, watch that shit. Still mine for the moment."

With no additional fanfare, I head to the parking garage and drive the five miles to Wicomico Regional Airport. Much as I wish I had a corporate jet at my disposal, I'm not quite that given to gratuitous excess, so I'm forced to check the departures board. There is a commuter flight to Boston, but it doesn't leave until almost 8:00, so I head over to charters. The agent behind the desk looks up from his newspaper. "Help ya?"

"I need to charter a plane to Boston. Doesn't have to be big, but it has to be fast. I'll be the only passenger, and I'd like to leave as soon as possible."

"Fast means a Learjet. That'll run into some money."

"I'm not concerned about the price. Can you do it?"

He checks his computer screen and enters the details. "Yeah, I can get you out of here in the next twenty minutes. Have you there in about two hours."

"Great. What'll that cost?" I ask.

He types a little more. "That comes to thirty-six hundred."

"Dollars?" I ask in surprise.

"They *are* the accepted unit of currency," he replies. "If that's too rich for your blood, I'm showing seats available on the 7:55. Get you there by 11:15 p.m. for $166 plus tax."

I pull out my personal credit card and put it on the counter. "I'll take the charter."

He offers a smile that might actually be genuine. "Excellent choice, sir."

I've never been the only passenger on a plane before, and it's a little strange. The pilot greets me before we take off and escorts me out to the six-seater Learjet. Now safely in the air, I have a chance to relax for the first time in hours. The universe must be satisfied that I'm on my way to answer the call, because the pain in my head has subsided, allowing me to think about this—what? Mission? Assignment? "Quest" sounds medieval. We'll go with "task" for the moment, until something more heroic steps up to take its place.

The flight allows me the luxury of being able to work through some of the logistics. I'll get to Boston after dinnertime, rent a car. I've got the family's address and instructions to warn the mother; not the father, not the child. Just the mother. I don't know why, but I guess I'm not allowed to know why. The child shouldn't have to know that his life is in danger. If I do my job right, he'll go about his day and never know how close he came to being a statistic.

So I'll tell the mother. Eileen Mansfield. How do I put it into words? And what will she say in response? Will she thank me? Believe me? Slam the door and call the police? I have to remember that it's not about me. It's about protecting this child from a kidnapper. *Child abduction by a stranger.* Those were the words that Kayla wrote down from my instructions. A stranger. Not a relative denied custody, wanting to live with his child. Not a friend of the family with unsavory intentions. A stranger, choosing a victim out of a crowd. An opportunist, finding an easy target at a museum. But I'll deliver my message, and that target won't be there to abduct.

And then what?

It's not like Logan Mansfield will be the only child at that museum tomorrow. The kidnapper will still be there, still have the same intentions. He'll find a different victim.

"I have to stop him myself."

"I'm sorry, sir, what did you say?"

I realize I've said the words aloud when the cabin steward comes over to see what I need.

"Nothing, I was talking to myself. Sorry. Could I get a bottle of water, please?"

"Certainly. Flat or bubbly?"

"Flat is fine, thank you."

He returns a minute later with a bottle of Fiji, and as I crack it open and drink deeply, I realize how very thirsty I am. *Oh my God, I have to stop him. I can't just go to that house and warn that boy's mother. Even if she did believe me, it would raise too many questions, ones I can't even answer. I have to be at that museum tomorrow. I have to find the kidnapper, and I have to see to it that he's captured.*

As if to scold me, my head starts throbbing, but I fight it back. *No, no, fuck this! I know I'm right. I'm still going to save that boy, but I'm going to do it on my terms. And you can make my head rage with pain or kick me in the balls or step on my foot, but I'm doing this. Do you hear me? I'm doing this!*

I feel like my thoughts are screaming. Strangely, though, it works. The pain subsides as if it was turning and running away. I'll be at that museum tomorrow morning. I don't know the abductor's name or even what he looks like—but I do know what Logan Mansfield looks like. His face came to me along with my instructions. I need to find the man who's going to try to take him. Unfortunately, that means Logan has to be there as bait. So I won't go to 12288 Persephone Court. I'll get a hotel in Boston for the night and finalize my plans. All of which, I now realize, means I've just spent thirty-six hundred dollars on a private jet I didn't need.

"Well, shit," I mutter aloud.

"What was that, sir?" the steward asks.

"I said this is delicious. Could I have another one?"

After we land and I thank my crew, I get a rental car for a day—just basic transportation; it's not like I need a convertible or anything. I make my way to a three-star hotel about a mile from the museum and secure a room for one night. As soon as I get the room key, I find the concierge on duty. He greets me with a pleasant smile.

"Good evening, sir. How can I be of service?"

"I'm wondering if you could set me up with a couple of supplies for my room."

"Sure. What did you need?"

"I'd like to get a large pad of paper, preferably twenty-four by thirty-six or larger, some masking tape, and a thick black marker. I have to take some notes tonight for a presentation tomorrow. And if I could rent a laptop computer with Internet access, that'd be perfect."

"No problem. I'll send those right up. What room are you in?"

I look at the key envelope to remind me. "Looks like 416."

"Right away, sir."

I take the elevator to the fourth floor and enter the room, which is spacious and comfortable, with a pleasant view out the window. I have no luggage to unpack, which saves time but means that what I'm wearing now I'm wearing until I get home again tomorrow. That's okay; on the eighth day, God created Febreze.

Before I can ponder that thought further, there is a knock on my door. I open it to see a member of the hotel's staff holding my requested items. "Here you go, Mr. Shays," he says, and I'm impressed that he greets me by name.

"Thank you," I reply, handing him ten dollars. Good service, knows my name. Winning combination.

With no further delay, I open up the pad and the marker and begin to scrawl notes. Anything that might possibly be useful for tomorrow's assignment goes down on paper. It's too late to visit the museum tonight, much as I would like to. But fortunately, I find a map of the place online, and I sketch it thoroughly, detailing the layout of the various exhibits. Unfortunately, I don't know exactly where the abduction is going to take place. I know the time, 11:35 a.m. If I get there early enough, I should be able to find the class, find Logan, and stay with the group. I hope.

By midnight, the walls of my hotel room are plastered with pages from the pad. On each is a sketch or a map or a timeline or a bulleted list. I ignore no detail; this has to go perfectly. I'm already going against the specific instructions I was given—again—so to prove my worth, I have to make this come out better than it would have if I'd obeyed.

I have to admit that the planning process felt good. Employing my rational mind and attacking the details comes very naturally to me, and I feel like I have everything I need to intervene at that museum in the morning. The one detail I've not yet worked out is whether or not to bring the Boston police in on this. Their presence would certainly make me feel safer as I try to capture the kidnapper. But weighing heavily on my mind is the inevitable question, the one for which I have no answer: How did you know this was going to happen?

If this were a magical world full of elves and wizards, the answer would be easy. "It's simple, Officer. I receive visions of strangers in peril, and an overwhelming compulsion to warn them before it's too late." Sounds simple enough; it's a reasonable explanation, and my very presence at the scene suggests that it's true. Ah, but this isn't a magical world full of elves and wizards, so my explanation offers two other possibilities: crazy person or accomplice. Not wanting to be branded as either of those, I decide to leave the police out of it. If things get ugly at the museum, someone will have a cell phone and can call the police from there.

A yawn makes me realize just how long this day has been. I've done everything I can for now; it's time to get some sleep.

Mercifully, I am spared the dreams I was dreading before turning in. I was relatively sure I would be plagued by nightmares of reliving the assignment over and over, failing each time in a new and spectacular way. But I awaken at eight in the morning with no recollection of any such dreams. I actually feel refreshed this morning, and as I look at my self-made wallpaper all around the room, I'm struck with a confidence in my plan. I'm also struck by how very peculiar it would look to anyone who finds it, so I take great pains to shred each page and stuff it into the hotel's dumpster.

Equally noteworthy is the absence of pain in my head. By the strictest definition, I have rejected the exact terms of my assignment by not informing Eileen Mansfield last night. Whoever or whatever brought me here must have seen the complexity and sincerity of my revised plan and chose to spare me further agony. I try not to think what awaits me should plan B go awry. *Visualize success.*

Now all that remains is to be there, find the man, and stop him somehow. It could be dangerous. I'm putting myself at risk. *But why?* What's in this for me? Yes, there's the whole avoidance of agonizing pain thing, but I could have talked to the mother last night and been done with it. What's driving me to take this step? Is it about fame? Reward? Personal satisfaction? Helping other people? I'm not one of those people who dresses up in Spandex and runs around fighting crime, believing I'm some kind of superhero. *Super* aside, I don't even think I'm any kind of hero. Sure, I give generously to charities I believe in, but I don't think that qualifies. So what is it? Maybe I won't know until I finish what I have to do today.

The drive to the museum is short but exceptionally tense. With each passing block, the reality of the situation grows ever deeper. I wish I could take my pages of notes with me, but their sheer size makes that impossible. Having checked out of the hotel this morning, all I could do was study them one more time and then throw them away. Besides, no matter how good the notes, reality always has a way of demanding some improvisation.

I park the rental car in the museum's parking lot and make my way to the main entrance just before 10:00. I leave early to give myself extra time to get a feel for the actual place before anything happens. I can feel my pulse quickening with each step I take closer to the entrance. It's important that I don't look nervous; don't want to give off the wrong vibe when there's an actual predator on the premises.

"One adult," I say to the young woman behind the desk.

"Eleven dollars, please," she says pleasantly, and I hand her the cash. She gives me a receipt, a ticket, and an unnecessary map.

I may have thanked her; already I don't remember. I'm hyper-aware of my senses and my surroundings. Just past the ticket desk is the museum's main hall, home of a few dinosaur skeletons and stuffed mammals. The building is not overly crowded, as it would be on a weekend. There are a few school groups making their way through, as well as some single people, couples, and families.

As I proceed deeper into the building, I am relieved to see several security guards stationed throughout, and further pleased to note that each is packing a firearm at his side. With no police backup, it's good to know that some semblance of law enforcement is only a shout (or, if necessary, an emasculating shriek) away.

With more than an hour before the moment of truth, I decide that there's time to do a full walk-through of the building. I wish more than anything else that I knew exactly where the crime is going to take place, but because I'm going against orders, that information isn't available to me. So I'm left to look for a man whose appearance I don't know in a building consisting of twenty huge rooms. What could possibly go wrong?

Chapter 7

Museums fascinate me; always have. Whether they celebrate natural history, science and technology, the oceans, space, or the oddities of the world, I'm a rapt audience. Thus, it pains me a little to have to disregard so much of the bounty of wonder and information before me as I travel from exhibit to exhibit. I'd love to learn more about Himalayan mountain goats or the people of the Ituri Rainforest of Africa or early proto-mammals, but I don't have the luxury. Instead I'm concentrating on faces, trying to figure out which individual looks like he's here to steal a child.

Complicating the matter is the troublesome fact that I don't even know if the kidnapper is here yet. He may arrive a few minutes before 11:35, which would make it much harder to track him down. But no, odds are good he's arrived early, in plenty of time to stake things out on his own. *Think like he'd think.* Clothing—he'd want to look utterly forgettable. Nothing with splashy colors, corporate logos, or distinctive markings. Race—I heard once that criminals tend to hunt within their own race. Logan Mansfield is white, so most likely, the kidnapper is white. Age—that gets tougher. I don't even know if his intentions are sexual in nature. If so, he's probably young enough to engage in that behavior. An old, frail man wouldn't risk such a public abduction anyway, so we'll narrow it down to ages eighteen to sixty; still a very wide range of years to choose from. Does he look like a predator, or does he look like somebody's neighbor? Like the man who sells produce at the grocery store?

How do I find a man who doesn't want to be seen?

The minutes pass so slowly as I wait for something to happen. I have to at least make a show of looking at the exhibits, lest I be mistaken for having dishonorable intentions myself. But I am so distracted by my task, I can't really take in anything of informational value. Besides, my head is so full of notes from what I've prepared over the last day, I don't want to threaten it with new information.

At 11:00, I find myself back in the museum's main hall, and I watch as a group of about twenty students is led inside by a young female teacher. My heart races a bit as I realize—*it's them. Logan Mansfield's class is here.* Then I get a glimpse of him, the boy whose face was sent to me in the vision. He's with them, and he's safe, for now. The group is about an even mix of boys and girls, and their teacher appears to be the only adult chaperoning the group. She can't be older than twenty-five; she looks intelligent, kind of pretty. *Shit, focus … focus!*

It's too soon to make anything resembling a move. I need to wait until closer to 11:35. But I can follow the class from a distance, and I do. I have a small notepad and pen, so—in the guise of taking notes on the exhibits—I record details about every man who could possibly be my suspect. And there are so many. How many of them are looking at me as I follow a class of ten-year-olds and wonder the same thing about me? *Who watches the watchmen?* As if in answer, I look ahead and into the unblinking glass eyes of *Homo neanderthalensis,* who stares back as he scans a diorama landscape for predators.

You and me both, pal.

The class moves on, and at each glass display case, hands and faces and tummies press in tight, to get as close to the occupants as possible. I remain close enough to see and hear what transpires, but far enough away to stave off suspicion. I overhear enough to learn that the teacher's name is Miss Snyder, and she is indeed the only adult on the trip. As the minutes tick by and I find myself with eight possible suspects, I realize that the moment of truth is fast approaching, and despite all my planning, I still don't have an effective plan in place.

At 11:27, the group makes its way over to the restrooms and water fountain. I am about twenty feet away, still watching, and then I see him. While I cannot say with absolute certainty that the man I see is the kidnapper, the moment I spy his face, I'm overwhelmed with a feeling of icy familiarity— like I know him somehow. Yet, this is impossible, as I am equally certain we've never met. He sees me, and his eyes meet mine. His reaction will tell me everything I need to know.

For just a few seconds, he locks on to my face. I see a range of emotion— at least, I think I do—visit his features. It starts with surprise, but then a look of expectation replaces it. I'm at least twenty feet away from him, so I can't really be sure; but I still can't shake the feeling that I know him, that I've somehow known him all my life, like a dark figure from a nondescript but profoundly disturbing dream. By now, it's too late to try to avoid arousing the kidnapper's suspicion; what's most important is protecting these kids. It's time to do something.

I grab my wallet from my pocket and approach Miss Snyder, who stands outside the restrooms, waiting for the students inside. When I reach her, I open it long enough to flash my company photo ID badge before closing it and saying, "Miss Snyder, my name is Mark Smith. I'm an agent with Massachusetts Child Safety Services. Ma'am, I don't want to alarm you or the children, but my agency has been tracking the activities of a suspicious individual, and we have reason to believe that he's here at the museum today and may have an interest in one or more of your students."

"Oh my God," she says quietly, trying not to frighten her students. "What should I do?"

"The best thing to do would be to cut the field trip short and return to the school. That's what I'd recommend."

"Well, I would, of course," she says, fear starting to make her voice quiver, "but the bus has left, and it won't be back for over two hours."

Shit, I didn't count on that. Now what?

I catch the eye of a nearby museum security guard and wave him over. The man joins us and says, "Yes, sir? Can I help you?"

"Officer, I'm with a child safety advocacy group, and we believe one or more of Miss Snyder's students may be at risk here in the museum today. I'm working to track the suspect, but I need to do so without arousing too much suspicion or starting a panic. The students aren't able to leave the museum for a few hours. Could you arrange to have a docent accompany them to the exhibits, preferably a young man?"

"Yes."

"Excellent. And could you yourself remain in sight of them as they complete their tour?"

"I'll have to ask my supervisor, but I believe so."

"Very good. Would you make those arrangements, please?"

As the guard gets on his radio, I listen to myself saying these things, this pastiche of truth and falsehood, and I wonder where the words are coming from. Massachusetts Child Safety Services? What the hell is that? And why is no one asking to see a badge or any paperwork?

Rule number one of bullshit: look and sound like you belong there, and people usually won't ask questions.

As all this is happening, I look over at my suspected perpetrator, and I see him watching this added fuss with what appears to be consternation. Good;

consternation is good. It serves to suggest that I'm right. Maybe it'll dissuade him from trying anything.

The guard says to me, "I've got the approval to accompany the students, and one of our museum tour guides will be here in a minute to give the group a guided tour."

"Thank you," Miss Snyder replies with a sigh of obvious relief.

"What about you?" the guard asks me. "What will you do?"

"I'm watching a couple of suspects," I answer, not wanting to make him think that I've found exactly the person I'm looking for.

"Shall I call the police?" he asks.

"No," I reply quickly, but then say, "Actually, yes. Let them know what's happening, but don't have them come in until further notice. Please ask them to wait outside, and I'll try to flush the suspect out."

I'm forced to cut the conversation short, as I see my guy walking away from the general area of the group. As briefly as I can, I turn back to the teacher. "Stay close to the students and to the security guard. Officer, be vigilant. If something looks wrong, odds are good that it is."

Quickening my pace, I follow in the direction that the suspect went, toward the Animals of Africa room, a room filled with subdued light for dramatic effect. Swell.

I've done it. At least I *think* I've done it; it seems that Logan Mansfield is safe from this kidnapper. The man would have to be suicidal to risk approaching the school group now. But there's still my earlier suspicion that he's an opportunist, and another victim would serve him just as well. So now I have to follow him, having dispatched a willing security guard to help someone else. It's time to end this, one way or another.

He goes to a far corner of the room. I watch from a distance as he lingers too near a girl of about twelve, alone. I see him stare at her, with a fascination both ancient and deviant. Now I'm close enough to see him clearly. He's in his forties, dressed—as I suspected—in nondescript shirt and slacks, muted earth tones. He looks clean and well attended to, like he could be anyone. Someone you'd see for a second and forget just as quickly. But in the recesses of my mind, his image burns like something unspeakably evil, even more evil than the act he intends to commit.

Cautiously I approach. Fifteen feet away; twelve; ten; eight. Close enough. This is the moment, but how will it go down? His back is to me, as he is still watching the substitute victim he has scouted. Do I tackle him? Grab him and immobilize him until help arrives? I have to do *something*.

"Hey!" It is a single word, a warning. I am surprised to realize that it is I myself who have uttered it. I only hope that I don't look too stupid as he turns around at the sound of my voice. "Let her go."

The girl, witnessing this, now seems to realize her plight, and she makes a hasty exit from the room. This, combined with my verbalizations, has drawn the attention of the few museum guests in this exhibit hall. More attention is better at this point, so I decide to raise the stakes. "I'm with the FBI," I announce to the onlookers. *It's only a felony if I get caught, after all.* "I'm here to take this man into custody. I need someone to go alert museum security that the suspect is here with me, and I need some assistance."

That about does it. Everyone but him clears the room. He faces me with no fear evident on his expression. "FBI?" he says disdainfully, with a look that resembles disappointment. "Lies make the baby Jesus cry, you know."

"What makes you think I'm lying?" I ask, internally terrified but refusing to show it.

"It's what you do. It's who you are."

"I know why you're here," I tell him. "I know about your plan to take Logan Mansfield."

"Of course you do." It's not a sarcastic response, but a proclamation which suggests that my statement is obvious. "What's the matter? Mommy didn't believe your warning and sent the little tyke anyway?"

This is the moment when it truly gets weird. His question suggests that he knows of my mission—and more, my deviation from it. I have to get him off this line of thinking. "I've been tracking you for weeks. The whole agency has. Your face is plastered all over the state. Police are outside. Come along quietly and you've got a chance at a deal."

"Oh, spare me the bullshit! There's no agency. I'd be hugely surprised if there's even police waiting. Hardly your style. Where's your friend, anyway? Guarding the exit, in case I make a break for it?"

I assume he's referring to the security guard. Freaked out as I'm feeling, I want to keep up an air of control, so I reply as confidently as I can muster, "He's out there. Right where he needs to be."

The man smiles oddly at this. "*He?* Don't let her hear you say that. With a body like that, I suspect she'd be pretty offended." All I can offer is a look of confusion. *What the hell is he talking about? Genevieve? That doesn't make any sense; there's no way he could ever have seen her.* My expression gives away too much, and I lose the control I need. "You're alone," he continues in a tone of delighted realization. "Of course. It's 2007. You haven't even— Oh, this is rich." A bit of mockery enters his voice. "I'm not your *first,* am I? That would be so special. I should make a speech or something."

My shit is officially wigged. All I can ask is, "What is this? Who are you?"

"You don't *know.* I love it. Here I thought you'd found me at the height of everything, her by your side, you all full of yourself. But you don't even know who I am. And I am *loving* this."

"Tell me!" The anger building in me won't be denied.

"No, no. Not yet. There'll be time. Many times. Different places, different circumstances. But many chances." He hesitates and looks into my eyes—drills into them with his own—and I see the strangest combination in his features. Hatred; contempt; disdain; and yet, I'd swear I see respect there as well.

Her by your side. Her ... who?

"Our first meeting," he says with something that, puzzlingly, sounds like nostalgia.

"Correction," I counter. "Our last meeting. It's over."

He laughs at this. "Oh, Tristan, you don't know how wrong you are."

"How do you know who I am?" I demand.

"It's simple," he says. "I'm standing over you when you take your last breath."

His words are utterly without humor or irony, and they are enough to freeze the blood flowing within me. I can't speak, can't move, overwhelmed as I am at what he has just told me. Before I can begin to make sense of it, there is a loud click and all the lights in the museum go out. In the second or two before the backup lights turn on, a horrible sound fills the place—a mechanical howling sound, endless and repetitive. *The fire alarm.*

I look for the man, who seconds ago was just a few feet away, but amid the darkness and noise, I can't see him anywhere. Moments later, to my horror, I hear him whisper in my ear, "Till next time."

I have an enemy. Worse, I have an enemy who knows me, while I don't know the first thing about him. An enemy who knows who I am, knows about allies I haven't even met, apparently. An enemy who will watch me die. How is that even possible? How can he know things about my future? I realize this question feels a bit absurd after everything that's happened to me already, but it defies everything I know and understand about the world. Time is linear; the future isn't written yet. *Is it?*

I keep harking back to his words: *her by your side.* But who is she? A partner? A wife? "Sidekick" makes me sound like Batman, so I dismiss that one. These unanswerable questions rattle through my mind on a very inexpensive, very regularly scheduled flight from Boston to Baltimore this evening. After the alarm sounded at the museum and my quarry escaped my sight, I joined the rest of the guests in exiting the building. I searched for him for twenty minutes, but he was long gone. Something tells me he orchestrated the darkness and the noise somehow, to cover his escape. Outside in the parking lot, police and firefighters were plentiful, and I was alone—with no suspect and a lot of unanswerable questions. I had done what I came here to do: protect Logan Mansfield from a kidnapper. Now it's time to come home.

Sitting in the plane, staring absently out the window, I have to wonder if Logan was ever really in danger. Was he just bait? A way to lure me there, so this man could—what? Kill me? Not from the way he was speaking. He said he would be there when I die, but he didn't speak like today was that day. What, then? Meet me? I was encountering him for the first time, but he certainly wasn't encountering me for the first time. His tone said that we'd met before, maybe even that I'd defeated him.

Defeated him. The very words sound preposterous. Two weeks ago, I was living a normal life, running a successful business, and the worst pain I had experienced was at the dentist's office. Now I have a fucking nemesis apparently, with whom I've had spectacular battles that haven't even happened yet. Where does a person go to get a handle on that kind of situation? The answer is obvious, of course, but I have to wait until we land before I can call.

As soon as wheels touch tarmac and the flight attendant tells us we can use our cell phones, I am dialing. "Genevieve? It's Tristan. Something's happened; things I can't explain. If I buy you an airline ticket, can you come to Maryland this weekend and spend a couple of days with me? I really need your guidance."

SATURDAY, AUGUST 4, 2007

Genevieve catches an early-morning flight to Baltimore and then a commuter plane to Wicomico. At 10:30 in the morning, I stand on the tarmac, watching her plane come in. It taxis to a stop, and the crew lowers the staircase. A few people deplane, and then I see her stand at the top of the stairs for a moment; she looks around and sees me, and she shields her eyes from the sun with one hand and gives a big, exaggerated wave with the other. My heart actually flutters a little. She's positively adorable.

I approach the plane as she's retrieving her overnight bag from beside the cargo hold. "Welcome to Maryland," I offer warmly.

Without hesitation, she throws her arms around me, a feeling I very much need right now. "It's so good to see you," she says. "I'm glad you invited me. Next-day flight couldn't have been cheap, though. I hope it wasn't too expensive."

"I wouldn't worry," I reply. "You're here. That's worth every penny and more." I grab her bag and begin to walk toward the parking lot as she follows about a pace behind. "I think we may have caught a break from the heat today."

On the half-hour drive to Ocean City, I ask her about how her week has been. I don't want to launch into mine until we're back at the house; I'll need time, and room to pace as I talk. She's more than happy to talk about the past seven days, and I listen with genuine interest, even though I have more on my mind than I've ever had on my mind before.

As we draw to within a mile of my home, I recall that I haven't yet told her the details of my work or my home life. Now seems as good a time as any. "Genevieve, I wasn't entirely forthcoming about how I live when we talked last weekend."

"It's okay if your place is a mess. I understand the life of a bachelor."

"Yeah, that's not exactly where I was going with this."

As we pull into the driveway, I watch as her face goes pale at first sight of the house. I think her jaw drops just a little. "Is there something you wanted to tell me?" she asks quietly.

We get out of the car, and she continues to stare up at the house in disbelief. "It's not something that's easy to talk about, the first time I meet someone," I explain. "People sometimes get the wrong idea. I'm sorry I kept this from you," I tell her, opening the front door.

She stares in wonder at the front room for a moment, before replying, "Apology accepted." I lead the way and she follows me. "So now comes the part where you tell me who you really are."

"I'm who I said I am. The part I left out is that I'm the owner and CEO of Shays Diode. My father invented the LED, and I'm running the company now that he's gone. So you see, your airline ticket was not a hardship."

I watch as she wrestles with her emotions. "You could have told me about this last weekend. It wouldn't have changed how I feel about you."

"I know that now. Please understand, it wasn't a judgment of you in any way. I'm just … very private when it comes to talking about myself. Believe me, if I didn't want you to know this, I wouldn't have brought you here."

"Okay."

"So, am I forgiven?"

"No. Because you're right; there's nothing to forgive."

"Good," I answer with a smile. "So, here's what I'm thinking. It's a pretty day, and in my refrigerator I have salad and wine and cheese. I'd really enjoy going out to have lunch with you on the beach."

"Private beach?" she asks with a slight smile.

"Of course!"

"You've got a deal."

I put together our makeshift picnic—I say *makeshift* to imply spontaneity, knowing full well that I orchestrated all the ingredients early this morning—and bring everything down to the beach. Genevieve brings the blanket, and we find a peaceful spot far enough from the water that each new wave won't soak us. Once all the components are in place and the wine is poured, Genevieve takes a deep breath and says, "Okay, now tell me everything that's happened."

And I do. I recount the events of the past week in great detail, focusing on the assignment and my excursion to the museum. She listens attentively without interrupting and with no visible signs—God bless her—of disbelief. Precisely the reason I chose her to consult with about this whole thing. Once the details are out in the open, she remains silent for several seconds, taking it all in. The first word out of her mouth, understandably, is "Wow."

"Wow as in 'seek a mental health professional at once'?" I ask.

"No, wow as in 'you've had a strange and amazing experience that I'm trying to wrap my brain around.'"

"Well, that's a start. So you don't think I imagined the whole thing?"

"I don't see how you could have. You were in that museum. You talked to other people; security videos would back up your claim. This man, whoever he is, was there with you, and I'm sure he said all the things you heard him say. One thing I've learned about this world of ours, Tristan: just because something sounds unbelievable doesn't mean it's impossible."

"Thank you for that. It's what I needed to hear."

"There's some bits of it I can't work out yet, though."

"Talk them out with me," I reply. "Let's brainstorm this. Between the two of us, we might be able to make a little sense of it."

"For me, the two big questions are who is he, and what does he want with you."

"I've got two others of my own," I tell her. "How does he know me, and how did he do that?"

"Also good questions. Your two are tied to my two. Once we know who he is, we might be able to find out how he knows you. Once we figure out what he wants with you, it could lead us to how he did that. Bizarre as it sounds, the words 'time traveler' come to my mind. He sure sounds like he showed up from your future."

"I thought about that, but it seems to me—and I can't believe I'm saying this—that a time traveler from the future would have a better account of what's happened in the past. The way he talked to me—it was like he was surprised that I didn't know him; like he's remembering things out of order."

"I see your point," she says, "but if we remove 'time traveler' from the table, what does that leave in terms of options for an explanation?"

"Yeah, I haven't worked that part out yet. I don't have a great answer. Maybe … well, you know how I get visions of things to come, and I'm supposed to go and warn people before they get into trouble? Maybe he's got a similar situation—he can see things in the future, but instead of warning people, he chooses to mess with them."

"Could be. Go on."

"So, he and I both get a message that there's a ten-year-old boy who's going to be kidnapped at a museum in Boston at 11:35 on a Friday morning. I drop everything to go to that museum and prevent it from happening. *He* goes to that museum to make it happen."

She looks intrigued. "I like it, but I'm finding one possible flaw in the theory: why would a supernatural force for good go to the trouble of sending two of you, working at exactly opposite purposes?"

"Who says we're being sent by the same force?"

The question is as sobering to me as I imagine it is to her. "Shit," she says. "Does that mean what I think it means?"

I down some wine before replying, "It suggests a God figure and a devil figure, duking it out, with earthbound assistants caught in the middle, doing their dirty work. Is *this* what I have to look forward to? Someone standing in my way every time I go to help somebody?"

"That would suck."

I stand up quite suddenly and take a few steps toward the water. Seconds later, I feel Genevieve standing behind me. "I can't do this," I tell her. "I'm fighting the devil now? I can't. It's just—it's not who I am."

From behind, she puts her arms around my shoulders and just holds me. "We don't know anything for certain," she says gently. "That's a very big conclusion to jump to. It's just one possibility, and not even a likely one. I've seen and heard a lot of things in my time, and I've never found any good evidence that the devil even exists."

"Then what is this? Who is he, and why is he doing this?"

"I don't know. But I brought some of my psychic-girl stuff, and we can see if there's a way to find out." She turns me to face her. "For right now, I want you to show me your house and your town and anything else you want to show me. I want you to put this all aside and be *you* for a little while. Will you do that for me?"

I kiss her for the first time in a week; it feels wondrous. "Yes. I'll do that for you."

We start with a tour of the house, which to me is just a house, but to Genevieve is a very big deal. I'm gently embarrassed by this; the last thing I want to do is show off. But she takes it in stride and tells me not to be ashamed of the benefits of my success. Fair enough.

Next we take a drive along the coast, and I show her the rest of Ocean City. It's a beautiful day and the car windows are wide open; it makes me wish I had a convertible. Someday, maybe. I truly let my mind depart from the very serious thoughts that have plagued me for the past two weeks. The more time I spend with Genevieve, the more entranced by her I become. I'm ashamed to admit that I did initially have my doubts about her because of her occupation, but she's proving to be sophisticated, intelligent, funny, and very caring. My attraction to her grows stronger by the hour.

We haven't discussed what happens tonight; I declined her advances last weekend with the excuse that I didn't want it to feel like a one-night stand. But now she's back, and it's clearly not a one-night stand. Could I sleep with her tonight? I imagine she'd accept the gentlest offer. Still, I've never had sex with someone I didn't love. I don't *think* I love her. I think I could someday, but is that enough to put aside my—

"Yoo-hoo."

Her voice snaps me out of my thoughts. "Yes?"

"You got quiet there. I wanted to make sure you were still with me. Since, you know, you're driving and all."

"Oh, I'm still with you. Thinking about you, as a matter of fact."

"Lost in thought over little me? I feel special."

"Well, good. You *are* special. I was just wondering how long you can stay."

"I have to be back at work on Monday," she says, "but I'd love to spend the night, if you'll have me."

Curious choice of verb. "Of course. I know a wonderful place for Sunday brunch tomorrow."

"Sounds great. Where are we headed now?"

"Salisbury. I want to show you my office, if that wouldn't bore you to tears."

"I'll suppress them as a matter of courtesy. Lead on."

As we pull up to the building twenty minutes later, she marvels at the size of the place. "All this from LEDs?"

"All this. My father's invention has served me well."

"I'd say so. Are we gonna raise any eyebrows if you walk in with me?"

I smile a bit at her very valid question. "I'll take my chances."

We enter the building, which is sparsely populated for a Saturday. I'm not a huge fan of overtime when we're running on schedule and according to plan. But a few people are in, doing their thing, and they greet me as I pass in the corridors.

"Afternoon, sir."

"Afternoon."

"Hi, Mr. Shays."

"Hi, good to see you."

"Afternoon, Admiral."

"How are you?"

Genevieve turns to me, holding back a little smile. "Admiral?"

"Long story."

"Well, aye-aye, sir. You'll have to tell me that one later."

We take the elevator up, and I lead her into my office. To my surprise, Kayla is at her desk. She appears equally surprised to see me. "Tristan, I didn't know you were coming in today."

"Neither did I," I reply.

"How was that thing you did in Boston? Did it go okay?"

"I think it did, yes." I'm forgetting my manners. Introductions. "This is Kayla Reilly, my executive assistant. Kayla, this is my friend, Genevieve Swan, who's visiting from Virginia for the weekend."

"Nice to meet you," Kayla says to her, and I'd swear I catch the briefest hint of a *who's-this-then?* expression cross her face.

"And you as well," Genevieve replies.

"Anything going on that I should know about?" I inquire.

"Nothing out of the ordinary, but I'm glad you're here. You got a voicemail this morning—early, before I got here. I saved the recording. There was no name, no number on the caller ID. Just a message. It sounds like the caller knows you, though."

With a few keystrokes, she pulls up the recording on her computer and plays it through the speakers. In seconds, I know the voice.

"Good morning, Tristan. It was good to see you yesterday. You're looking so youthful. I have to apologize for my rudeness in leaving so quickly. I had hoped we could spend some more time together, this being such a momentous occasion. But things didn't go exactly according to your plan, as you know. Don't worry; we'll meet again soon. See you then."

All I can do is stare at a fixed point in space. I stand there—I don't know how long—until Kayla breaks the silence. "Do you know who he is?"

"Not exactly, no."

"Do you want me to delete the message?"

"No, e-mail it to me. Business and personal addresses. I want to refer to it later."

She sends the e-mail and then asks, "Is … is everything okay?"

"I wish I knew."

The rest of the visit is brief and quiet. The voicemail is as disturbing to me as the encounter at the museum. He knows where to find me; he knows so much about me. And always that calm about him, that terrifying calm.

Arriving back at the house, I enter, with Genevieve a step behind me. Courtesy has eluded me, and she knows it. "Tristan, talk to me. You barely said a word all the way back here."

"I don't know what to say. I'm scared, and in trying to be rugged and not show that in front of you, it's turned me silent and sullen and unpleasant. I'm sorry about that."

"It's all right to be scared. I don't think less of you because of it. It's a frightening situation."

"I just want to know who he is."

She goes to her overnight bag on the living room chair, unzips it, and pulls out a short rectangular box. "Then let's find out."

"A Ouija board?" The disdain is obvious in my voice.

"With everything you've been through, it's a bit late for skepticism. Now, you can try this with me, and maybe we can learn something about your mystery man, or you can doubt it and go on wondering."

"Okay, let's try this."

She opens the box and puts the familiar-looking board on my dining room table. At the top two corners are the words Yes and No. The bottom two are occupied by Hello and Good-bye. In the middle are all twenty-six letters of the alphabet above the numerals zero through nine. Onto the board she places the planchette, a wooden device in the shape of an oak leaf, with a glass window in its center.

I have never used a Ouija board, but I'm familiar with the basic premise. Two people put their fingertips on the planchette and open their minds to the influence of outside forces, which move it around the board. Users can ask questions and get answers from the spirit world. Fundamentalist groups love to decry it as an instrument of the devil. I'm more fond of the theory that one of the two users manipulates the device via wishful thinking to spell out what the group wants to hear. But I'm willing to give it a try. I don't think Genevieve wants to deceive or mislead me, so I figure the worst that'll happen will be that the thing sits there and does nothing.

We sit next to each other at the table, with the board in front of us. "You know what to do?" she asks.

"I put my fingers on your thingie and let my mind go blank."

"No, that's later, if you ask nicely. For now, you rest your fingertips on the edge of the planchette, while I rest mine on the other edge. Open up your mind to all thoughts, and let yourself lose the sensation that you're touching it. You'll feel it start to move. Don't fight it, and don't try to influence where it goes. It may spell things out. Even if you know what's coming, don't consciously go to a specific letter. Let the board do the work. Even if it spells T-R-I-S-T-A, don't move toward the N. Okay?"

"All right. I don't know about this, though."

"Then I'll make a believer out of you. Here we go. Put your fingers on it."

We both touch the controller, and Genevieve speaks aloud in her best psychic-y voice. I know it seems silly to doubt when I've already received the kind of messages I've received, but this feels damned weird. "Spirits that dwell beyond this world, we come to you seeking knowledge. We apologize for disturbing you, and we humbly thank you for speaking with us today. If there is one among you who will join our realm, please send us a sign."

Before I can even work to suppress the witty comments I'm developing, I feel the device move beneath my fingers. I give Genevieve a look that asks *Are you doing this?* and she shakes her head no. The planchette moves over the word *Hello.*

"We welcome you," she continues, "and we ask you this question: Who is the man stalking Tristan?"

For many seconds, nothing happens. We both sit there with our fingers on the device, waiting for any sign, any answer. After almost a full minute, when I'm just about certain it won't work, I feel it begin to move again. It slides as if it is on a cushion of air, stopping at the letter E. A second or two later, it moves again, this time to P. I know for a fact that I am not consciously moving it. It travels to H. Genevieve closes her eyes and begins reciting words I can't make out; this confirms that she's not actively manipulating it. The planchette stops on R. Seconds later, it moves over to A. Ephram Zimbalist Jr. is stalking me? No, that's not even the right spelling. It continues on to the letter I and then almost immediately to the M, where it stops.

Genevieve opens her eyes as I say aloud, "Ephraim? That's his name?"

Though I am asking her, I react with surprise when the device scoots over to Yes.

"Who is he?" I ask. "What does he want?"

My heart sinks a bit as the pointer scoots swiftly over to the word Goodbye.

"Wait! Don't go yet! I have more questions." I look to Genevieve for hope, but she just shakes her head a little.

"That's all they'll say," she tells me. "For whatever reason, they know his name, but they won't tell you more about him."

"That's bullshit!"

"Tristan, please. There are very powerful forces at work here. We don't want to risk offending them."

"But I'm no better off than I was. All I have is a first name? That doesn't tell me anything important."

"Try to calm down. You're very agitated."

"Yes, I'm agitated. I tried this Ouija thing, and all it gave me was a lousy, useless name. I'm frustrated, and my back hurts from sitting in this chair."

"Why don't you move to the couch."

"My back hurts a lot, actually. Almost like …" As I stand up to make my way to the couch, the pain hits with full force, shooting up and down my spine with enough intensity to throw me to the ground, rolling in agony. I am dimly aware of Genevieve rising to try to help me, and the look of fear and confusion on her face.

"Oh my God, Tristan! What's happening? What's going on?"

I'm barely able to get a few words out. "Get … pen … and paper. Take … this … down."

She rushes to the kitchen to find something to write with and to write on. I'm still on the dining room floor when she returns. "I've got it," she says. "Tell me whatever I need to write."

Once again, far too soon for my taste, the images return. As clearly as I see them in my mind, I describe them aloud. "Washington, DC. Dulles International Airport. Sunday, 1:45 p.m. Consolidated Airlines, flight 9526. Sixty-three people on board. Mostly children. Refugees from the flooding in Haiti. They're going to a relief agency in Miami. But something's wrong … a mechanical failure. The plane will crash on takeoff, and sixty-two people will die."

The pain becomes too much, and I can't say anything more of what I've seen. Instead, I just close my eyes and lie there, trying to regain my strength. Genevieve puts the pad and pen down and begins to stroke my forehead. I open my eyes a little to take in her blurry form as I offer a wan smile. "Aren't you … glad you … came … for the weekend?"

She laughs a little at this, even as tears form in her eyes. "Yes. I *am* glad. I needed to see this, to see what you go through when this happens. Now I know."

"Lucky you."

"How can I help?" she asks.

"Supporting me as I get to the couch would make you my very best friend."

She helps me to my knees and then to my feet, and together we get me to the couch, where I lie flat on my back, in a position that yields, if not comfort, at least reduced agony.

"How long will you hurt like this?"

"Until I accept the assignment."

"Okay. I'll bring you the phone, and you'll call whoever you need to call."

"No," I reply, "no calls. It didn't work with the church, and this is far too important. I have to be at that airport tomorrow afternoon. I have to warn them in person."

"But that's a three-hour drive."

"Two and a half if I speed."

"That means you're going to be in pain all night."

"Some, yes."

"That's awful," she says. "Because I had some really amazing things I wanted to do to you."

"Yeah, just my luck. There are some really amazing things I would have let you do to me."

She holds my hand. "I'll stay by your side all night. Anything you need, just ask me."

Chapter 8

I ᴀᴡᴀᴋᴇɴ ᴇᴀʀʟʏ Sᴜɴᴅᴀʏ morning feeling a bit disoriented. Memories of the night before are clear, but the fatigue and discomfort are not being kind to my poor brain. It takes me a moment to realize that I am still on the living room sofa, still dressed in the clothes I wore yesterday. Looking down, I see Genevieve seated on the floor in front of the sofa, resting her head next to me. *She didn't leave my side.*

My stirring rouses her, and she looks around, doubly disoriented I'm sure at being on the floor of someone else's living room. "Are you all right?" she asks.

"I'm tired, but I'm okay. Did you get any sleep?"

"Some. I wanted to be alert in case you needed anything."

I sit up enough to position myself so I can kiss her. "You are everything I needed, and I am sorrier than you can possibly know that I wasn't able to make last night more special for you."

"Tristan, you don't have to apologize."

"The apology isn't entirely altruistic. I'm sorry for what I missed out on too. But if you can take a rain check until the next time we see each other, I will make it up to you."

"Are you still in pain?" she asks, watching as I struggle to stand.

"Not as bad as last night, but still not great. They need to be sure that I'm accepting my assignment before they let me be."

"They?"

"My employers, whoever they are. They're not big on introductions."

"So do we have time to get some breakfast before we go to Washington?"

"*We?*" I repeat.

91

"Yes, I'm going with you."

"We've talked about this. It could be very dangerous, and I don't want to risk you getting hurt."

"Stop and think about this from a practical standpoint. I have to go home today anyway, and I don't have a return ticket yet. You've got a three-hour drive, and you're still not out of pain. It makes the most sense for me to go with you to the airport. Once we're there, if you want my help with this, I'll stay long enough to help you. If you don't, I'll rent a car and drive home from there."

"Drive? Why not fly?"

"Richmond is only two hours from DC by car. It's a pretty day, and I have the time. You can't talk me out of this, so here's what's going to happen: I'm going to take a shower—to which you're invited, if you so desire. Then I'm going to let you take me out to breakfast at your favorite place to have breakfast. And then, I'm driving us to Dulles Airport. Any questions?"

"I can really take a shower with you?"

I do, of course, take her up on that invitation—telling myself that it is for reasons of safety. I want to have a spotter there with me, in case the pain in my back makes me fall. Once we are upstairs in the shower, with our clothes intermingled in a pile on the heated bathroom floor, warm water cascading down upon us, there is no pain and no question of safety. I melt into her arms and she into mine as leg meets leg, shoulder touches shoulder, and our faces find each other.

She's beautiful—not in the way that Hollywood and the advertising industry insist that a woman must be. And not in that "on the inside" way that you tell homely people to make them feel good about themselves. Her beauty is classical, endowing her with soft curves in all the right places, delicate yet simultaneously strong features, and what is to me the most attractive feature a woman can possess—self-confidence.

The water feels wonderful on my pain-wracked body, but not half as wonderful as this woman's touch. She discovers me with her fingers, her palms, her nails—in touches alternating gentle and firm. For several minutes, I keep my hands at my sides, allowing her to explore me uninterrupted. Then a glimpse a look in her eyes that says the invitation is mutual, and I reach out to her as well. There is a softness to her skin, and yet a solidity to her muscle tone that makes me want to touch her for hours without stopping.

She brings her lips to mine and kisses me like no one ever has. If I were unable to breathe on my own, I believe entirely that her kiss would return life to my body. Strangely, powerfully, I am aware that each kiss, each touch removes a small fraction of the pain that came from this new assignment—as if surrendering to physical pleasure with Genevieve Swan was part of what I must do. I emit an audible moan, and in an instant, she stops, pulling back from me.

"Is it too much?" she asks.

"No," I manage in a gasping exhalation. "Well, yes, but in all the right ways." I pull her gently back to me to kiss her some more, which she welcomes. When I do withdraw slightly, I look in her eyes and tell her, to my surprise, "I really think I could love you."

"You do?" she says. "I mean, you could?"

"I know, it sounds crazy."

"No, not crazy. A little fast, a little impulsive, but not crazy."

"What about you?" I ask her. "What do you feel?"

"I don't know. I have a personal rule that I never tell someone I love them for the first time when I'm naked. Okay, it's a strange rule, but it's worked well for me. Because naked makes you say things. Naked makes you believe things you might not believe when you're dressed and sitting in a chair and … I don't know … eating Pop-Tarts."

"Pop-Tarts?"

"For example. So I don't know," she says. "Because I'm here with you, and we're naked, and I know I shouldn't feel things like that because I met you a week ago. But then you … you touch me, and you kiss me … and you tell me these things—and all I can think is that loving you feels right and natural. They say you shouldn't love someone until you've seen them at their worst. I think I've seen you at your worst last night; what you went through. That didn't scare me away."

"Then … are you saying …?"

"I might be, Tristan. Let me get close to you, to the real you, so I can find out?"

With a nod, I accept her offer, and we continue our powerful embrace.

It is nearly 8:00 in the morning when we get out of the shower. We dress in separate bedrooms, which gives me a few minutes to come to terms with what I've just experienced. She makes me feel strong and cared about. But beneath it all, a voice haunts my thoughts, a voice I've been working diligently to suppress all morning. It is the man from my dream, the very dream I had moments before I met Genevieve. The man who told me, "Without you, she will die. Someone you love. And she will be the first of many."

The reality of my life is changing. I am always on call now, on these assignments, which can take me anywhere, to do any number of things. Dangerous things. And then there is the matter of Ephraim, if that truly is his name; this mysterious figure who knows my future, while I don't even know his present. If he is dangerous to me, he could be dangerous to someone I love. But at the same time, he acted as if he expected someone with me—someone female. Was he speaking of Genevieve? Is my future to be by her side? Could I put her in that much jeopardy? Conversely, am I to be denied human companionship simply because my circumstances are potentially dangerous?

My thoughts are interrupted by the touch of her hand on my shoulder from behind me. Startled, I jump a little, before realizing she's there.

"Sorry," she says. "Didn't mean to scare you."

"It's okay. I was just lost in my own thoughts."

"You look better. Much better than last night. Is the pain gone?"

"I wish I could say you healed me completely. But in truth, on a scale of one to ten, it's down to about a three. Just enough to remind me that changing my mind would be bad for my health. Good news is, the closer I get to Washington, the less it'll hurt."

"That's so strange. I wish I could begin to understand how and why this happens."

"You and me both," I reply. "Now, if I recall the details of our agreement correctly, there was talk of breakfast at my favorite establishment before hitting the road. It's called the Golden Door, and it's a ten-minute drive from here. So, get your stuff together, and let's get this Sunday drive underway."

She smiles and heads downstairs. My chipper demeanor is an act; inside, I'm quite scared. I haven't forgotten the importance of what today brings. A plane filled with children; more than sixty deaths, if I can't stop them from taking off. How can I possibly stop them? How is this a reasonable thing to ask, to expect, of anyone?

The Golden Door is a locals' establishment, largely overlooked by the flock of tourists who descend on Ocean City every summer. It is owned by a married couple in their sixties. Joseph works the kitchen, while Irene is hostess, cashier, and head waitress. They are the nicest people anyone could meet, and the breakfasts they serve are nothing short of amazing. As we enter the restaurant, Irene looks at Genevieve discreetly and shoots me a look that says, *And who is this?* My expression does its best to convey that I'll explain later, and she gives a knowing nod of acceptance.

As she seats us and gives us our menus, Irene asks, "In from out of town, dear?"

Genevieve, realizing that she is "dear," replies, "Umm, yep. Just visiting Tristan for the weekend. Heading home to Richmond, Virginia today."

"Well, I hope you've enjoyed Ocean City. We're pleased to have you here. I'll be back with coffee."

She walks toward the kitchen, and Genevieve looks at me with an expression of bemused wonder. "You didn't tell me your mom owned a restaurant."

"My …? You mean Irene? Oh, she's not my mom, although I suspect she'd be happy to adopt me. I've just been coming here for a very long time. Irene and Joe are like family to me. My mother's been gone for a long time."

"Oh, God, I'm sorry. I had no idea. That was insensitive of me."

"No, not at all. I had my grieving period. I'm fine."

"What was she like?"

"My mother? She was good to me, but she had a very tough exterior. She was an attorney, so she had to be strong in a very male-oriented field. But I knew her softer side."

"How did she die, if that's not too personal?"

"It's all right," I reply, bringing up the memory from long ago. "She died in a work-related accident."

Before I can elaborate, Irene returns with coffee, and we place our breakfast order.

Ten minutes later, the food is on our table, and it's everything I need to get me through this day. I opt for the omelet with ham, tomato, feta cheese, and spinach, which comes with hash browns and pancakes. Genevieve gets the banana french toast with a side of oatmeal and fresh strawberries. Her first bite registers as pure heaven.

"Did I tell you?" I ask with a smile.

"Oh my God. Does she want to adopt *me?*"

"You can ask on our way out."

After a few more wondrous bites, she says, "I suppose we should talk about the day ahead."

"Yeah, I guess."

"Do you have a plan? How you're going to approach this?"

Though I've thought about it in general terms, the specifics have been elusive. "Not exactly. I'll go to the airport, and I'll talk to someone official, someone in charge. I'll tell them what I know and see if they'll stop the flight from taking off."

"What you know is less important than *how* you know. Have you thought about how you're going to explain it?"

"No. That's the part I haven't figured out yet. Before, I lied to people and told them I was with a government agency. That won't work at an airport, not without flawless fake ID, which I can't even begin to contemplate getting. I'm just afraid that a safety tip from a private citizen will hold absolutely no weight with airline officials."

"But a flight filled with children? If there's even a chance that you're right, wouldn't it make sense for them to cancel it, to be sure?"

"That's what I'm hoping. I'm scared; I'm scared of what happens if they don't believe me and that plane takes off."

"If you give it your best effort and they don't believe you, it's not your fault. You have to understand that."

"I'm trying to," I tell her. "But I have an overly developed sense of guilt. If I screw this up, I'm going to feel like every death is my responsibility."

After a very satisfying breakfast, we get on the road for Washington. Despite my objections, Genevieve takes the first driving shift, to give my back a chance to heal for a while. Though I won't admit it outwardly, I am grateful. I like to drive, but it feels good having someone else do it for me.

We're both quiet for about the first ten minutes of the drive. I know I have no idea what to say, and I imagine Genevieve doesn't either. Eventually, she starts the difficult conversation we need to have. "Have you decided if you want my help during this thing?"

"I don't know yet. If there's a way you can help make it happen without putting yourself in danger, then yes. But if it looks troublesome, I'd rather you were nowhere close to it."

"That's very noble of you to say, but I'm good at taking care of myself. Besides, if I could choose how things go, I'd rather have *you* nowhere near danger either. You may have noticed that I'm growing rather fond of you."

"I noticed in the shower this morning," I reply with a little smirk of satisfaction.

"Yes, well, the feeling appeared to be mutual. And I'm glad. I just don't want you feeling like you have to protect me today, when things go down. Remember, part of my job is helping the police track down killers. I've been known to laugh in the face of danger."

"Laugh in the face of danger? Who talks like that?"

She gives me a little smack on the head. "I do, thank you very much. I'm a wild woman; stick around long enough, you'll find out."

"I'd like that."

"Yeah," she says quietly, "I'd like that too. So please promise me you won't do anything foolish, like boarding the plane that's supposed to crash and convincing the crew not to take off."

"You've clearly mistaken me for someone heroic. The plan is to do all my persuading from a very safe place. Dying in a fiery puddle is not part of the plan."

"Well, I'm glad to hear that. I had visions of you standing in the cockpit as the plane was taking off, pleading with the pilot to land before it's too late."

"Wait—you had visions, or ... *visions?*" The final word is presented in a relatively awful Madame-Vanya-sees-all voice.

"The former, not the latter. It's courtesy of my active imagination, not gifts from the spirit world."

"That's a bit of a relief. I'd hate to think I was destined to do something brave."

We fall into a lull in the conversation for several more minutes. Several times, I contemplate turning on the radio to cover the silence, but it feels wrong. So we drive on, and we let the silence persist. When it starts to feel overwhelming, I gently attempt conversation again. "What I said this morning ..."

It is a start, but not enough of one to carry us, so she prompts me. "Yes?"

"About ... well, about loving you. I don't want you to feel pressured."

"I know."

"I know it feels fast, telling you that I love you—"

She interrupts. "I believe your exact words were that you *could* love me."

"Did I say *could?*" My memory of the moment is unreliable.

"That was the word."

"Could is good," I answer. "Could suggests promise. Possibility."

"Growth?" she suggests.

"Yes, growth too. What I mean is ... I kind of suck at being in touch with my feelings, and I don't want to lead you on, but at the same time, I don't want to make you think that what I said was just because of the circumstances. I mean to say, I feel just as strongly about you now as I did when we were in the shower and you had your fingers on my—"

"Tristan."

I've been blathering; I sense this.

"I understand. And it's fine, really. This is new ground for me as well. We don't have to rush anything. Something tells me this isn't going to be a traditional relationship. I'm okay with that. If it gets too weird, I'll let you know."

"There's something else that's making me hesitant," I confess. "You remember when we first met, how I'd been dreaming? You remember what the old man in the dream said to me?"

"That someone you love will die unless you prevent it. Yeah. It's been on my mind since this morning."

"I don't want that someone to be you."

"I'm not too keen on the idea either," she says with an anxious smile. "But at the same time, I don't want to miss out on what could be a wonderful relationship with a wonderful man, just because of something heard in a dream. Because I believe in my heart that you would never hurt me."

"Never." The very thought of it is abhorrent to me.

"And that's not a guarantee I get with every relationship."

Her voice catches just enough to make me ask, "Has someone hurt you before?"

She shakes her head, not fully enough to be a *no,* just enough to dismiss the question. "Everyone's been hurt at some point. The crazy thing is, even though I'm traveling with you to a strange city to stop a plane crash, while you're being stalked by a disturbed man with knowledge of your future, I feel safe with you."

This evokes a laugh from me. "Lady," I reply gently, "you've got some strange concepts of *safe.*" She laughs at this too. "But thank you. One thing I've always believed is that I can get a good feeling about a person as soon as I meet them—right away, I know if there's goodness in them or something else. And when I met you, all I could think was, *Who is she? I want to get to know her.*"

"I thought the same thing about you. Different pronouns, of course."

"Of course."

"I trust that feeling, and I want to see where it takes us."

"Well, right now, it's taking us to Washington. If we're not slaughtered horribly, maybe I can call you sometime."

"You always know the right thing to say to a girl."

"It's a gift," I reply.

After about an hour and a half, we switch drivers. My back is feeling better, as I expected, and I feel like I can take us the rest of the way to Washington. With the absence of pain comes a growing sense of dread. Along the way, I have pictured a number of different ways this could play out, and they all end badly. I've heard that in order to succeed, you should visualize yourself succeeding, and I tried that, but it's just not happening for me. I want to believe that I'm being sent here because some otherworldly power feels I can make a difference. I'm even following the instructions this time. So why can't I envision myself victorious?

"You're going to do fine," Genevieve says, interrupting my thoughts.

"Hey, no fair," I reply gently. "You reading my mind?"

"No, just your face. Your self-doubt is like a road map."

"I'm just so scared. There's so much at stake this time, and I feel unprepared. I know what's going to happen and when it's going to happen. But like every time I get this information, the big X factor is how to explain how I know. If the world were different, I could just walk up to people and say, 'I get warnings from an unknown source, but they come true, so you should do what I say.' But if I said that, ninety-nine people out of a hundred would like at me like

I'm crazy and disregard me. So I have to tell lies and make up stories to make it sound like I have this knowledge from reputable places. And if I'm lucky, people believe the lie, so I don't have to tell the truth."

"I understand, really I do. Look at what I do for a living. Half the time, when I meet people, I tell them I'm an executive assistant or an office manager. Because I know if I tell them I'm a psychic, they'll look at me like I'm nuts or like I'm some kind of charlatan. So, yeah, I know where you're coming from. I wish I had a good answer for either of us, but unfortunately, I don't. In their private lives, millions of people in this country believe in ghosts and angels and the devil. They go to psychic readings and fortune-tellers. They believe in heaven or reincarnation or a hundred other things that can't be seen or heard or touched. But get those same people in an official capacity, and the skepticism comes through. So the woman who comes to see me to get a psychic reading every two weeks won't be my friend in the world at large because of my job. And the airport security official who prays to Jesus for the lottery numbers each week can't accept your explanation that you get precognitive visions that tell you he needs to ground that plane."

"Thank you. I didn't think anyone could understand what I'm going through."

She gives my hand a squeeze. "Better than you know."

When we arrive at Dulles International, I head right for the short-term parking lot and find a good spot. I shut off the engine and take a deep breath. "Okay, this is it."

"It is indeed," she says.

I reach into my pocket and produce my wallet. "Before I forget …" I pull out two hundred dollars and hold it out toward her. She looks at me like I'm holding a decomposing piglet.

"Why are you giving me money?"

"Oh, Jesus, it's not for *that!* In case we get separated and you need to get home without me, this will cover your airfare or your rental car, whichever you choose."

"I really don't need it. I can cover it, honest."

"I know you can, and I respect your independence, but the fact of the matter is, I agreed to pay for your trip out here. God knows the weekend didn't go exactly as planned, and I would feel like a total shitburger if you ended up having to pay your own way home. So, pretty please, take one little thing off my very beleaguered mind and accept the money. If it makes you feel better, you can buy me a fancy Christmas present, provided I'm not killed today."

She takes the money from my hand. "You hopeless romantic, you."

"Humor me. I'm new at this."

As we get out of the car, another thought comes to me. "One more thing." I dig a business card out of my wallet and hand it to her. "This is my attorney's card. If something goes wrong in there, please call him. Tell him what's happened to me, and that I need him to come here in person. I'll cover his travel and all expenses."

She looks at the card. "Steven Atkinson, Esquire. Baltimore, Maryland. Kinda far from you, isn't it?"

"I usually don't need to be in the room with him to conduct business. If things go south today, I will. Fortunately, his office is less than an hour from here."

She pockets the card and the cash and takes her overnight bag. "Well, fortunately, you won't need him, because everything's going to go smoothly."

"Here's hoping."

As we make our way to the terminal, the seeds of a plan begin to sprout. "I'm working it out," I tell Genevieve discreetly. "No matter what I say to anyone, agree with it. Deal?"

"Deal."

As we enter the building, I glance at a clock. It is 12:20 in the afternoon; tighter than I would have liked. I next go to the departures board and find Consolidated Airlines flight 9526. Destination: Miami. Departure time: 1:45 p.m. Status: On time. Gate: B41. Seeing this makes everything feel very real, very immediate.

"We don't have much time," I say to her. "Follow my lead."

Moving quickly, I seek out the nearest uniformed TSA officer. Fortunately, there is one just a few feet away. I try to get his attention; he is an older man, probably in his mid-fifties. He looks very serious. They always look very serious. "Sir, excuse me, officer? I'm sorry to bother you."

"Yes, sir?" he asks. "What do you need?"

"My friend and I were in the parking lot just now, and we heard a man talking on his cell phone. It … well, I can't be sure, but the things he was saying—"

"What was he saying?" the officer asks.

"He was talking about a Consolidated Airlines flight to Miami this afternoon. Saying things about how he couldn't let it take off or some such. Now, I don't know if he was an air-traffic controller or an employee or *what*, but he sounded kind of nervous, and when he saw us getting closer, he stopped talking."

"Do you recall what he looked like?"

Gotta be careful here. I need to be nondescript enough to keep them from bringing someone in, but at the same time not sound like a screaming racist. "He was white, about my height, maybe a little shorter."

"Brown hair," Genevieve says.

"Right, brown hair."

"What was he wearing?" the officer asks.

Nondescript, nondescript. "Dark slacks and a short-sleeve light-color dress shirt."

"Sir, ma'am, I want to thank you for coming to talk to me. You're right, it may be nothing, but I'll let my department know, and we'll investigate this. Can you stay with me for the next half hour or so, in case we find the person?"

Hadn't thought about that. Too much time in his presence could lead to the unraveling of details. If they believe me, they believe me without my being present, and they'll ground the flight.

"Oh, I wish we could," I tell him, "but we have to catch our plane. I'm very sorry."

"That's all right," he replies. "I understand. You've given me good information. We'll look into it."

"Thank you, sir. God bless you. God bless America."

Genevieve starts to lead me away from him as I add, "You're doing a fine job for our country."

Once we're out of hearing range, she asks, "What was that last bit?"

"Stage decoration. Patriots aren't suspicious people. Scary terrorists are suspicious people."

"Duly noted. What do we do now?"

"We hang out in a quiet part of the terminal, and we watch the boards. If this goes well, our TSA man will radio it in to his office. His office will put someone on the surveillance video of the parking lot, looking for the person matching that description, talking on a cell phone. Meanwhile, other officers will get in touch with Consolidated Airlines and turn in a credible threat report, prompting the airline to first delay and then cancel the flight. All of which we can monitor from the nearest departures board. Once we know it's canceled, we can leave."

"You know, for a guy who didn't have a plan fifteen minutes ago, you made that sound pretty effortless."

"Correction: I didn't have a *finished* plan fifteen minutes ago. What you'll learn about me if you witness any more of these escapades is that I make this shit up as I go."

"I'm impressed."

"Yeah, well please save your applause until all the graduates have their diplomas and the departures board has a big old 'canceled' sign on our dear flight 9526."

I find a mostly unoccupied sitting area in sight of an arrival and departure board, and we sit, casting subtle glances at the board regularly, while trying not to look too obvious about it. The last thing I want is for TSA guy to still find us here after I told him we had a plane to catch.

Five minutes pass with no change in status. Then ten. Each new minute brings a different fidget to my regimen. Fifteen minutes pass and still the departure status reads On time. "Something's wrong," I announce with a shake of my head. "It should have changed. They should have changed it by now."

"So what do we do? Go back to talk to the TSA officer again?"

"No, it's too risky. Besides, if our first contact with him didn't move them to action, I don't think a second contact will do anything."

"What's plan B then?"

"We have to get airside. We have to get to gate B41."

"Wait, they won't let you do that without a ticket."

"Well then, it's a good thing I have a lot of money, isn't it? Come on, let's go to ticketing."

As we make our way through the terminal, she says, "Maybe we should split up. We don't have to buy tickets on the same flight or even the same airline. That way, if something happens, one of us can get through and warn them."

"Good thinking. I'll try to get on the Consolidated flight. You buy a ticket on Northeast. We'll go through security separately and meet on the other side of the checkpoint."

"Good luck," she says.

"You too."

With that, we separate. She heads to the Northeast Airlines ticket counter, while I make my way to Consolidated Airlines. When I reach the ticket agent, the woman at the desk asks, "Can I help you?"

"Yes, I need to get to Miami right away. I believe you have a flight leaving in the hour."

She checks her screen. "Flight 9526, yes. I'm sorry, but that flight is full."

I shouldn't be surprised by this, yet I am. I am on the verge of asking for a ticket on any upcoming flight, but I realize how that would sound, so I change my tactics. "Do you have another flight to Miami today? I really need to get there."

She checks again. "There's a flight leaving at 4:30 this afternoon, and I have seats available. Do you need business class?"

"No, coach is fine, thank you."

"Round-trip?"

"Uh, no … one-way. I'm not sure when I'll be returning."

"Okay, with tax it comes to $138. What card would you like to use?"

"I'll pay cash, if that's all right."

"Sure. I'll just need to see a photo ID."

With no small degree of trepidation, I hand her $140 and my driver's license. I feel very exposed, very watched, as I buy this airplane ticket that I have no intention of using. The agent takes the money and the license and processes my ticket.

"It's $25 for the first checked bag," she says.

"Ah, I don't have any bags to check."

"Ten dollars for carry-on."

I offer a little smile and shrug. "Don't have one of those either. I have a business apartment in Miami, so I have clothing waiting for me."

She gives a little nod that doesn't really convince me that she believes me. Why should she? I don't believe me. Still, within a minute, my boarding pass is printed and in my hands. "Here you go, Mr. Shays. You still have quite a while before your flight, so you're welcome to make use of the airport's amenities. Have a good flight."

"Thanks. Here's hoping."

Without another word, I head toward the security checkpoint. I manage to get in line right behind Genevieve. At this point, I don't know whether it's better to pretend we don't know each other. But there's information I need, so I engage in discreet conversation. "Did you get what you need?"

"Yep. Ticket to Richmond, just in case. You?"

"Barely. Flight 9526 is full, so I got a ticket to Miami for later in the day."

"That's nice. If this goes well, you can treat yourself to a little vacation."

"Yeah, I wish. I just booked a flight, paid cash, and told them I don't even have a carry-on bag. If I'm not already on the FBI's Most Wanted List, I'll be very surprised."

"Well, nobody was suspicious of me," she says, "so we've got a fallback plan."

We wait our turn, and she goes through the scan with no problems or issues. I hand my boarding pass and license to the TSA agent. He looks at my paperwork and then at my face and then at his computer screen and then at my paperwork. "Step to the side, please."

Oh, I'm fucked.

"Everything okay?" I ask, trying to sound as not guilty as humanly possible.

"You've been randomly selected for additional screening," he says.

Yes, randomly. That's what they tell travelers of Middle Eastern descent these

*days. I now look forward to the impending body cavity search that I am certain
awaits me.*

And so my journey through the world of homeland security begins. It
starts with the wand, waved up and down, left and right, all around me, as
if some magician were trying to transform me into a rabbit. When the wand
yields no unsavory noises, my shoes come off, and it is time for the pat-down.
I hope for an ideal situation: a pat-down by someone young, female, good-
looking, and lonely; but alas, it is humorless middle-aged security man who
gets to know the various bumps and bulges of my body. Satisfied that I am
not carrying weapons of any flavor, I next go into a little chamber that closes
around me. It looks futuristic and gently scary. I look around to make sure no
flies get in there with me, lest I emerge transformed. But no, I am alone.

Lights light up, motors hum, and a puff of air hits me, making me
wonder in my own curious way just what the living hell this thing is doing
to my genitals. Before I can give it too much thought, the chamber opens,
and I emerge, one step closer to trustworthy in the eyes of the federal
government.

By this point, I am fully prepared for the trip to the little room for the
strip search, but to my surprise, the agent says to me, "Thank you for your
cooperation. Have a good flight."

That's good enough for me. I skip the God bless America part this time
around and high-tail it gratefully out of there to catch up for Genevieve, who
is waiting for me just around the corner.

"Get felt up?" she asks as we continue our walk.

"You did better this morning."

"Glad to hear that, at least. Have you been deemed non-threatening?"

"For the moment. Until they get a load of my announcement at the
gate."

"So that's the plan?" she asks. "Go directly to B41 and tell the crew?"

"I think if anybody would be interested in the risk of a plane crashing
and burning, it would be the person who's about to fly it."

"Are you nervous?"

"The fact that I have bladder control at this juncture is nothing short of
a miracle."

We proceed via the walkway to terminal B. Of course, gate 41 is at the far
end of the terminal from where we enter, so there's a very long walk ahead of
us. As we draw near, I see that the flight has not begun boarding yet. In the
gate area are a few adults and dozens of Haitian children, some as young as five
or six. They look weary. From what I learned while receiving this assignment,
they were flown from Haiti to Washington yesterday for official processing.

Today, they'll fly to Miami to be housed by an international relief agency, who will then try to find them permanent homes in the United States.

Looking at their faces, the importance of what I have to do rushes up and kicks me in the head once more. *Their lives in my hands.*

Genevieve sees them and sees my expression. "The children are right here. We should do this quietly."

"On the contrary. If they don't believe me, I'm going to do this as loudly as I can."

"What? Why? You'll scare them."

"Exactly. Do you think they're going to want to put sixty frightened, crying children on an airplane, even if they think nothing's wrong with it? One way or another, I'm not leaving here until I know that those kids aren't getting on that plane."

"Okay, good luck."

"Hang back," I instruct. "Watch what happens. If it goes wrong for me, you're their last chance."

She nods, and I walk over to the agent at the desk for gate B41. "Miss, I'm sorry to bother you," I begin in a conversational tone. "Have you heard anything from Consolidated or TSA about mechanical problems with this plane?"

Clearly not a question she gets often, she looks surprised to hear it. She checks her computer screen and replies, "No, sir. Is there something wrong that I should know about?"

"There might be. I was just in the terminal, and I heard two maintenance workers talking about this flight. It sounded like there might be something wrong. Can you check with someone?"

"Yes, sir. Thank you." She picks up the phone and dials a four-digit extension. "This is Keisha at 41B. A passenger said he overheard maintenance talking about a problem with the aircraft for 9526 outbound. Are there any alerts or C.O.E. requests in? We're supposed to start boarding in the next ten minutes." I watch as she listens. "Okay, thank you." Hanging up, she tells me, "I spoke to a maintenance supervisor, and he says there's no reports of problems with the aircraft. We should be able to take off on schedule."

I don't understand it. Somebody should have done something by now. How could they all ignore this?

"I need to speak to the pilot."

"Sir?"

"Please, it's very important. I need to let the pilot know what I learned."

"That's not going to be possible. The pilot is on board, preparing for takeoff."

"I understand that, but there's a real threat to this aircraft, and I want to make sure the pilot knows about it, so he can make the decision whether he feels it's safe to take off."

"This is highly irregular," she insists.

"You don't know the half of it. I really don't have time to convince you that I'm the good guy here. I just need two minutes to talk to the pilot and tell him what I know. If I can't do that, I'm going to start talking to the passengers and telling them what I know. Which of those scenarios do you see ending better?"

She looks at me intently, a look of concern on her face. I watch as she makes the difficult decision. Without saying a word, she goes through the jetway toward the plane. I breathe a sigh of relief, truly hoping that the pilot will be the first person here to take my warning seriously and come here to learn more.

Almost three minutes pass—confirmed by the frequent checking of my watch—and the door to the jetway opens again. The gate attendant returns with two other men, both of whom appear to be in their forties. She points me out and the men approach me.

"I'm Captain Mims," he says. "This is my co-pilot, Harris Bower. I was told you have some information you need to share with us."

The words are a blessed relief. I've spent the last day feeling so anxious and so frustrated that the words that follow flow of their own accord, with very little control from me. "Please, listen to me, if there's any part of you that loves your life and values the possibility of tomorrow. What I'm going to tell you is the truth. Don't let this plane take off. Things are not right, and this airplane will not take you to your destination. On the tail of the airplane, the elevator has failed. A maintenance worker was careless in his work, and it will function long enough to begin your takeoff. But before you get to cruising altitude, that elevator will fail. Your plane will crash, and all but one person on board will die."

It's out. I've said it. I've done what I came here to do.

The men stand pondering what I've told them for seconds that feel like hours. "Assuming you're correct about the maintenance worker," the pilot says. "Assuming you're correct about the elevator. How can you know the last part? How can you know there'll be only one survivor?"

Shit, I've said too much. No more bluffing. "I receive warnings. Visions of danger that come to me and compel me to share the warnings with the people who most need to hear them. I've driven here from Ocean City, Maryland, today to tell you this. And I can't say or do anything to convince you I'm not crazy. If you're a man of faith, I can tell you that God shares these warnings with me. If you're open to the paranormal, I can call them psychic visions. All I can tell you is that I've never been wrong. I gain nothing from telling you this. I just need you to make the decision to abort this flight until another plane is available and use that plane instead."

The two men again stand and ponder what I've said. Then a look comes to the co-pilot's face. "Seattle."

"What?" the pilot asks him.

"What he just said—the elevator failing and all but one person dying. I felt like I'd heard those words before, and now I know where. Seattle, 2003—the TransWest flight. A man showed up at the gate and warned the passengers that the tail elevator would fail and that the plane would crash. Do you remember, Captain?"

I know I certainly don't remember anything about this, but the similarity is eerie. The pilot searches his memory and replies, "You know, I *do* remember now. The same kind of circumstances."

"This could just be a copycat, someone trying to get attention," the co-pilot continues, apparently unconcerned that I'm standing right here and can hear every word.

"Maybe so," the pilot says, "but think back, Harris. That plane *did* crash, and there was only one survivor. That's good enough for me." He turns to the gate attendant. "Keisha, call ops. Tell them pre-flight doesn't check clear and we need a change of equipment. Have them change the board to delayed, and try to find us a new plane ASAP."

"Yes, Captain," she says.

A wave of relief washes over me, for a few seconds, anyway, until the pilot further instructs, "And call TSA. I want this man taken in for questioning."

"What?" I exclaim.

"Standard procedure," he tells me. "Thank you for the information. We have to let TSA know any time there's a threat against an aircraft."

"But this isn't a threat. It's a—"

"Warning, I know. You're not under arrest. Just some questions."

Two TSA agents approach me, and one actually puts my hands behind my back in handcuffs. "Really?" I ask him, my voice laced with disbelief.

"Standard procedure," he says unemotionally.

"You know," I say to Captain Mims, "for not being under arrest, this sure feels like being under arrest."

"Standard ..."

"Yeah, yeah, yeah, I know." I turn the other way to meet the eyes of my awestruck companion. "Swan, now would be an excellent time for that phone call!"

Chapter 9

Sunday, August 5, 2007

I AM LED LIKE a common criminal through the terminal of Dulles International Airport. I now understand why actual common criminals work so hard to cover their faces with clothing while on camera. The looks I am getting from people are soul-crushing. They stare at me, with my very put-out expression, no doubt wondering what awful thing I've done to warrant this treatment. Was I drunk and unruly on a flight? Did I punch a flight attendant? Am I a terrorist, planning an overthrow of the government? Sorry, contestants, the answer is *none of the above.* I saved a plane full of orphans from exploding. So naturally, I need to be taken into custody.

They take me to the TSA office in the main terminal building, away from the gates, and put me in what appears to be an interrogation room. I am momentarily surprised to see that an airport needs an interrogation room, but it occurs to me that there are some genuinely bad people out there who need interrogating. Sadly, at the moment, they believe I am one of them.

Once I am seated, the agent removes the handcuffs, and I do that thing people do in movies when they get handcuffs removed—the wrist-rubbing thing. The damn things are uncomfortable. Without a word, the agents leave me alone in the room.

Oh, so that's how it's going to be, huh? Psychological games? Disorient me, leave me alone in this room until it breaks my spirit. No food or water. No bathroom. Just me, alone with my thoughts, until the pressure of solitude and deprivation makes me talk? Well, bring it, bitches. I can last a couple of days. Give me your worst.

About a minute later, the door opens, and a man of about sixty enters, wearing a suit and a TSA badge. "I'm Agent Forrester," he says. "Do you want some water or anything?"

"Uhh, no. I'm fine, thanks."

"I didn't get your name."

"Tristan Shays. S-h-a-y-s."

He writes that down. "And did you say *Kristin?*"

"No no, *Tristan.* With a T."

"Oh, that's good. Would've been strange if you were called Kristin."

"Yeah, look who you're telling."

"Mr. Shays, I should start by informing you that you're not under arrest. I need to ask you some questions, and based on your answers, you could be placed under arrest later, if we determine that you've committed a crime. Do you understand?"

"Yes. And no. I really don't know why I'm being detained. All I did was report to the flight crew that there was a mechanical problem with the plane, and I asked them to consider switching planes. I didn't threaten anybody."

"Since 9/11, airport security is a new ballgame. You've flown; you see this. The Transportation Safety Administration is a central part of keeping the skies safe. When we receive word of a safety risk, we act swiftly. You were identified as a person of interest, and we need to get a statement from you about what you know and how you know it."

"I have to question the acting swiftly part," I reply. "The TSA agent I spoke to when I first got to the airport heard what I had to say and did nothing. There was no report, no delay of the flight. If I hadn't gone to the gate, the flight would have taken off."

"What agent did you speak to, and when?"

"It was at 12:20 in the main terminal. I told him what I had learned about the flight."

"Which agent was it? What was his name?"

I try to recall but can't.

"What did he look like?"

"Well, he—" The strangest feeling comes over me. Though I met this man an hour ago, I can't recollect his physical features. There is a mental block when I try to picture his face. "I'm sorry, but I don't recall. With everything that's happened, I'm blanking. I'm pretty sure he was Caucasian, but beyond that, I—for some reason, I couldn't go into more detail."

"Mr. Shays, there was no report of any issue with flight 9526 until you spoke to the flight crew. Are you sure the man you talked to was a TSA agent?"

"Yes, that part I know. I sought him out because of his position."

"What did he say to you?"

At this increasingly anxious moment, I am startled by the ringing of my cell phone. I look at the screen and see a familiar name. "This is my attorney calling. Can I take this?"

Forrester nods, and I answer. "Steven? Thank you for calling me back. Do you know what's happened? … Can you come and talk the TSA people with me? … Okay, good. Thank you. I'll give you more details when you get here. How soon before you arrive? … That's fine. I'm in the TSA office in the main terminal. See you soon. Thank you."

I end the call and speak to Agent Forrester again. "My attorney can be here in about half an hour or so. I'd feel more comfortable talking with him present. Is that acceptable?"

"Yes, that's acceptable. I need to review statements made by the personnel you spoke with, so we can continue when your attorney arrives. I need to take your phone until then." I surrender it to him. "And you're allowed to have a meal while you're waiting."

"That's better than I'd get on the plane," I quip with a morbid laugh. He laughs a bit in acknowledgment. "Seriously, though, if someone wouldn't mind going to Subway, I could do with a six-inch turkey and cheese on wheat bread, with lettuce, tomato, and mayo, and a bottle of water."

"I think that can be arranged. When your attorney arrives, I'll give you two some time to confer before we continue with the investigation."

As he starts out of the room, I say, "Agent Forrester?" He turns back to me, halfway out the door. "I'm not a bad person. I'm a respectable businessman who cares a great deal about his country."

He nods a little. "My job is not to judge you, Mr. Shays. Just to ask some questions and get some answers."

With that, he disappears, presumably to put in my unexpected lunch order. Breakfast was good, but it was five hours, one warning, one non-arrest, and one possibly fake TSA agent ago. That part bothers me. Though I can't for the life of me picture his face, I know the man I talked to was an agent; at least he looked like an agent. I wish I had my phone so I could call Genevieve and see if she remembers him.

Genevieve. Where is she now? Did she do the smart thing and head for home? Or is she out there somewhere, waiting for me to emerge? Painful as it is, I can't focus on her now. I have to concentrate on what to tell these people.

Lunch arrives ten minutes later, and as I eat my sandwich, I try to decide if honesty is the best policy in this circumstance. I've told so many different stories since arriving at the airport, it's difficult to keep them straight. I said one thing to the person I thought was a TSA agent, but that information apparently never reached the others. I told the gate agent one story and the flight crew another. If TSA is taking statements from both, the end result is going to sound pretty jumbled. That may actually work in my favor; it could make the witness testimonies sound confused and unreliable, leaving me free to insert whatever I deem to be the truth. We'll just have to see how that works out.

About thirty minutes later, the door opens and in walks a rather flustered Steven Atkinson, my attorney and friend. "Tristan, what the hell is going on?" he asks, clearly not presenting himself as the voice of calm in a crisis. "I get a call from a woman I've never heard of ..."

"That would be Genevieve," I tell him.

"Right, and she tells me you were taken away by the TSA at Dulles for telling them that a plane was going to crash? What's this all about?"

"Sit, and I'll tell you." He sits and gets out a pad and pen from his briefcase. "Steven, something's happened to me in the past two weeks, something remarkable. It's going to sound strange, maybe even crazy, but you have to believe me. I'm receiving messages."

"Messages?"

"In my mind. Warnings that bad things are going to happen to people. I'm told who and where and when, and if I don't warn them, I'm afflicted with terrible pain. That's what brought me here today."

He pauses to take it all in. His face is decidedly stoic and thoughtful. Almost a full minute passes before he replies, "Tristan, I've known you for a very long time. In all those years, I've never known you to be not right in the head. As your friend, I'm going to set aside any personal doubts and believe that what you say is happening is actually happening to you. As your attorney, I'm going to say that I hope you haven't told that to these people."

"Not ... all of them. I may have mentioned it to the pilot."

"All right. I'm here now, and we'll see what they have to say. They told me you're not officially under arrest."

"But I could be if things don't go well."

"You'll have to do the talking, because you know what happened and I don't. But I won't let them ask you anything that incriminates you."

There's a knock at the door, and Agent Forrester returns with a few sheets of paper, one set he keeps for himself and another that he gives to Steven and me. No introductions are made, so I'm guessing they met outside of the room.

"Mr. Atkinson," Forrester begins, "did you have enough time to confer with your client?"

"Yes, I did. Thank you."

"Since Mr. Shays hasn't been arrested, he wasn't advised of Miranda rights. Under the guidelines of the Patriot Act, we have a deeper breadth of questioning that we can engage in during this investigation."

"That's fine. I'm just here to ensure that Mr. Shays's constitutional rights aren't infringed upon. I trust that's acceptable."

"Yes, sir, it is. However, if we don't receive answers to the questions we ask, it may be necessary to place Mr. Shays under arrest and transfer him to a federal facility offsite."

"Understood," Steven replies.

Gee, everybody has something to say about this but me.

"Mr. Shays, the first question is what brought you to Dulles Airport today?"

I look at Steven, who nods his acceptance of the question. "I needed to catch a flight to Miami to see a friend."

"When you arrived at the airport, what happened?"

"As I was approaching the terminal, I heard someone talking about a problem with a Consolidated Airlines plane. They said that they couldn't get the tail elevator working properly, but it worked well enough to pass the preflight check, so he hoped that everything would be all right."

"Did you engage this individual in conversation?"

"No, I did not."

"What did you do instead?"

"I entered the terminal, and I notified someone who I thought was a Transportation Safety agent."

"This would be the individual whose appearance you can't recall?"

"Yes."

"And who never filed a report of what you told him?"

"So it would seem," I reply.

"Mr. Shays, if the problem you heard about was mechanical, why would you notify TSA, rather than an airline employee?"

"I don't know. Time was of the essence, and I believed TSA could notify whoever needed to know about this."

"Did you believe the mechanical problem was in any way related to criminal or terrorist activity?"

Steven jumps in at this point. "That's speculative. Beyond what's reasonable for my client's knowledge base."

Forrester rewords the question. "Mr. Shays, did it sound like the person you overheard was talking about a mechanical problem or an outside threat?"

"A mechanical problem," I answer.

"Thank you. What did you do next?"

"I went to purchase a ticket to Miami."

"You didn't come to the airport with a ticket or a reservation?"

"No, it was a last-minute trip. I wasn't concerned about the cost."

"Mr. Shays, did you attempt to purchase a ticket on Consolidated flight 9526, the very aircraft you heard was potentially imperiled?"

"Yes, I did. But it was a full flight."

"Here's where I get confused," he says. "If you had knowledge or even suspicion that this aircraft might not take off safely, why would you choose to book passage on that very aircraft?"

He's caught me in the first part of my story that doesn't make sense, and it's a very valid question. It will require the finest top-shelf bullshit, delivered with confidence and credibility. "After reporting the problem, I thought the aircraft would be serviced or swapped out, which would make it safe enough to travel, and I wanted to get to Miami as early as I could."

"But you ended up purchasing a ticket for a later flight."

"It was all that was available."

"What happened then, Mr. Shays?"

"I went to the gates, and when I passed the gate for flight 9526, I saw that they were going to start boarding soon. I was concerned that they hadn't been told about the possible mechanical failure, so I spoke to the gate agent."

"I have her statement here, as do you. Please look it over and see if it accurately reflects your interaction with her."

Steven and I read it at the same time, and I see his eyes widen at the accurate account of what I said. "It does," I report.

"You demanded to speak to the flight crew during their preflight check, and you threatened to make a scene if you couldn't."

"*Scene* is a harsh word …"

"You threatened to frighten refugee orphans, Mr. Shays. What word would you use?"

"Scene is good," I answer sheepishly.

"Now please look at the statement of the flight crew and tell me if it accurately reflects your interaction with them."

Again Steven and I read, and again it's on the money. I think my attorney is going a little green around the gills at this one, which includes my more prophetic ramblings. "Yes, sir, it does," I tell him.

"Well then, Mr. Shays, I'm looking forward to one hell of an explanation for what you told Captain Mims and First Officer Bower. Would you please explain to me why you used the words from a similar incident from four years ago in Seattle, and why you told these men that almost everyone in their care was going to die today?"

"It was a moment of desperation," I answer, reaching for my A material. "There was so little time left before takeoff, and everything I was hearing suggested that the crew was unaware of the danger. At that moment, I would have said anything to make them decide to delay the flight and either inspect the equipment or change planes. I see now that I used poor judgment and that my actions were ill-advised. I apologize to the airline and to the TSA, and I promise not to make trouble in the future."

The two men sit there, taking in what I've said. Steven looks quietly impressed at my ability to improvise. Forrester, to my pleasant surprise, looks satisfied by what I've said. *Could I have gotten away with it?*

"There's one piece of paper I haven't shown you yet," he tells us, sliding it across the table to us. "It's a mechanical inspection report of the plane in question, performed immediately after the pilot called for a change of equipment. It found that the tail elevator was defective, and that if the plane tried to take off, it would have failed within the first three minutes, likely resulting in a controlled flight into terrain. A crash, in the vernacular."

"So Tristan was correct?" Steven says, holding back what I think is surprise.

"It would seem. We're certainly interested in knowing just what you heard to alert you to this."

Given my cover story, I can't tell him the real truth, so the fabrication continues. "One Consolidated maintenance worker was talking to another. Apparently, the company's having financial issues, and all the maintenance staff had to take a 10 percent pay cut. One of their colleagues was very upset and distracted by this, and he was the one working on the plane for flight 9526. They were concerned that their co-worker didn't address the problems with the elevator."

Apparently, this explanation is good enough for him, as he asks, "Do you know the name of the maintenance worker in question?"

"No, I'm sorry. I didn't hear it."

"Well, Mr. Shays, I've been in this job for many years, and this is the strangest situation I've ever encountered. Your actions at the gate constitute interference with a flight crew, and in the strictest terms, they would be enough to get you arrested. But under these highly unusual circumstances, and given the fact that you very likely saved the lives of these children, I'm going to ..."

His sentence is interrupted by a muffled boom that shakes the table and everything in the room that's not nailed down. Forrester looks gently alarmed, which is nothing compared to how I'm feeling. "What was that?" I ask him.

"I don't know," he says. "Stay here, both of you."

He opens the door to the interrogation room, and in the three seconds before he slips out and closes it again, I hear considerable agitation and confusion in the TSA office outside.

"Steven, what's going on? What could that have been?"

"Nothing good. Just sit tight and stay as calm as you can. If it's bad news, react naturally. Be upset, but don't sound panicky. And whatever you do, don't respond with the words 'I'm sorry,' even if they are an expression of sympathy."

Ten full minutes pass before Agent Forrester returns to the room. His expression has graduated from alarm to genuine shock and anger. Before he can speak, I ask him, "What is it? What happened?"

"Consolidated Airlines flight 9526 exploded as it was taxiing for takeoff."

The news brings me to my feet. "What? How is that possible? The pilot said they weren't going to let that plane take off."

"They didn't," he answers. "That aircraft was grounded. The passengers and crew were put on a different aircraft. *That's* the one that exploded."

"Were there any survivors?" I ask, dreading the answer.

"Only one."

The implications of this impossible news wash over me. Clearly, Forrester has implications of his own, as he walks right up to me and says, "I want some answers. I don't know what you've been telling me so far, but I want the truth out of you."

This prompts Steven to stand as well. "Now, just a moment …"

Forrester is unmoved. "Save your objections, Mr. Atkinson. I was seconds away from letting your client walk out of here. This changes everything. What he told the flight crew came true, down to the single survivor. I want to know what he knew, how he knew it, and what his connection is to that explosion."

"You can't be suggesting that foreknowledge equals complicity."

"The term is accessory before the fact. I'm sure it's one you know, Mr. Atkinson."

"Yes, Agent Forrester, I learned it the same day I learned innocent until proven guilty. That's one term that the Patriot Act tends to gloss over these days. Now, before my client is convicted in your court of hurried conclusions, I suggest you remember that Mr. Shays has been in your custody since before the change of planes. He had no access to that aircraft, let alone knowledge of which one would be chosen."

"Which again leads to the theory that he is an accessory. A diversion to keep TSA busy while the actual aircraft is targeted."

"That's absurd!" I chime in, finally ready to speak for myself. "If I were responsible for this—which I'm not—why wouldn't I just let the damaged aircraft go up? Why would I risk putting myself into your custody by actually warning the flight crew not to take that aircraft?"

"Means, motive, and opportunity, Agent Forrester," Steven continues.

"Mr. Shays had no access to those planes, either of them. He has no motive to want to hurt anyone. And with security at the airport as tight as it is, the opportunity for my client to be the person you're looking for never presented itself. To say that his foreknowledge and warning are tantamount to guilt is the same as suggesting that picking the winning lottery numbers is grand larceny. You have no evidence linking Mr. Shays to this incident—which forensic investigators may learn is an accident—and as such, you have no grounds to hold him. I'm going to ask you to do the right thing now and let him go. If you don't, I can secure a federal writ of habeas corpus with one phone call. I don't want to have to do that, sir. It's been a bad day, and I know you've got a lot of work to do. Mr. Shays will give you his full contact information, and I assure you he'll cooperate with you in the follow-up investigation. But he's not responsible for this. As much as you want to believe you're holding the guilty party, I can see the truth in your eyes. You know he didn't do this. Can I count on you to do what's proper?"

There is a pause, long enough for me to be impressed once again by my attorney's skills. Then, in a tone suggesting muted defeat, Forrester says, "Wait here. I'll process his release."

After he leaves, I smile at Steven. "You are good."

His reply is deadly serious. "God damn it, tell me you didn't do this."

"Steven, no. Of course not. If you had doubts, then why—"

"It's my job to defend your interests. And I didn't want to doubt. But I had to hear it from you."

"You know me. You know I could never do something like this."

"I know. It's just that the things you told those people—they're not things you should be able to know. It scares me that you know them, and it scares me more that you feel compelled to act on them."

"This isn't what I wanted," I tell him. "I didn't choose this. I literally woke up one day knowing that bad things were going to happen, and if I don't give these warnings, the pain I suffer is so terrible, it cripples me. Believe me, if I didn't have to do this, I wouldn't."

"So you're going to continue, even after this?"

"I don't think I have a choice. I don't know how long I'll be expected to do this. It might be for the rest of my life."

"Just *please* be careful. This sort of thing could land you in big trouble, and I won't always be here to help. I was close to DC today, but what if you're many states away? What if you can't stop someone who's going to be killed, and you get arrested for murder, God forbid?"

"Steven, I appreciate your concern, but that scenario is pretty unlikely."

"At least let today's events give you something to think about. You came here, you put yourself at risk, and the flight exploded. What does that mean?"

The starkness of his words affects me. I haven't allowed myself to think of the implications yet. I suspect that when I do, it won't go well for me. "I don't know. Something feels wrong. I feel like my warning should have worked. It should have prevented this. Otherwise, why send me, if it was going to happen anyway? I think someone or something interfered this time. I just don't know what it was."

Forrester returns to the room. "You're free to go. There's some paperwork at the front desk that you'll need to fill out before you leave. Thank you for your cooperation."

There's nothing to say in reply. I know he's suffered a loss today, and I know he wanted me to be the guilty party. That's human nature. It's easier, somehow, if there's someone tangible to blame; someone you can look in the eye and say *You did this. Now I'm going to punish you for it.* To believe that it's random, that it's the act of a God who destroys at a whim, is a frightening thought. I get that.

Steven bids me good-bye and heads out. His services for today will be expensive, but it's worth it. He kept me out of trouble, and I appreciate that.

At the TSA office front desk, I give them my full contact information and sign a form that states that I will cooperate in any ongoing investigation. And with that, my time in federal custody comes to an end.

I open the office door and step out into the main terminal building. I don't even know if Genevieve is still here; a quick call to her cell phone brings up her voicemail immediately. "It's Tristan. I'm safe; they let me go. But something went wrong, and I want to talk to you about it. Call me when you get this. Let me know where you are. I'm sorry I got you into this. I'm so sorry."

As I end the call and pocket the phone again, I look up to see a figure about twenty feet away from me. He's just standing there, across from the TSA office entrance, staring at me and shaking his head slowly in what looks like disapproval. With painful slowness, recognition comes to me, and I realize that this is the same TSA agent I first reported to when I arrived hours ago. I approach him, saying, "It's you. Why didn't you tell them? Why didn't you tell the others what I told you about that plane?"

"Because it was a lie," he says. "Like I said before, it's what you do. It's who you are."

The words freeze my blood. And with them, he begins to peel off his face. In seconds, I realize that it is not actually his face, but theatrical prosthetics, a mask of sorts, and when it comes off completely, I am looking into the eyes of my enemy—the same man who eluded me at the museum in Boston just days ago.

My reaction is instantaneous and instinctive. "Security!" I shout. "I need help!"

He remains calm. "Haven't you had enough fun with them for one day?"

He's right; the last thing TSA wants to see right now is me. So it's time to switch gears and try my luck with a theory that Genevieve and I built together. This man is evil, and evil can be dispelled. "I reject you!" I say boldly to him. "I cast you out and send you back to the darkness and the depths from which you came. Return to your foul master and never pollute this world with your machinations again!"

For several tense seconds, he stands there, looking me straight in the eyes. Finally, his expression breaks. First a little smile, then a look of disbelief, culminating in hearty laughter. "Really?" he asks. "Foul master? Holy shit, that was priceless! I wish I had a video camera. If I get a video camera, would you do it again? I mean, it was beautiful. 'I cast you out and send you back.' I can't do the voice, but you get the idea. Did you rehearse that, or was that improv?"

"Don't mock me, Ephraim."

The mention of his name stops him in his tracks. "So you've learned my name." He actually sounds impressed. "That was quick. That wasn't supposed to happen yet. Good, good. I was hoping you had the ability to change things. Did you get the name from your little fortune-teller friend? She's not really your type, but hey, a piece is a piece."

His callous attitude is pissing me off. "What do you want from me?" I ask through clenched teeth.

"We need to talk. Especially if you're running around thinking incantations will send me away. Have you got an old priest and a young priest waiting in the car, too?"

"I'm having a very bad day, and you're not helping."

"On the contrary. You're having a very bad *month,* and no one on this planet can help you more than I can. There's a coffee shop about a mile away from this terminal. Not very good, but fairly private. Give me an hour of your time. Let me explain the new facts of your new life to you. Answer all those annoying questions you must have. When that hour's over, you can tell me to go fuck myself … or you can try something different. I won't stop you; I won't hurt you. I won't interfere with you in any way."

I'm searching desperately for the deception, for the angle, for the elusive other shoe to drop, but I can't find it. All I see in this walking enigma is a sincere offer, a chance to learn about what's happening to me. And in all honesty, if it is a trick and he plans to kill me, I'm not sure at the moment that it would be such a bad thing.

"One hour," I reply.

"Good."

"And you're buying the coffee."

"I'll even spring for a muffin."

My pulse is rapid as I accompany this man out of the chaos of the terminal. The explosion of the Consolidated plane has travelers in a panic, flights delayed, and authority figures everywhere. It takes every bit of my effort not to dwell on what's happened and how my actions may have been responsible.

We go to the parking lot, and he lets me drive us in my car about a mile and a quarter to the Café Javanese. There are only a few customers inside, offering a relative degree of privacy for what he plans to say. Those who are there are speaking anxiously about the explosion of the small plane. True to his word, he orders me a sixteen-ounce Jamaican blend—the best of a bad lot, he says—and a banana-nut muffin, getting the same for himself. *How can he know so much about an out-of-the-way coffee shop near an airport?*

We sit at a small table in a corner of the establishment, two travelers pausing for refreshment before or after a flight, as far as the rest of the world knows. Could they read on our faces how absolutely *other* we are? How unlike the rest of the world our abilities make us? I certainly hope not.

He extends his hand to me. "This is a good place to start. Hi, my name is Ephraim." Tentatively, I shake his hand. It is neither hot nor cold, not extraordinary in any discernable way. "But you knew that. And you are Tristan Shays. *The* Tristan Shays. I, uhh ... I don't usually get star struck, but this is special. You are one of a kind, my friend."

"Friend?" I repeat. "Is that what you are to me?"

"I can be," he says, a smile coming to his lips. It's not the wicked smile of a body with no soul. It has warmth, invitation, even compassion. "I can be a good friend, but it's going to take some suspension of disbelief from you. It's going to take a level of trust that defies your strongest intuition. And that's not easy. I respect that."

"Who are you?" I ask him flat out.

"Who am I? Complicated question. I guess you could say ... I'm you."

My answer is instantaneous. "Bullshit."

"Okay, I'm oversimplifying. Of course I'm not *actually* you. But our paths are so similar that you could look into my eyes and see what you'll become." He sips his coffee. "Needs more sugar." He rips open two packages and stirs them in, tasting again. "Better." Ephraim looks at my face. "You're here, warning people, so it's obvious that it's begun for you. How long ago did it start?"

"Two weeks," I reply.

"And how many have you done since then?"

"This was the fourth."

"Four in two weeks?" he asks in astonishment. "Christ, they don't waste any time! They have big plans for you, boy-o."

"Who are *they*? Who's making me do this?"

"I suppose it wouldn't be too dramatic to call it God. If you believe in that sort of thing. Or has this shit made you an atheist yet?"

"Disgruntled agnostic," I reply.

"Good start. It's the American way, hating your boss. Especially when he makes you work hard with no performance reviews. So tell me: why do you take the assignments?"

"If I don't, the pain is overwhelming."

He nods knowingly. "I remember the pain. Like having balls all over your body and constantly getting kicked in them, isn't it?"

"Yes." It feels so strange to have someone understand. "So you were chosen too?"

"Oh, yes. Twelve years ago. I had a life before that. A wife who I loved; a career; a home. Then the assignments started. I thought I was losing my mind. The pain drove me to distraction. My wife tried to help me time and time again. Eventually, the pressure was too much for her, and she left. I haven't seen her since. But I took the assignments. No matter where they were, I answered the call faithfully. If it was close enough, I went in person; if it was far away, I phoned. But always I accepted. For eleven years, I did everything they told me to do.

"Then one day, last winter, the assignment hit too close to home. I received a warning about my sister, Hope, a dire warning. She was going to be involved in a fatal automobile accident if she was on Highway 67 on a given day at a given time. All I had to do was warn her not to be there at that time. I was very anxious about the assignment; I hadn't told my family about what I was chosen to do for people, and I didn't know how to warn her without telling her. So I told her I had a dream about her being in an accident. I told her I knew how silly it sounded, but I would rest easier if she stayed off of Highway 67 on that day. But there was a problem. In my anxiety, I forgot the correct highway number, and I asked her to stay off of Highway 76. And she did. She took Highway 67, just as she would have anyway. And the accident happened."

He pauses in the telling of his tale, and a look of anguish and guilt overtakes his features, eliciting such pity from me that I wouldn't have thought possible for him. Composing himself, he continues. "I fell into despair. Self-pity, misery, every negative emotion you can name. I stopped accepting assignments. And yes, the pain came, like nothing I'd ever known. I took it, even relished it. It was my punishment, after all, because my stupidity cost my sister's life.

"Deciding that it was my faulty memory that was to blame, I experimented with parapsychology and the black arts. I studied with people you wouldn't want to meet, in places too unspeakable to describe. But these people treated me like long-lost family; taught me things. Showed me ways to unlock my own mind to everything it's capable of doing. One night, they injected me with something—to this day, I still don't know what it was—and put me in a sensory-deprivation chamber and left me there for four hours. I had a breakthrough, a moment of supreme clarity like nothing I'd ever experienced. I unlocked my memory, giving me access to every moment I'd ever lived in my life. But I realized there was more to it. I had memories of things that weren't familiar—things I'd never done. I realized at that moment that I now had access to memories of events that hadn't happened yet."

"But how is that possible?" I interrupt. "The future doesn't exist yet."

"Doesn't it?" he replies. "Time isn't linear, Tristan. We perceive it as such because that's the way we live it, minute by minute. But the future exists. Every moment in time exists simultaneously. Think about it: we can sit here and discuss events that transpired in 1959 or 1776 or 1538. To us, all of those periods of time existed. But to people in those years, 2007 doesn't exist yet. How can the same moment exist for one individual and not for another? The simple answer is, it can't. In the same way, people in 2015 or 2750 or 5011 can speak of us in 2007 because they exist. Time isn't a line; it's a network stretching across everything. I've been given a view into events I shouldn't be able to see yet. And in those events, I've seen you, Tristan Shays, delivering messages big and small, year after year—rising so high and then falling so fast. But I digress."

He pauses long enough to take another bite of muffin. By now, I'm too fascinated to eat or drink. "With my new perfect memory, I left my teachers and determined to return to my life. But the forces that controlled me wouldn't let me go. No hardship discharge for me. They kept sending me assignments, and week after week, I kept refusing them. I don't know how many people suffered or died for my refusal, and I didn't care. I hoped that if I refused enough times, they would fire me and replace me with someone who did care. And then came you. The museum in Boston? That was my assignment, and I was there. But by that point, I'd made a decision. I decided I was going to become the instrument of whatever chaos was supposed to take place. We were sent to stop a child abduction, so I stepped in to take the abductor's place. In my memory, I saw you there as well, and I knew it would be our first meeting."

A realization occurs to me. "And you were there today, at that airport, just like I was."

"Yes," he says, "I was."

"Does that mean that you were also sent to stop this plane crash?"

He gives a half-smile and a noncommittal shrug as he sips his coffee.

"You blew up that second plane, didn't you?" I realize that I have risen and said those words loud enough for people in the coffee shop to hear.

Calmly he says, "You should sit down. You're making a scene."

A glance around shows me that people are indeed giving me uneasy looks. "Then answer me. Did you cause the explosion that killed all those people?"

"It's funny, isn't it?" he says, still so unemotionally. "By all societal definitions, you're the good guy and I'm the bad guy. Yet, look at who these people are afraid of right now."

"Why won't you tell me what I want to know?"

"Because it doesn't matter!" And for the first time, a hint of controlled anger seeps into his voice. "There's the answer that eludes you. It doesn't matter if that explosion was caused by me or by you or by a bird in the engine. It happened. And how dare the Lord God Almighty, creator of this world, send the two of us, equal and opposite forces, into this melee to battle for the outcome? Do you see the arrogance in it? Do you see the detestable futility of it all? It's like a game to him. He takes his finger off the piece and then wants to call back the move anyway. And thanks to an accident of genetics, your life is given over to being the instrument of that celestial mulligan. Is that how you want to spend your life?"

The enormity of his words is so overwhelming, I can't even fashion a response. *An accident of genetics? What does that mean?* Before I can even ask, he continues.

"I see it on your face. It's not what you want. And it's not what I wanted. That's why I did something about it. It's why I want you to do something about it too. I got God's attention with my actions, but he considers me an insignificant threat. He has to. Otherwise, why would he let me live? But with two of us—two of his trusted foot soldiers, particularly the one he sent to offset me—think of what we could accomplish. I could teach you to use your mind in ways you never knew were possible. Remember my little escape from the museum with the lights and the fire alarm? Child's play, compared to what I can teach you."

I pause long enough to take a breath and gather my thoughts. "First of all, thank you for the information. It does help me to understand what's happened to you and what's happening to me. And I really hope you don't take offense when I tell you that you're insane."

Apparently, he takes no offense, based on the cordial tone in his voice when he replies, "Of *course* I'm insane! How could I possibly know everything I know and not be insane? We're all insane, Tristan, every human who walks this Earth. We're all inbred from a single mother and father, cousins fucking cousins fucking cousins, pumping that same guilty blood through generation after generation of tragically flawed veins. In every mind there's madness at work. How we function in this life is entirely dependent on how well we accept it and what we can do despite it."

"You say you can see your own future," I tell him. "Then surely you already know the outcome of this conversation. You know I'm about to tell you that there's no way in hell I could ever help you, join forces with you, or work with you in any manner."

"That's the good part—I *didn't* see that outcome. Yes, the future already exists, and within it every decision we're going to make until we die. We have free will, but the results of that free will already exist in the annals of future history. But a few people, a precious, gifted few, have the ability to transcend that, to rewrite what will happen next. It's what I've given my life over to doing now. And it's something you can do as well. Flip fate the bird and do things differently. You see? You see how powerful we could be, working together? You see why I want you working with me, rather than against me?"

"Of course I do. Because now that I know this, I'm going to work even harder to stop you."

"But why?" he asks. "Why spend all that effort essentially negating what I do?"

"Because what you're doing is evil, and I can't sit back and do nothing."

"Evil? Is there really even such a thing, Tristan?"

"Uh, yeah. I'd say snatching little boys from museums and then blowing up airplanes full of fucking orphans qualifies as evil. Call me old-fashioned, but yeah."

"The point of all of this," he continues, "is to stop the exploitation. Mine, yours, and everybody else's out there who's being used against their will. I'm not asking you to molest kittens and knock down hospitals. Help me find others like us who are tired and want their lives back. We'll band together, make a stand, say enough is enough. And none of us will have to do acts of good or acts of evil. We'll simply get our lives back. Maybe we won't be able to warn some people that bad things are going to happen to them, but answer me this: when you give these warnings to people, does it feel natural?"

The answer doesn't require much thought. "No."

"Do people get this news and say, 'Thank you, kind stranger. I'm glad you appeared out of nowhere to save me from this'?"

"No."

"Or do they treat you like you're out of your mind, like you're intruding into their business, and you feel like you should hurry out of there before they call the cops or a shrink?"

"Yes," I answer quietly.

"The very people you're sent to protect, and their first instinct is to treat you like you're crazy. And why? Because they think they're immortal. Because they think bad things can't happen to them. Because their lives have taught them that God doesn't send people to give warnings of impending danger. Because that's not how the world works. So tell me, Tristan Geoffrey Shays, is this how you want to spend the next forty years of your life? Running frantically from place to place, trying to beat a deadline and deliver a message to an ungrateful stranger who treats you like you've just spit on his shoes, when all you're trying to do is save his life?"

What other answer can I give? "No."

"Then join me. Work with me to end this injustice, and let the world operate as it's meant to, with no one interfering."

I sit in silence, watching him. For a moment, it sounds reasonable. For a moment, it feels right and proper, like a resistance movement against human trafficking and indentured servitude. For a moment, the temptation to learn from this man is captivating; the chance to unlock the powers of my own mind and transcend who I've been all along.

But then I remember who I am.

"No," I tell him resolutely. "I won't. You can sit there and dance around the truth all day, but I know better. You killed sixty children today, to prove a point. Make all the pretty speeches you want about your intentions, but I know evil when I see it. You want me on your side because you know how hard I'm going to fight you. And I will. You were courteous enough to give me an explanation. Now I'll return that courtesy. I'll give you sixty seconds to get out of here before I call 911 and tell them who you are."

Without making a fuss, he stands and looks at me for a moment. "You're missing an amazing opportunity."

"Fifty seconds."

"We'll see each other again soon. Next time, I might not be so courteous."

"Forty-five."

He puts a hand on my forearm and gives a gentle squeeze. For a second, a flash runs through me—like a brief lightning storm of energy running through my head. Not pain; I certainly know what that feels like. Something different; something powerful and infinitely frightening. For a second, I get a vision in my mind—a vision of me standing on an old fishing boat with people I don't recognize, and yet they are familiar to me. In an instant, it is gone.

He makes his way out of the coffee shop without another word. I sit there, not even watching him go. I can't tell the authorities what I know; not with what I've been through today. They would detain me again, and rightfully so. Ephraim knows this; he has to. He knows he's won. And as soon as I'm free to process the implications of what that means, I know it will destroy me.

Chapter 10

THREE HOURS LATER, I am back in my own home. The drive home was on autopilot; I couldn't describe what I saw or heard. My cell phone may have rung during those hours, but I didn't answer it. I couldn't rid my mind of the thoughts that overwhelmed me. More than sixty lives; children who had just survived a natural disaster, now snuffed out by a different kind of disaster, and I was in the middle of it.

I keep trying to determine what would have happened if I hadn't showed up at all. It's a futile exercise, I know, but three hours alone in the car give me far too much time to think. Ephraim and I both got the assignment. His intention, all along, was to cause the crash, whether or not I was there. I stopped them from using the first aircraft, but I did so after alerting Ephraim himself that there was a problem. What did he do from there? Did he tamper with the first aircraft? The second?

That's just it—he never answered my question whether he was responsible for the explosion. But he had to be, didn't he? The odds of two planes in a row, for the same flight, destined to crash…. Then there was the whole matter of destiny. Ephraim's little speech about time made me wonder. Does destiny exist? Is everything already written, and does the future exist somewhere, simultaneous with every other moment in history? If so, does anything we do matter? And why am I—and others like me—being sent on these fools' errands?

Ephraim succeeded in one aspect: he confused me about the way the world works.

I am jarred from my thoughts by the ringing of my home phone. I pick it up with a listless "Hello?"

"Tristan, thank God." Genevieve's voice sounds very relieved.

"Oh, hi."

"Oh, hi? That's the best you can give me? I've been trying to call you for hours. I keep getting your voicemail. Are you all right?"

"I don't know. At the moment, I don't even care."

"Oh, sweetie, I'm sorry. Tell me everything."

I do tell her everything, from the moment she lost sight of me. My interrogation, Steven's assistance, the explosion of the second plane, my release, and my bizarre conversation with Ephraim. My narrative lacks energy, because I do as well, but it gets the information across.

"I'm so sorry I had to leave you there," she says. "I knew there was nothing else I could do to help you myself. Your attorney told me he would handle everything, and he advised me to get on the plane and go home, to avoid being implicated. I hope you can forgive me."

"There's nothing to forgive. You did the right thing. You would only have complicated your own life by staying there. I'm just glad you're home safely."

"I heard the news about a plane blowing up at Dulles," she says, "but I thought that somehow, it was the first plane. The news report didn't say anything about the change of planes or the second plane crashing."

"I failed," I tell her weakly. "I was sent to stop this from happening, and I failed."

"No, no you didn't. From what you told me, this Ephraim guy blew up the second plane. You did everything you were supposed to, and he's actively working to thwart you. Tristan, what are you going to do about him? If he's going to be there fighting you every time you get an assignment, how are you going to continue?"

"I don't know. He seemed so determined. But he also treated me … I don't know … like he respected me or even liked me. Like I was a big deal to him."

"Maybe in the future, you are."

"So you mean to tell me you believe what he said to me about the future?"

She counters with, "So you mean to tell me you don't?"

"I don't know. It seems impossible."

"Says the man who receives the visions. The rules have changed, Tristan. There's stuff at work here we had no idea about. If what Ephraim said is true—and I'm ready to believe that it is—there are some powerful forces struggling for control, and unfortunately, you're caught in it."

"Yeah, I guess I am. Lucky me."

"What are you going to do?"

"I really don't know," I reply. "I'm tired, more tired than I've felt in years. I don't think I can go in to work tomorrow. I don't know if I can go back there at all. If the last two weeks are any indicator, I'm not in any condition to run that company. I'm called away at a minute's notice, and there's a good chance I could be killed during any of these things."

"Don't say that." She says this with some urgency.

"I don't want it to be true, but I know it could be. When Ephraim touched me at that coffee shop, I started ... seeing things."

"What kind of things?"

"Tiny movies inside my head; visions of things I don't recognize, but they're still familiar somehow. I think he may be letting me see brief glimpses of my own future."

"What did you see?"

"It happens so fast, I'm never quite sure. But I saw myself standing and watching a terrible storm on the horizon. And I've seen men with guns, and a tall man with empty, dangerous eyes. I've seen gravestones and fishing traps. And in all these visions, I'm not alone, but I can't see the person I'm with. I really want to see who it is, but there's something blocking me."

"Do you really think it's your future?"

"I don't know. I don't want it to be, because it looks terrifying."

"I want you to call me every day," she says.

"Genevieve, really, I'll be fine."

"Great, then you should have no trouble calling."

"Really, it—"

"Please," she says quite firmly, "do this for me. For better or worse, I'm in your life now, and I care very much about what happens to you. Hearing your voice each day will make me feel better; it'll help me know that you're safe."

Her sincerity disarms me. "Of course I'll call. I like knowing you're safe too."

"Thank you."

I make the decision to say more. "I don't think anything will happen, but please be watchful. Ephraim mentioned you—not by name, but he knows about you, and the last thing I would ever want was for something bad to happen to you because of your association with me."

"I'll be careful. I promise."

"I'm glad."

"Rest up. As much as you can."

And then, as they say, depression sets in. Not the full-blown, can't-get-out-of-bed, what's-the-point variety, but relatively speaking, for me being me, I feel depressed. As I expected, I don't feel like going to work. Daily calls to Esteban prove to me that he's doing fine and the company's doing fine without me. He would never say so in as many words, but there's a comfort and a confidence in his voice that tells me he's adjusting to life in the captain's chair.

I, on the other hand, seem to be more content on the couch. It's where I spend much of my days and most of my evenings for the next four days. The lack of energy and the lack of enthusiasm for life in general feel very strange to me; this isn't who I am, and I know that. The trouble is, I can't do anything about it.

I've quit watching the news. The day of the crash, I watched for hours, following the details of what happened. The FAA did a thorough investigation of the second plane. There was no bomb or explosive device found, but the aircraft was definitely tampered with. Someone had rerouted wiring and safety systems in a way that would cause an overheat as the plane approached takeoff velocity. And it did exactly that. Someone with access knew exactly what he was doing. I shudder to think that it was Ephraim, but based on what he told me at that coffee shop, how could it be anyone else?

The media interviewed tearful family members of the refugees who would now never live to see adulthood. Many turned to God for solace in their grief; if only they knew what I know. Others wished for swift justice against the person or persons responsible. For a brief, reckless moment, I considered contacting one of the families and telling them what I knew, but common sense prevailed. It would do nothing to assuage their grief, and it would very likely put me in the public eye again as a suspect, something I can ill afford, now or ever. Ephraim would be only too happy to cast me in the role of culprit in his misdeeds, that's for sure.

Mercifully, no assignments come to me in these four days. In my present state of mind, I don't know if I have the strength, mentally or physically, to be anybody's hero. And to tell the absolute truth, I really don't want to. With all due respect to the forces of goodness and mercy, fuck others.

With one exception, of course. I do talk to Genevieve every day, and she is a source of limitless patience and comfort for me. I'm sure I must be coming across as pathetic and whiny, but never once does she judge me, cajole me, or otherwise try to make me do anything other than whatever I need to feel better.

On the fifth day of my self-imposed exile, I realize that I'm in fact *not* getting better on my own, and it's time to seek outside assistance. Having never sought this type of assistance before, I ask the company's HR coordinator for a recommendation, and she gives me the name of Dr. Jacob Kellner, psychiatrist. The concept is both alien and a bit aberrant to me. To make the appointment is to admit, in some small way, that there may be something *wrong with me.* But, truth be told, I've stepped away from my job, I'm mulling around my house, and when you get right down to it, I'm doing shit because God tells me to. Not the hallmarks of a brain at its happiest.

So I swallow what passes for my pride these days, put on my big-boy clothes, and drive to Dr. Kellner's office. Either there aren't many crazy people in Salisbury, Maryland, or I get the special CEO pass to the head of the line, because immediately after completing my new-patient registration, I am invited in to see the doctor himself. He is young, by which I mean roughly my age, with a look of kindness and compassion about him. Necessities of the trade, I imagine.

I don't know if I look as uneasy as I feel upon entering the psychiatric inner sanctum, but he does his best to put me at ease. "Mr. Shays, welcome. I'm Doctor Kellner."

I offer my hand. "Thank you. You can call me Tristan. I'd prefer it, I think."

"Thank you, Tristan. Would you prefer to call me Jacob?"

"No, that's fine; Dr. Kellner offers a degree of professional courtesy. So, where do you want me? Chair? Couch? Fetal position under the desk?"

He offers a polite laugh. "Wherever you're most comfortable. I'll have to move some things if you opt for under the desk, though."

"I'll start with the chair and see how the hour progresses."

I sit; he's done a good job of putting me at ease so far.

"You'll have to forgive me," I tell him. "This is my first time."

"Perfectly all right. Believe me, I hear that a lot. It looks like you're the CEO of a large corporation."

"Yes. Though I've put myself on a bit of a sabbatical."

"We could start, if you'd like, by talking about what brought you to see me today."

And so it begins. "It's not easy to talk about. It's not easy to understand."

"Take your time, Tristan. Anything you tell me is between us, and I'm not here to judge. I want to help you feel better about life and about yourself."

It takes me many seconds, I'm not even sure how many, to get the first words out. But once they begin, it feels easier to continue. "About three weeks ago, I started having … I guess you could call them visions."

From there, the narrative flows. I spend the next twenty minutes talking nonstop, about everything that's happened to me since that morning when I first learned about Esteban. From time to time, I glance up at my doctor. He takes notes as I talk, working to keep some eye contact as well. He does not interrupt me or even try to ask clarifying questions. He just lets me finish, which I do with the question, "So, do you think I'm crazy?"

"First of all, thank you for sharing your story with me. I imagine that wasn't easy to share. Let me add that you are not crazy. That's not a word I like to use, as you might expect. From what you just described, this is very real to you. These are things you're seeing and hearing, and you're acting based on them. I think the first thing we need to establish is whether they're accurate or not. I suspect that'll go a long way toward making you feel more at ease. If they're not accurate, you'll feel better about ignoring them. If they are accurate, you'll want to make the decision whether you're the person who's meant to set things right."

"But how could they be accurate? That's not the way the world works."

"Who are we to say?" he replies. "My understanding is focused on how the human mind works, and listening to you talk to me, I feel like I'm dealing with a mind in good working order. That, to me, suggests that you're not hallucinating these things and you're not making it up. The alternative that leaves is that this is actually happening somehow. And if we determine that to be the case, it goes beyond my field of specialty. I'm very happy to stay on as your doctor, listening to you tell me about anything you want to tell me. But I won't treat you with medications for a condition unless I'm convinced you actually have one, and so far, I'm not seeing one."

I take a moment to absorb all this. "Well, I suppose that's good news," I reply. "Although, when I came here, I think I wanted the exact opposite answer. I wanted you to tell me that I have some medical condition that you can drug me through, so I never have to get these visions again."

"I'm not a religious person," Kellner tells me in a tone ironically reminiscent of confession. "But I've read up a bit on the lives of the biblical prophets. From what I've learned—in a historical context, at least—they struggled too. They were persecuted, ridiculed, distrusted. Now, I'm not saying this is the same situation with you. But if you are the recipient of some sort of divine gift, it's quite possible that it comes with certain trials and tribulations. Together we can work on some coping strategies for you. Unfortunately, I don't think there's anyone who has a cure for prophecy."

"I'm feeling so much guilt right now."

"For the children on that flight?"

"Yes."

"Then let's talk about that for a while."

I talk through the rest of my appointed hour, and I appreciate that Jacob Kellner is a good man and a good doctor. I also start to understand why therapists and psychologists and psychiatrists make such a good living. But at the same time, I realize that I will not be needing his services on an ongoing basis. Because despite my wishes to the contrary, it feels increasingly clear that I do not have a medical condition that can be remedied. I have, for lack of a better word, a calling—a gift of unknown origin that few people throughout human history have had. I have been chosen to alter the course of events, to prevent bad things from happening. I didn't choose it, and I may not even want it, but it is mine to do.

Ephraim will try to thwart me at every turn; I know this. And I realize how absurd it is that the words *thwart me at every turn* are now part of my thought process. This may not be who I was, but if I'm going to survive with my sanity intact, I have to make it who I am.

I thank the good doctor for his time and his words, and I politely decline his offer to set up a follow-up appointment. He keeps the invitation open, for which I am grateful. Odds are good in the days ahead that I will experience things that will bring me to the aforementioned fetal position under his desk. Welcome to the life of a twenty-first-century prophet.

Tuesday, August 14, 2007

I awaken this morning actually feeling like I can face the day, a sensation I have not experienced for more than a week. Dr. Kellner's wisdom, however wise, was not enough to restore me to a feeling of being who I was before all of this started. It took several more days of introspection, coupled with encouraging calls from Genevieve, before I could go to sleep last night knowing I would be well again.

The drive in to work feels right, feels familiar. As I enter the building, I am greeted warmly by my employees, most of whom probably thought I was on a business trip—a frequent occurrence in the days before these days.

I will admit that it is gently disconcerting to walk into my office and find Esteban at my desk. Upon seeing me, he stands quickly, reminiscent of a child caught in his parent's favorite recliner. I give an understanding wave. "As you were," I tell him gently. "You're fine."

"Didn't want you to think I was taking over," he says.

"Why not? That's precisely what I asked you to do. And from everything I'm hearing, you're doing a damn good job of it."

"Thank you. How have you been?"

I smile and cock my head a bit. "I've had easier months."

"I imagine."

"Can I ask how things are between you and Annalisa?"

"I've decided to give her another chance. We're in couples therapy, and she's seeing a doctor on her own as well. It's unfortunate that this is what it took to get us to work through our problems, but at least we're working through them."

"I'm glad for you. I really hope you can work things out."

"Tristan, I don't know if I ever thanked you properly for saving me the way you did."

"You did. Trust me. Now it's my turn to thank you for saving this company in its CEO's absence."

"Well, you're welcome, but it's good to have you back."

"Yeah ... about that."

"Tristan, don't say what I think you're going to say."

"These past weeks have given me a lot to think about. You're privy to information that most of this company isn't. Our employees and our clients deserve our best, and that includes a CEO who will be here when he's needed. Despite your insistence that you're not the man for the job, I beg to differ. I'm here today to draw up the papers to name you as my successor."

He receives the news with quiet professionalism. "Thank you. I ... uh, I will do my best to uphold everything you've created here."

"I never doubted that."

"I have a difficult question, though. What happens if in two weeks or a month you stop receiving these visions and you have time again to run this company full time? Will you come back, looking for your position again? I'm sorry if that sounds rude, but it's something I should know."

"No offense taken. It's a very valid question. The fact is, visions or no visions, I need some time to be me. Because of the arrangement with the patent, I receive a small payment anytime an LED is manufactured anywhere in the world. Realistically, I never have to work another day in my life. There's really no way to say that and sound humble, and I apologize for that. Part of the unpleasant reality of our world: money is important. If I didn't have the finances to make this possible, I'm not sure what I'd do. But I do, and it's time I did this."

"How do we present this to the world without making the company look weak?" he asks.

"I have an acquaintance at the *Wall Street Journal*. I'll let her scoop this for tomorrow's edition, and I'll have Kayla send out a press release tomorrow morning. I'll let it be known that I've decided to dedicate my time to philanthropic work, and the readiness of my finest vice president will make the transition smooth and a very exciting time for the company."

"I have questions. A lot of questions."

"I'll answer as many of them as I can. Even after I leave."

"When do you want this to happen?"

"I'll call a companywide meeting for 3:00 today and announce it there. Your first day as CEO will be tomorrow."

"I don't suppose if I decline, it'll convince you to stay?"

"If you decline, I'll just have to give it to someone less qualified than you. And I don't think either of us wants to see that. I need you to trust me that this is good for you and good for the business. I promise I won't leave you hanging."

"I trust you."

The rest of the day passes like a blur for me. It takes two hours to draw up the paperwork naming Esteban as my successor. The board of directors is no problem; though they give me the obligatory "please reconsider" speech, they all know me well enough to know this isn't something I'm deciding lightly. So in the end, they wish me well and sign off on the decision. I let Kayla know, both because she works so closely with me and because she'll need to write up the press release for tomorrow. I then spend forty minutes on the phone with Susan Spencer at the *Wall Street Journal*. She's busy, but when she learns what I have to tell her, she's able to put things aside and listen to my story.

My story is, of course, a story. While it's true that what I'm doing is philanthropic in a sense, it's not as if I'm headed to Africa to feed hungry villagers or to Central America to bring drinking water to drought-ravaged areas. *Not yet, anyway.* But to tell the world that Tristan Shays is stepping down as CEO of the company his father built up from nothing because he has visions of strangers in peril and must go and help them would sound a bit insane to most people.

As it does to me.

So for now, vagaries are the order of the day. This is also the case as 3:00 arrives all too quickly and I must face the hundreds of employees who trust me to run this company each day. It's all in the presentation, so I have to make this right. I let them get settled in the auditorium on the second floor, and when they're quiet, I step to the podium. "Thank you all for coming on short notice. I'm not a fan of big speeches, so I'll keep this as short as I can; I know we all have work to do. After a great deal of thought, I have decided to step aside as CEO of Shays Diode Corporation."

This elicits a wave of murmuring throughout the room. I hear no cheering and see no high-fives, so I'll take that as a good sign. "Lately, I've been doing some charitable work, and it feels very much like what I need to be doing for a while. Running a corporation is an amazing opportunity, but there are days when I feel like I'm serving stacks of reports, rather than people. There are people out there who need me, and I'm in a position to help them, and that's what I'm going to do."

A professional round of applause starts up among the employees, and I accept it for what it is before continuing. "Now, when something like this happens in a business, there are questions that people often think but seldom say. I'm going to ask them and answer them right now. Has the company been sold? No. Are we in financial trouble? No. Will a bunch of jobs be sent to India or the Philippines? No. Will Shays Diode become the moneymaking tool of some off-site venture capital team? Not at all. I'm pleased to report that the man who will be taking over as CEO is a familiar face to you, and someone I certainly hope and believe has been earning your trust and respect for years. He's definitely earned mine. As of tomorrow, Mr. Esteban Padgett will be taking over the responsibilities of CEO for this corporation. Please be as good to him as you've been to me. It's not an easy job, but thanks in large part to everyone in this room, it's a very satisfying one. I'll take questions if you have them."

At 6:35 p.m., for the first time in my adult life, I am unemployed. It is by choice, of course, and I want to feel liberated by my decision, but there's a work ethic in me that's crying out *Slacker!* every time I think about it. And I think about it plenty on the drive home, with three cardboard boxes of my personal possessions in the back seat of my car. *I've handed my company away.* Granted, it's to someone I trust, someone very deserving, but I have to wonder what my father would say. I'd like to believe that he'd understand, that he'd support my decision, knowing that I made it for all the right reasons. But he was all business from the start, with a never-quit attitude, and quitting is what I've just done.

Safe at home, and with a glass of wine in my hand, I decide to call Genevieve.

"How are you doing?" she asks.

"I went to work today," I tell her.

"That's great. I'm glad you did."

"And then I quit my job."

She is silent for several seconds in the face of this news, finally saying, "That's a big step. Are you sure about this?"

"I'd better be. The paperwork is signed."

"I have no doubt that you set the wheels in motion, but my original question still stands: are you sure this is the right thing to do?"

"I wasn't this morning, but I am now. Did you ever feel … did you ever feel like you were waiting for something important to happen to you, but you needed to be in the right place before it could happen?"

"Yes," she says, "last month. Right before I met you."

That's a big compliment, and it deserves a big response, but the best I can manage is, "Thank you. That's how I'm feeling now. The job was great, and the company is amazing, and … at the risk of sounding artificially profound, we're bringing light to the world. But I've got bigger business now. Life-changing stuff. So what do you think? Can you still respect me after this?"

"Lovely, foolish man. First of all, thank you for believing that my opinion in this situation is that important. And secondly, the fact of the matter is that I'm falling in love with you, and part of that is because of how much I trust and respect you. You want to leave the world of big business to travel the country, saving people you've never met. Tell me precisely how I could not respect that?"

I laugh a little; she makes a good point. "Well, when you put it that way."

"That doesn't mean I won't worry about you. Every time you're away, helping someone and putting your own needs and your own safety last, I'll worry; and I'll live for that phone call from you that says you're all right, and for my next opportunity to see you. On that subject, when do you suppose that might be? Now that you're a man of leisure and all. What about this weekend? Come down to Virginia, and let me show you my home. It's not as luxurious as your digs, but it's comfortable."

"Genevieve, you know you don't have to impress me with your home. You've impressed me with you, and that's what matters. As for this weekend? Yeah, if I'm not off saving the world, I'd very much like to spend it with you."

"That's great. I'd love to have you."

"To have me … or to *have me?*"

"Your choice."

"Thank you for being my voice of reason during this whole thing. It's made a huge difference."

"You're welcome," she says. "You've made a huge difference to me too, and when I see you, I hope to show you that."

TUESDAY, AUGUST 14, 2007

I am awakened just after 5:00 a.m. with pain. *Great, first day off the job, and I can't even sleep in.* As consciousness returns to me, I realize that this pain is unlike any I've felt in the last month, yet there is a familiarity to it—something I experienced about ten years ago during a trip to the Caribbean: sunburn. The sensation is identical to a full-body sunburn, and I am jarred from my bed by the absolute agony of any part of my body touching a horizontal surface. Even the ordinarily comfortable silk sleepwear I use feels like flames against my body. So I hurriedly pull it from me and stand naked in my bedroom. In the dim light of morning, I know that something feels wrong, so I hurry into my bathroom and turn on the light.

To my amazement and horror, I realize that I not only feel like I have a sunburn, I look like I have one too. My face, arms, legs, and chest are bright red, and though I can't see it, I know my back is too. "This is different," I say aloud.

Immediately, I rummage through the bathroom cabinets, looking for relief. I find it in the back of a drawer: a bottle of aloe gel with lidocaine. Quickly I slather it on to every body part I can reach. It offers the barest minimum of reprieve, inasmuch as my sunburn isn't an actual sunburn but God's little simulation thereof.

Within a minute, the details arrive, momentarily allowing me to put the burning sensation aside to concentrate on where I must go and what I must do. As each new detail emerges, I see a picture that is very grim. Again, lives are at stake, and unless I do exactly the right things, it will all end very badly.

I make a decision at this moment, motivated by the relief of pain but also sincere in what I say. "I will do this."

My voice sounds strange in the emptiness of the bathroom. For reasons unknown, I repeat myself. "I will do this."

Almost immediately, the pain eases back; it doesn't disappear completely, but there is a feeling of soothing that follows my words, as if a reward for my acceptance. I fully understand that they could well and truly fuck me over should I disappoint in any way. Checking my reflection, I see that the faux sunburn has faded somewhat, though I still resemble an imprudent vacationer. "You know," I say aloud, "if I'm going to be in the car for hours, a burn like this is going to hurt."

It may be my imagination, but the pain seems to subside once again—just a bit, but it's an acknowledgment that the mysterious, unseen "they" are listening.

By 7:30 a.m., I decide that it is late enough to make a phone call. Genevieve answers on the second ring. "Didn't expect to hear from you again so soon."

"What can you tell me about Plouton, Virginia?"

"Plouton? Not much to tell, really. Nothing worth seeing there. Just a bedroom community for Kensington, about fifteen miles away. Planning a vacation?"

"Not exactly."

"Oh my God, you got another assignment, didn't you?"

"Yes."

"When is it?"

"Today. This evening."

"Can you give me details?"

"From what I saw, it's a domestic dispute gone wrong. A family with a husband, wife, and two small children. Tonight, he's going to have some sort of psychotic episode, come home, get a gun, kill his family, and then himself."

"Unless you stop him," she says, more of a statement than a question.

"Unless I stop him."

"Can you call the police in for help?"

"That's part of the problem. From what I saw, the police make things worse. They upset the man so much, it pushes him over the edge and into violence. So I have to do this alone, with no law-enforcement intervention."

"Well, I'm glad you called, then," she says. "I can take a half day. Plouton is about an hour past Richmond. You can swing by and get me, and we can arrive together. What time is all this supposed to happen?"

"At 8:30 tonight. But back up. Swing by and get you?"

"Of course. That's why you called, isn't it? So I can be there with you."

"I called to find out what you know about Plouton. I don't want you to be there with me."

"Why not?" she asks, sounding hurt.

"I hark you back to the part about the crazy man with the gun killing everyone around him. I don't want you anywhere near that."

"And I hark you back to the part where you stop him from doing that."

"I'd like to remind you of my recent track record. I'm not exactly what you'd call undefeated. If this goes wrong—as it very well might—I couldn't live with myself if something happens to you."

She takes a resolute breath. "Tristan, our relationship is still young, so I'll forgive you the presumption, but there's one important thing you should know about me: I don't need protecting. Going with you may not have been your idea, but it certainly is mine. Think about it: you've got the husband and the wife and kids. Your main task will be trying to calm the husband. I need to be there to keep the wife and children from upsetting him further."

She makes a lot of sense. It would be helpful to have someone else there, and she's right; I'm playing the alpha male card, shielding her when she doesn't need to be shielded. "Okay. I'll pick you up. E-mail me your address and directions to your house, and I'll be there by 5:00."

"Thank you. You won't regret this."

"I hope not. I don't want to see anything happen to either of us."

"Tristan … do you think Ephraim is behind this somehow? Remember how he told you he's getting the same assignments you are, but he's working to make things worse?"

"I thought about that, but in the visions I have of what's going to happen, I don't see him anywhere. He's not the man with the gun, and there's no one except the family involved. It sounds like a basic domestic situation gone wrong. I'll go in, talk to him, try to talk him out of doing anything rash, and hopefully, everybody gets to keep living."

"What are you going to tell him about why you're there?" she asks.

"I haven't worked that part out yet, but I have a few hours to figure that out. I'll come up with something. In the meantime, you head on over to your job, and I'll see you at the end of the day."

"I know this sounds stupid, given that we're walking into a violent situation where people may be killed horribly, but I'm really looking forward to seeing you."

"Yeah," I reply, hiding a little smile. "I'm looking forward to seeing you too."

Chapter 11

A FOUR-HOUR DRIVE TO Richmond awaits, with another hour to the town of Plouton. As I get into my car just before 1:00 p.m., it strikes me just how much driving I've been doing, and how much lies ahead if this becomes my new circumstances. I hate to put so much wear and tear on my personal vehicle. I may have to start considering the wisdom of renting cars for these missions. A different car every time sounds appealing; I could try out new makes and models, change things up a bit.

One thing at a time. Take it slowly; focus on today.

I feel deeply unprepared for what lies ahead. In Boston, I had everything laid out, every detail mapped and charted and planned for—and things still fell to shit. Now I'm headed into a violent domestic situation with no plans to speak of, no advance strategy, no backup plan. I'm bringing Genevieve with me, which—despite my open-minded, empowering acceptance—disturbs the hell out of me in a primal, me-Tarzan-you-Jane kind of macho bullshit way. And to frost this particular tasty cupcake, my brand-new nemesis might be there waiting for me, working his hardest to screw things over.

Why did I quit my $525,000-a-year job again?

I think too much; I know this. I've always overthought things, always been the classic type-A personality. This isn't a fault, per se, certainly not in the CEO of a major corporation. It's served me well over the years, both in my business life and in my private life. But this blessing is also my curse, because I can't turn it off. I can't *not* think. Even now, as the miles of Maryland and then Virginia pass beyond my windshield, my mind races at twice the speed of the car. I'm always thinking about something, even when I sleep. My dreams have always felt real to me. Never could I tell myself, *It's okay, you're only dreaming.*

What must that feel like? To subdue the terrors of your unconscious mind with the power of your conscious will.

I truly believe the terrors of my dreams will be nothing compared to what awaits me today, in the little one-story house in Plouton, Virginia. I've seen the place in my instructions; I saw the people too. The wife, Trish, thirty-two years old and frightened and confused by her husband's actions. Their children, eight-year-old Annabelle and six-year-old Michael, too young to truly understand what's unfolding before them, but watching their mother for cues on what to feel. And the man at the center of it all, thirty-four-year-old Benton Tambril. My age. I don't have access to his thoughts, but I can see his face, with eyes wide and distant, sweat beading on his forehead, despite the air-conditioning I can feel cooling the house.

What's haunting him? What would drive a husband and father to pull a firearm off a high shelf in a closet, load it from a box kept two rooms away, and then turn it on his family and then himself? That's not a crime of passion; it's not a moment of weakness. It's deliberate, calculated, measured. He sees their faces, and then what remains of their faces; he must, because I can. And then, finally, when his atrocity spree is over, he makes the decision to end his own life—not as a reaction of shame and horror over what he's done, but ... something else. I can't tell what it is, and that scares me too. It makes his actions feel unpredictable; a strange word to use for someone who can see in advance what will transpire, but that's how it feels to me—like despite my foreknowledge, anything is still possible.

Just after 5:00, I arrive in Richmond. The directions Genevieve gave me lead me through a variety of neighborhoods into a quiet residential area, dotted with modest but tasteful bungalows and a few two-story stick-builts. At last, I pull up in front of her house, and I find, to my surprise, that I am actually nervous. She's seen me in my home, even seen me vulnerable, but this is the first time I'll be seeing her home, and I'm scared of saying the wrong thing. Come across nonchalant, and it sounds like I think her place is too shabby. Come across too complimentary, and it sounds like I'm being artificial and condescending. She's the closest thing I've had to a girlfriend in a long time, and I don't want to screw this up.

Building my courage, I get out of the car, proceed briskly up the walkway, and ring the doorbell. A few seconds later, she opens the door and smiles, which looks just as beautiful as I realize she is every time I see her.

I offer a little smile of my own. "I made it."

"You sure did. I'm glad you're here."

"I'm glad I'm here too."

"Please, come in."

I enter the house and put my arms around her, as she puts hers around me. The ease with which we kiss each other seconds later surprises me a bit; I'm not sure which of us initiates it, and in this rare instance, I decide not to overthink it and just enjoy the sensation.

When the kiss ends—too soon for my taste—she says, "Well, this is the place," in precisely the way that people do when they're not proud of their home but it's the best they can do.

"I like it," I say sincerely. "It's very you."

She smiles at this. And it's true—the living room is decorated with artwork and objects of a spiritual nature. No, the place isn't fancy, but neither is she. She's earthy, and so is her home.

"I was nervous," she says, in a tone of confession. "After seeing your place, I was afraid mine couldn't compare."

"Well, fortunately, it's not a contest. If your home makes you feel safe and centered, it's the right space for you."

"It does," she says. "So, are you hungry or anything?"

I check my watch—not my typical measuring device for hunger, but it displays the very pressing reality that we need to scoot, and soon. "A little, but I think we'd better get something on the road. I want to get to Plouton before our boy comes home. If I could use your bathroom, I think that'll be all I need before I'm ready to go."

"Down the hall, on the left," she replies, pointing the way.

My necessaries completed five minutes later, I emerge to find her holding two bottles of water and an overnight bag slung over one shoulder. "I didn't know if this would be finished in a single day," she explains.

"I packed one myself," I tell her. "Same reason."

"Guess it's time then."

I exit the house, and she follows, locking the door behind us. "You'll have to come back when you can stay longer," she says.

"I'd like that."

We climb into my car, putting her bag in the back seat next to mine. I start the engine and turn to her. "Still not too late to change your mind."

"Left at the stop sign," she answers simply. I nod and take us to the corner.

As we approach the highway to Plouton, she asks, "Do you have a plan?"

"When I got my vision of the house, one of the things I saw inside was a pledge envelope from a place called First Church of Plouton. I think that might give us an in, if we claim to be from the church."

"Plouton's not a big town," she tells me, "so I can't imagine the church is very big either. Odds are good they know everybody in that church."

"So we're new members, on an outreach committee, there to talk to the family about what's coming in the months ahead."

"You think that'll work?"

"All we need is a way inside. Once we're there, we can say or do what we want, as long as we come between the husband and his family."

"What time is he supposed to get home?"

"I don't know. All I know is that 8:30 is when everything ends—badly. If we can be there by 6:00, we can help shield the family, maybe talk some sense into him."

"Tristan, do you think this will work?"

"Honestly? No. I think this will end in violence and tears, possibly with one of both of us being killed too. Sorry you asked?"

"A little. So why are you doing this?"

"Because I absolutely know how it will end if I don't."

A minute of silence passes between us, and she declares, "I'm not afraid to die."

It is a bold statement, a proud announcement of her inner strength. Rather than answer honorably, I choose to answer honestly. "Well, you should be. It'll help you live longer."

This greeting-card-perfect moment serves as a conversation killer for the remainder of the drive. I know I should be glad to see her and thankful for the assistance on this difficult task, but I'm afraid for both of us. That feeling overwhelms everything else I feel, and I really hope it doesn't distract me from what I have to do.

Just before 6:15, I see a roadside sign: Welcome to Plouton. Population 8,256.

Plouton. Another name for Pluto or Hades, ruler of the underworld. Charming name for your quiet little town. *Hey, where ya livin' these days? Found a little house out in Satan, Virginia. You really should see it.*

Within three minutes, we pull up to the Tambrils' house, looking just like it looked in my vision: a little one-story brick structure with a well-kept lawn and a white mailbox at the curb. As we park at that curb, I look at the house, and flashes from my vision assail my senses. Gunshots; the smell of black powder; children's screams. So much blood. I am God's guest of honor at a private nightmare. Unless …

"Are you all right?" Genevieve's question breaks the cycle of awful thoughts and images.

"Yes. Sorry. I think I am."

We exit the car, and she says to me, "You take the lead. I'll follow what you start."

I work hard to subdue my nerves as we make our way up the walk to the front door. Taking a deep breath, I ring the doorbell. In less than a minute, the door opens, and a woman appears. Ah, the security of small towns. "Hello," she says.

I put on an artificially large smile. "Good evening, Mrs. Tambril. I'm Charles Goodman from the First Church of Plouton, and this is my wife, Sarah. We're actually new to the church, having just come from the district headquarters, and we're visiting with local members. Do you have a few minutes to talk with us about some good things coming this year?"

"Well," she says, appearing to buy the story but not looking entirely comfortable, "my husband's not home from work yet, but he should be soon. Yes, come on in."

The two children enter the room, and my saccharin smile extends to them. "Well, this must be Michael and Annabelle. Nice to meet y'all." *Did I actually just say "y'all"? Holy shit.* "We're Charles and Sarah, from the church. New to town and talking with folks from the congregation."

"Can I get you some sweet tea?" Trish asks politely.

"That would be lovely," Genevieve answers, bringing out a Virginia accent I'm hearing for the first time.

"If y'all'd like to sit at the dining room table, I'll bring that out."

She disappears into the kitchen, and Genevieve and I exchange a look that suggests that all is well so far. The two children remain in the dining room with us as we sit, watching us with eyes that instinctively see through falsehood. In a quiet voice, six-year-old Michael Tambril asks me, "Are you here to help Daddy?"

For the sake of preserving our cover, I have to play dumb. "We're here to get to know your whole family. Does your daddy need some help?"

The boy gets shy for a moment, and we watch as he decides whether to answer. His face speaks of family secrets betrayed. "He gets sad sometimes."

At this moment, Trish re-enters the room with three glasses of tea. "Michael, you and your sister run along outside and play while the grown-ups talk." She delivers this Tennessee Williamsesque directive as naturally as breathing. I guess it ain't proper to talk about Big Daddy.

Handing us the tea, Trish offers a little smile of apology. "Children say things, and you don't always know where they come from."

Except I do know.

"How are you enjoying living in Plouton?" Genevieve asks.

"Well, it's home. I was born in Kensington, and truth be told, I've never been more than fifty miles outside of this area. Benton—that's my husband— he went to Washington, DC last month to take the cure."

"The cure?" I repeat.

"Yes. He's got the lung cancer, from all those years of smokin'. But he signed up for a new treatment the government is tryin' out. He had to spend three days in Washington. Said it was nice there. He got to see Arlington Cemetery, where his daddy is buried. He was a war hero, you know."

"I'm certainly sorry to hear that Mr. Tambril is unwell," I reply. "I hope the treatment is having some effect."

She looks uncomfortable at this, and she hesitates a bit before answering, "It's helped with the pain, some, but … it's made him—moody."

Genevieve and I exchange a look. *Moody* might not be such good news. I was counting on being able to talk some sense into Benton Tambril, make him see that life is worth living. But if today's actions are the result of a drug-induced psychotic break, all the calming talk in the world won't make a difference.

Sensing a gap in the conversation, Genevieve takes the lead. "We have some new programs that we're working on at the church this year. Some support groups for people dealing with this or that. We're planning one for people who have trouble with alcohol, one for people who have a chronic illness like cancer, and one for families experiencing domestic troubles like violence in the household."

Clever girl. She's opening the door wide for Trish to share any history of violence in the past.

"That all sounds very good," Trish answers unemotionally. "I imagine Benton'll be interested in that one for folks with chronic illness. He doesn't have anyone he can really talk to about what he's going through. And those others …" We both watch with great interest, ready for her to tell us what we need to know. "I don't mean to play the gossip, but I know that some of the men in the church drink, and they've been known to raise a hand to their women. I've been blessed, but some not so much."

I try not to look disappointed at this revelation. The patented Tristan Shays completely unscientific lie detector tells me that she's not covering anything up. Her husband is not a violent man. What happens here tonight will most likely take her completely by surprise. Part of me hoped Trish would let Genevieve take her and the kids out of here, so I could face Benton Tambril alone, but without a good reason, it doesn't seem likely to happen.

The conversation is interrupted by the opening of the front door. Into the fray walks the man of the house, the reason we are here, looking just as he looked in the first part of my vision. A chill sweeps through me, being in the room with a man who may kill as many as six people today—including me.

Genevieve and I rise, as does Mrs. Tambril. "Hello, Benton," his wife says with a smile. "How was work?"

"It was fine," he replies noncommittally, eyeing us. "I didn't know we had guests."

"This is Charles and Sarah from the church. They're new to town and doing some community work, I guess you'd call it. They came to tell us about some new programs at the church."

"They stayin' for dinner?" he asks, clearly sounding unenthusiastic at the prospect.

"No, sir," I answer for her. "Just here for a few minutes of your time, and then we'll be on our way."

"That's for the best," he replies.

The vibe I'm getting off of him is unsteady and dangerous. I need to get the others out of here. "Sarah, why don't you take Mrs. Tambril and the kids on a stroll around the block and talk to them a bit while I get to know Mr. Tambril here in the dining room."

"That'd be lovely, Charles," Genevieve answers. "Shall we?"

Trish Tambril has to be the definitive example of Southern patience and grace, not to be completely wigged out by the bizarre nature of this intrusion. She rounds up the children and dutifully follows Genevieve out the front door, to listen to made-up programs from a church we've never been to.

Benton, however, subscribes to no such social grace. As I sit at the dining room table, he stands over me, eyeing me with all the affection he would bestow on one of the 9/11 terrorists. "You should know I think the church is bullshit," he drawls, savoring the last word for all it's worth. "And God can kiss my white ass for all he's done to me. Givin' me the cancer."

"God and all the cigarettes you've been smoking since you were, what, fourteen?"

"Twelve," he retorts in defiance. "What of it? I went to your church every Sunday, sang your damn hymns, said your bullshit prayers. Where's this God now when I need him?"

"Closer than you might think. Tell me about the treatment."

"What treatment?"

"The one you went to Washington to get. The cancer treatment that takes the pain away but leaves you moody."

"What is this?"

"The most important conversation of your life." My goal is to sound portentous, but to my ears, it just comes out ominous.

He takes a few steps toward the front door. "Where did she take my family?"

"Away from you, Benton. Don't worry; they're safe. A lot safer than they'd be in here with you."

"That's crazy!"

Sitting isn't working for me anymore, so I stand and face him. "Is it? I'm not so sure."

"Who the hell are you?"

"A messenger. It turns out the God who can kiss your ass actually sent me to save it. You. Your wife. Your children."

"No! I wouldn't hurt them."

"I want to believe that. Just like you want to believe that. And if we can get through this night and make that true, we'll leave here. Leave you and your family to live your lives in peace, the way it should be. But there's a problem. I'm here because if we don't change things, at 8:30 tonight, you're going to take the gun that's in the bedroom closet, and you're going to point it at your wife."

"No …"

"You're going to kill her in front of your children, and then you're going to kill both of them."

"I'm not …" he replies, his voice wracked with emotion.

"And when you do this thing, this unspeakable thing, there's no tears in your eyes, no pain in your expression. It's like—it's like you're switching off the kitchen light. And then, Benton, you turn that gun on yourself and you end your own life. Right here in this room. At 8:30 tonight, unless we find a way to stop that from happening."

The tears are in his eyes now; the pain on his face. "How can you stand here, a stranger in my own house, and accuse me of these things I haven't done? No man can know such things about another man."

"No, Benton. No man *should* know such things about another man. But a few of us do. And I think you're standing here now, crying about these things because these thoughts were already in your head before I even mentioned them. Weren't they?"

His answer is tiny as he buries his face in his hands. "Yes."

I go to him and place my hands on his shoulders in a show of support. "That's why I'm here."

He looks up at me through eyes wet with fear. "I love my family."

"I'm sure you do. And I would bet that on any other day, hurting them would be the last thing in the world you would ever do." He nods in agreement. "That's why I need you to tell me about the treatment. What did they do to you? Did they do something with your mind? Some kind of hypnosis or mind-altering substance?"

"It's not like that," he says, calm starting to return to his voice. "It's not a cure. Just a study for a new kind of pain pill for cancer patients. They interviewed us, and if we qualified, we got a supply of the pills each month. But they told us we couldn't talk about the details, not even with family. They said it was classified, and if we talked about it, we wouldn't get any more of the pills."

"Benton, I think those pills are what put the thoughts in your head about hurting yourself, about hurting your family."

"But they make me feel better …"

"Show me. Bring me the bottle, please."

He looks hesitant for a moment but then decides to trust me. "It's in the master bathroom. I'll have to go get it."

With that, he hurries from the room and toward a back bedroom. *This has to be it. It has to be those pills. But what could they be? I can find out; I can call the manufacturer or someone. Even if he gets removed from the study, it's better for everyone. Better than what those pills could make him do.*

He returns almost three minutes later with an opaque pill bottle large enough to hold about a hundred capsules. Before handing it to me, he looks at my eyes once more, searching, I would guess, for evidence of trustworthiness. He must find something there, as he hands me the bottle. Quickly I examine the label. Unlike a traditional prescription label, this one is very sparse, with the information looking almost coded: Subject 16,265. Tambril, Benton. Age 34. Plouton, VA. 500 mg CP117beta. Take one tablet by mouth three times a day with a full glass of water or milk. Lot 68552. Approv. SODARCOM.

It tells me almost nothing. CP117beta; the pre-branding name for the drug. Lot 68552 for tracking purposes. But who or what is SODARCOM? It's just not enough information. "Did they give you a phone number to call?" I ask him. "Someone to talk to if something goes wrong or if you have questions?"

"No. They call me once a week to make sure everything's all right. The call comes from Washington, but the number is blocked. I don't know how to reach them."

I open the bottle and pour three of the pills into my palm. Benton looks at the pills—stares at them, actually—with the expression of someone guarding a precious treasure. It's clear to me at this moment that he's addicted. "You have to stop taking them," I tell him.

"But the pain—"

"Is nothing compared to the pain you'll feel if you lose control of your thoughts and actions. When I leave here tonight, I'll take these with me."

"No!"

"I'll have them analyzed. I'll let you know what's in them. In the meantime, you can take other pills for the pain."

Benton reaches behind him and pulls a pistol out of the waistband of his pants, pointing it at me. *Shit, that's why he was gone so long. He was getting the gun too. Stupid, Tristan. Sloppy.*

"Give the pills to me," he says calmly, but in a tone that suggests that rage is on the way.

I manage to maneuver into the living room, pick up the telephone, and dial 911. At the first hint of someone answering, I say, "He's got a gun," and put the receiver down on the table, hoping like hell they can trace the call.

In just a few seconds, Benton moves into the living room and hangs up the phone, never letting me out of his sights. "You shouldn't have done that. Give me those pills."

"I'm sorry, Benton. This is the only way I can save you, save your family. If you take this pill tonight, you're going to kill your family, and I can't let that happen."

Rather than rage, anguish sweeps over him. "I'm a burden to them," he tells me through moist, ragged breaths.

"In sickness and in health. She's promised to love you through anything that happens to you."

"She has. And she never complains. But I see it. I see it in her eyes, how tired she is. How she—" Painful-sounding coughs interrupt his words for many seconds. "How she wishes she could have a husband again. Instead of this sick, dying thing that shares her bed."

"Whatever you think she's going through, you can work through it together. She won't abandon you."

Mercifully, in the distance, I hear a siren drawing near. Help may be on the way after all.

"She can deal with my body being sick. But now this? My own mind turned against me? Turned against her and the kids? Making me do things I would never do. How can I fight that?"

Something in his eyes suddenly conveys to me very clearly that I am not the one who's in danger. "Benton, no …"

"I suppose I should thank you for coming here and saving their lives. Because I think that's what you did. I don't know why God would pick me to get such a second chance, but here you are."

"I can get you help. I can take you somewhere, away from them, so you can get proper treatment. I'll even pay for it. Please—*please*. Don't make this their last memory of you."

"Don't tell my family what you saw. Don't tell them what it was I almost did."

I take a step in his direction, but it's too late. I watch in horror as he puts the barrel of the gun into his mouth. There is barely time to close my eyes and fall to the ground as I hear the overpowering sound of the gunshot and the indescribable horror of the sound that follows it.

I can't look at him. I just can't. I force myself to turn away, eyes still closed, and crawl in what I think is the direction of the living room. The siren that had been approaching has stopped, I now realize. Seconds later, I hear the front door open forcefully and a man's voice announce, "Sheriff's officer!"

Eyes shut tight, I get to my knees. "Officer, thank God you're here." I open my eyes to see the new arrival, and the sight of him freezes the words that were already forming.

Ephraim. He stands before me in the uniform of a sheriff's deputy, complete with stiff-brimmed hat, badge, and service revolver, which he holds in one hand. "It's not possible," I say in an emotionless whisper.

"I know!" he replies, his tone actually sounding jubilant. "You, me, two wacky guys sharing another misadventure. I mean, what are the odds? People are gonna talk!" He looks past me at the lifeless form on the dining room floor. "Yuck! That's a messy one. Did he do the family too?"

His question stirs a feeling of horror in me. "Yes. They're in the bedroom. You got what you wanted. Now go!"

Ephraim shakes his head at me. "You are such a terrible liar. The family's out with your little Beanie Baby. That's okay, Daddy's the important one in this little domestic saga. Lurleen and the young 'uns are free to live lives of pious humility and quiet desperation in this geographic shithole they call home. That reminds me ..." He looks around and spots the bottle of pills I have dropped in the next room. "There we go," he says, picking it up and pocketing it. "Evidence for my investigation."

By this point, I am too numb to speak. Ephraim, however, shares no such malady. He remains smug and even playful as he says, "I wish you could see your face. You look like someone just fed you your childhood pet. Cheer up, Sparky. You didn't fuck this one up."

Bereft of words, I simply point to Benton Tambril's body.

"What, him? I've got news for you: this was the best outcome. Without those pills, he had six painful months to live. With the pills, he had six *less*-painful months to live."

"What are they? The pills?" I manage.

"They are unimportant. Little details. Footnotes. And you know that nobody really reads the footnotes. The police report will say that a terminally ill man took his own life rather than dying slowly and painfully. At least it will after I type it up. The community will chip in to take care of the survivors, and everybody who was meant to live will live happily ever after. So listen to me when I tell you this: go home. Stop and have a drink first. Get yourself laid. For Christ's sake, you look like you need it."

What happens next is like a blur. Maybe it's motivated by his taunting or by his tone or by the very fact that he's here in the middle of such a colossal wrong. In a flash, I turn on my heel, dive into the dining room, and make a grab for Benton's gun. Ephraim won't suspect it, and I figure I can fire twice before he even realizes what I've done.

Except it doesn't go that way. I do turn on my heel; I even dive into the dining room. But in doing so, I slip in a puddle of blood and fall face-first onto Benton's body. Complicating matters is the fact that in reaching for his gun, I get a long look at what remains of his head. So as I stand up, gun in hand, and turn to face Ephraim, a wave of nausea overtakes me, and I vomit all over the floor, dropping the gun in the process.

For a moment, Ephraim just stares at me. He looks almost impressed at my efforts, but that quickly gives way to peals of laughter. "Oh my word, that was priceless! I think Bruce Willis did that same move in *Die Hard.* Stop or I'll puke!" The laughter begins again.

"Fuck you," I toss at him through the very bad taste in my mouth.

"I'm sorry, I'm sorry," he replies, curtailing the laughter a bit. "It was just ... I really didn't expect that move out of you."

Exactly the words I wanted to hear. "And that's why you need to be afraid of me, Ephraim. You think you know what's going to happen. You think you know everything I'm going to do. But I can change things up. And one day, I might just decide that I don't want you here anymore."

My tone is ominous, and it's not lost on him. He raises his revolver and points it at my head. "Now you listen. I've been patient with you, and I've let you go about your business. But don't go thinking you have any special treatment from me. I can end you at will. I'm letting you walk out of here today, but the offer isn't unlimited. Leave here. Find your little girlfriend, take her by the hand, and go. Fast. No explanations, just leave. Let the nice policeman tell the grieving widow what happened. Because I fucking swear to God if you're here when they get back to this house, I'll tell the family that you shot their husband and father."

It's no bluff; I know this. Without another word, I move swiftly through the front doorway and out onto the walkway. I spot Genevieve and the Tambrils a half block away, making their way more quickly back to the house now that they've seen the police car out front. I rush to her side and take her hand. "Come on," I say, "we have to leave. Police are here. We've done all we can."

"Wait!" Mrs. Tambril calls as we sprint away. "What happened? Where's Benton?"

I don't even look back; I just get in the car as Genevieve gets in the passenger side. As I start the engine and pull away, she looks at me, watching me intently as I sit in silence, completely focused on the road ahead. There are no words to tell her what I've just been through.

Chapter 12

Minute follows minute in the car, as we drive on in silence. In my peripheral vision, I see Genevieve sitting next to me, clearly confused, clearly uncomfortable, wanting to say something, anything. But I know she sees the expression on my face, the combination of disappointment, horror, and anguish. It does not invite conversation. So we drive on, back toward Richmond.

Fully ten minutes pass before she musters the resolve to say quietly, "You have blood on you. Are you hurt? At least tell me that much."

"No, I'm not hurt."

The readiness of my answer inspires her to ask, "Is Benton dead?"

This answer comes more slowly. It feels more like a confession than a reply. "Yes."

"How d—"

"Genevieve, *please.*" My tone is firm but not angry. "Let me drive. I'll talk to you when we get back to Richmond. For now, I just need to focus on driving. Please." It's harsher than I want to be, but I really don't have the words yet.

We drive on in silence, all the way back to Richmond, back to her home. I pull up to the curb, and for a moment, we just sit. "I should probably go," I utter quietly.

She hesitates a moment, perhaps finding her words. "No, you most certainly should not. When I went with you, I agreed to follow the plan. But this? I have to do this my way. I don't know exactly what happened inside that house, but I need you to stay here tonight. I need you to tell me what you've been through, and I need you to feel it. Whatever it's making you feel, express that. Get angry, get sad, scream obscenities. You're safe here. And you don't have to kiss me or touch me or eat my cooking, but you do have to sleep in my house tonight. Because after what you've been through today, I can't let you get back on that highway, drive to that big, empty house, and go through this alone. You don't have to answer me, because you're clever enough to know that this isn't a request. So, you can signify your understanding by turning off the ignition, grabbing our bags, and following me inside."

I turn off the ignition and grab our bags, following Genevieve inside. She's right; physically, emotionally, I'm spent. If I had to spend four more hours in the car tonight, it might just break me. Right here and now, I'm at a destination, a safe place where my beleaguered soul can find refuge for the night. My initial refusal is not for lack of desire; as usual, I just don't want to inflict my own unhappiness on others. But this woman, who I barely know and yet know so well, is offering me a chance to unburden, a chance to be held, a chance to sleep. The road will still be there in the morning, pushing me on toward home and probably the next assignment that's mine to conquer or fail.

Safely inside the house, I put the bags down, and Genevieve instantly wraps her arms around me. The embrace is not demanding, not sexual, simply protective and safe, as if her limbs could shield me from what I've just been through, even erase it from my memory. But I know she can't, and she knows she can't. All she can do is what she's doing: giving me some of her strength at a moment when I desperately need it.

I don't know how long we stand together this way. Time doesn't matter. When at last we separate, she goes right to the refrigerator, brings out a cold bottle of water, and hands it to me. I down it in seconds, surprised at how thirsty I am. "Would you like another?" she asks.

"No, no. That was what I needed. Thank you."

"We should sit," she suggests, leading me toward her living room. *Living room.* The words strike me as odd, as if the room is some sort of life-giving haven, after what I've seen in other rooms of other houses. Before my mind can go too far down that path, I lower myself to the sofa, and she sits next to me.

"I don't even know what to ask you first," she says. "Most important to me is that you're all right."

"I'm not hurt. Not physically. It was Ephraim; he was there, dressed like the local police."

"Can you tell me what happened?"

Over the next twenty minutes, we exchange stories of what we saw and did. Her tale is a lot simpler than mine. She accompanied the wife and children out of the house, spoke with them, listened to Mrs. Tambril's concerns and fears and her hopes for the future, for a future that now would not be.

Then she listens to my story, my interactions with Benton, his actions with the pills and the gun, his final, desperate decision, followed by the terrible realization that once again, Ephraim has intruded into my life. "And so he stood in the way of my successfully completing this assignment again."

"I wouldn't say that. You saved the wife and children. That wouldn't have happened without you there."

"But he killed himself, and I couldn't stop him."

"Who's to say he wasn't a lost cause?" she asks, with no hint of malice in her voice. "I had a friend who died of cancer five years ago. Her last days were agonizing. No one could do anything to help her through that. You heard what Benton said; I think he chose his own way out."

"Then why was I sent to save him as well?"

The question leaves her at a loss for a reply. After several tense seconds, she says, "I don't know. Maybe because whoever sent you doesn't accept loss well. But people die. All the time. Maybe you're like a doctor, and some of them you can save, and some of them you can't. If you keep doing this, you're going to lose some. If you grieve for them and blame yourself for their loss, it will destroy you. So please tell me now if that's what's likely to happen. Because I'm falling in love with you, and it would tear me apart to watch this hurt you that much."

What can I say in the face of this honesty? How can I explain to her the battle that's raging inside my own mind? At the heart of her words is the message *I love you, and I don't want to see you suffer.* "I just don't know. I want to believe that I can walk away from an assignment like this, win or lose, and just carry on with my life. But to see what I saw today … that's going to stay with me forever."

"I'm not asking you to forget it. I'm not even asking you not to feel what you feel. But I am asking you not to treat the losses as *your* losses."

"I'll try very hard."

She puts a comforting hand on my shoulder and offers a kind smile. "It's been an awful day. Take a hot shower, and let's go to bed. I know I could use some sleep, and I'm pretty sure you could too."

The water beats down on me. I close my eyes, turn my head up slightly as the drops cascade down my face and body. They could be a million uncried tears washing over me, trying to cleanse me for sins of omission. Chastisement for underachievement to a God I've never met and don't know. *Failed.* All my life, I have striven to escape that word—in my childhood, in my studies, in my professional life. Failure has never been an option; hard work, self-sacrifice, and personal work ethic have carried the day every time. And yet now, when so much is at stake, failure haunts my steps, threatening the delicate hold I have on my new circumstances.

How can I possibly consider today a success when a sick, frightened man ended his life as I watched? *Correction—didn't watch. Couldn't watch. Not strong enough to face the moment when everything became too real. Charles Goodman? What a farce. Not Charles, and not a good man. An alias; a walking falsehood, spinning lies rather than telling people honestly that you've received a gift and you're there to share it with them. What are you afraid of? Would Benton Tambril be alive if you walked up to him and said, "God wants you to live, and he sent me to save you"?*

I shake my head to clear these thoughts. They are not helping; more like self-flagellation of the mind. And they are directly counter to what I told Genevieve I would do. At this moment, I embrace the loss as my loss. I fucking own it, bought and paid for. Trish Tambril will have to bury her husband, but in my thoughts, he will never be laid to rest. He and the children from the doomed flight will walk unburied through my memories for the rest of my life. How many more can I lose before the legions of them drive me out of my mind?

Is that what finally pushed Devin Larimer over the edge? Maybe it wasn't all the ones he had to save; maybe it was all the ones he couldn't. And now I've left my job, walked away from my life as I knew it, ready to commit myself to the ongoing pursuit of this cavalcade of futility. What have I done?

What have I done?

I vaguely remember getting out of the shower and toweling off in the bathroom. In the next room, Genevieve awaits me. Exactly what will happen tonight, I don't know, but everything she's said suggests that there will be no pressure in any direction. I dress in a clean pair of gym shorts, hoping that's enough to wear. When I enter the dimly lit bedroom, I find Genevieve lying on top of the covers wearing a nightgown that's tasteful without being frumpy. "Is this okay?" I ask, gesturing toward the shorts.

"Perfectly," she says. "Is this?"

"Yes."

"If you're uncomfortable sleeping in here, I can make up the couch …"

"No, that won't be necessary. I'd like to sleep in here."

She smiles pleasantly at me. "Then come on over." She pulls back the covers and I slide in next to her as she gets underneath as well. I feel a comforting arm on my shoulders, a loving hand through my hair. "Can I get you anything?" she asks.

"No, I have everything I need right here. Thank you."

We lie there together for a time; I'm not sure how long, exactly. I can't see a clock in the room, and after the events of the day, I'm not at my sharpest. In fact, I actually start to drift off to sleep, because I'm aware of a sensation of being awakened by her voice, which tells me, "I want to spend more time with you."

At first, I have to be sure I'm not dreaming. Once I feel a level of certainty, I partake in the conversation. "What did you have in mind?"

"I know this is going to sound sudden, and I guess it is, but I want to be there with you, to help you on these assignments."

"Genevieve, you saw what happened today. You saw how dangerous this can be."

"Today was dangerous because we split up. If we stay together, we can be more effective. Ephraim might know what you're going to do, but I don't think he knows what I'm going to do."

"Even if I thought this was a good idea—which I don't—what about the disruption to your life? Who would take care of your house? What about your job?"

"My sister can take care of the house. She stays with me sometimes, and she's looking for a place to live. As for the job, I'm one of three partners in the shop. The other two can cover for me while I'm away."

For every reason I offer not to do this, she returns with rational possibilities. But she hasn't answered the big question yet. "Why? Why would you want to do this? You see what this does to me. Why would you deliberately choose to take this on yourself?"

"Precisely *because* I see what this does to you. It isolates you from the world, and it pushes you to limits you didn't know you had. At least if I was with you, you wouldn't be alone; you'd be with someone who loves you. And yes, sometimes it would be dangerous, but we'd look out for each other."

"And in between assignments?" I ask.

"You've got a nice big house."

"Move in with me? That's what you're thinking?"

"Not in a shack-up context. More in a base-of-operations context."

"G.I. Joe's mobile command center. You hopeless romantic you."

"Does that mean you'll do it?" she asks, the hope evident in her tone.

"I need to sleep on it. And on you."

"Oooh, I like the sound of that."

"Then come closer and show me."

And she does.

Darkness. I'm aware of a darkness that's so deep, it feels like a solid object. I am standing, but I can't tell where. Then I hear footsteps, a man's footsteps; not hurried, not urgent. Casually walking somewhere near where

I stand. They stop, and I hear a familiar sound: a pull chain on a bare-bulb light fixture. Following the sound, a dome of light appears about six feet away from me. Standing under the dome very calmly is Ephraim. I want to react, but I feel as if I don't know what reaction is right, so instead I stand and do nothing.

"Hello, Tristan," he says gently, as if we were old friends.

"Where are we?" I ask, looking around.

"We're nowhere, technically. I'm visiting your consciousness at a time when that impressive brain of yours is at rest. I can't hurt you here, and you can't hurt me."

"Why are you doing this?"

"I thought we should talk, after what happened last night. I feel bad for laughing at you."

"*Only* for that?" I ask.

"That's the part where I was rude, so yes. I mocked you in a moment of weakness, and I shouldn't have done that. I apologize."

"You don't have to do this, any of this. I'm not your enemy."

"No, you're not. But you work for my enemy. Your success is his success, so I find it necessary to insert a little failure in your path. I wish you could believe that I'm trying to help you."

"I don't believe you," I reply. "Every move I've seen you make is selfish, vindictive, destructive. Help me? All you try to do is stand in my way. And I expect that if I don't do what you want me to do, one day, you'll try to kill me."

"Oh, Tristan, you see things in such a straight line. Such cause and effect. Black and white. I could open your eyes to such *color*." On the final word, he extends his hand, and the room fills with light of a hundred shades and hues, surrounding us like a luminescent kaleidoscope. To me, it's just more parlor tricks.

"There's more to my life than color, Ephraim."

"Oh, I know. I know you so well. From moments when we'll be together; from moments when you won't even know I'm watching you. I know how much there is to your life, how much there will be. You may be the noblest person I've ever met."

"And that just sickens you, doesn't it?"

"Far from it. Nobility is on the verge of extinction. Look at the world, Tristan." Another wave of his hand, and the color fades away, leaving the darkness and a bare bulb. "Look at the people. Scurrying about, trying to grab everything they can before their personal extinction. Is it any wonder the religious idiots think these are the end times? Predicting the rapture in 2011, the apocalypse in 2012. Spoiler alert: *wrong!* No such luck. No self-respecting messiah would show his face in this evil age."

I actually laugh out loud at this. "You decrying evil? Might I remind you about the airplane full of children? The planned abduction at the museum?"

"Means to an end," he says without a hint of remorse. "Bigger picture; think bigger."

"Nope. Not seeing it. Thinking you've just lost your mind and this is how you act out."

"It's too soon. You won't be able to see it yet. But if you follow your current path, you'll find out very soon, and it will change you forever. You'll never again be able to be the person you were. It's not too late to change your mind, though. Turn away from what's about to come; don't pursue it. If you do pursue it, then what happens to you is on your own head."

"I'm prepared for that."

He shakes his head slowly. "No. You're really not."

"You can stand there and try to convince me that you're looking out for me, that you're doing this for my protection and my well-being, but I know the truth."

"And what truth is that?"

"I'm the only person in your life whose future isn't completely set in your memory. You're so used to knowing what comes next, what everyone's going to do. You thought that was the case with me, too, until you finally met me at the museum. Things didn't go the way you expected them to—the way you remembered them. I'm a wild card, and you don't like wild cards. I would pity you, but you don't deserve it. So I'll just ask you one more time: leave me alone, stay out of my way, and let me do what I do."

"You're making a mistake, Tristan."

"You can't talk me out of this."

"Thirty million," he says.

I look at him in disbelief. "Surely you know I can't be bought."

"It's not a sum of money."

"What, then?"

"Follow your course and find out; or allow yourself a normal life, and you won't even need to know."

"I want you to leave me."

"Be smart, Tristan. The way I know you can be. If not for you, then at least for her."

The circle of light expands to reveal Genevieve's sleeping form next to me, safe and comfortable in her bed—where I have been all along. Slowly, Ephraim recedes into the darkness, and I feel myself falling backward into sleep.

When I am next aware of conscious thought, daylight floods the bedroom. I open my eyes with full memory of the encounter with Ephraim. *Just a dream?* That's the logical assumption, given that it happened during sleep and outside of any known place and time. Yet I have doubts. Knowing Ephraim's abilities, it may very well have been real, which is a disturbing possibility. It means that even the privacy and sanctity of my own thoughts are not safe from his intrusion. I don't relish the idea of going through life wearing a tinfoil hat, though I suspect not even that would keep him out.

Genevieve stirs at my side and looks up at me with a smile. "Sleep well?" she asks.

"Like a baby," I reply. Unsure as I am about exactly what happened, it's best that I don't go into it with her. "Thank you for letting me stay here for the night."

"You can stay as long as you like, especially if you continue doing what you did to me last night."

Yeah, that was pretty good. It's nice to know that I haven't fallen out of practice. "What can I say? You inspired me."

"I'll make breakfast," she announces, getting out of bed with more energy than I currently possess.

Twenty minutes later, I am vertical, passably presentable, and even dressed. I'm a little proud of this, given that there is nothing pressing this morning. As I walk toward the kitchen, familiar, comforting smells rush to greet me—coffee brewing, sausage in a pan, cinnamon toast heating up. They are the smells of home; not my home, as I seldom indulge in such things, but a real home in which one is loved.

"Right on time," she says with a smile, plating the various delights.

"It looks great. You didn't have to go to any trouble."

"I wanted to. Where would you like to eat? Kitchen table? Back yard?"

"Actually, if there's local news on at this hour, I'd like to eat in the living room. I want to see if last night's events made the news."

"There's a local newscast starting in about three minutes. I'll get trays and we can watch while we eat."

Breakfast is good, beyond good. Lightly basted duck eggs, maple-flavored sausage patties, crispy hash browns, and lightly buttered cinnamon toast. More than just the flavors themselves—which are incredibly rich and satisfying— there's a certain life-affirming comfort in having someone you love make you breakfast. We sit in her living room with the TV on, the volume low as the local newscast starts up. A couple of stories run, and then they cut to a reporter in front of a familiar-looking house—the Tambrils' house—and I quickly turn up the volume.

"Not much usually happens in the small town of Plouton," the young, earnest-sounding woman says earnestly, "a suburb of Kensington, and home to just over eight thousand people. Last night, in this modest home, the peace was shattered by gunshots, as one of Plouton's own took his life." They show a photo of Benton and his family as the reporter continues in voiceover. "Thirty-four-year-old Benton Tambril was a devoted husband, father of two young children, and a respected machinist at TransAllegheny Foundries in Kensington. Then, last night, a call came in to the local police dispatcher." They play the recording. *"911, what is your emergency?"* *"He's got a gun."* My voice, my words, the only words I managed to get out before the phone was hung up.

We return to the young reporter in front of the house. "The voice on the call did not belong to anyone living at the house. Exactly whose voice it is remains unknown, but it was enough for the county sheriff's office to dispatch an officer to the scene. Unfortunately, he arrived too late. Benton Tambril was already dead of a self-inflicted gunshot wound. The other members of the Tambril family were out on an evening walk and were not harmed. Mrs. Tambril spoke of visitors from her church, strangers she did not recognize, coming to talk to her and her husband. Police found a suicide note written by Mr. Tambril, dated seven days before the incident, indicating that he had been planning this for some time. Tambril was suffering from lung cancer and may not have had long to live.

"In the midst of this tragedy, several questions remain unanswered. Why did Benton Tambril wait seven days after writing his suicide note before taking his own life? Who was the 911 caller there in the house with him? Who were the strangers that came to talk with the Tambrils just before Benton took his own life? And, perhaps most mysterious, where is the sheriff's officer who responded to that call? Officer Shep McGillicutty had only been employed with the sheriff's office for two days when he responded to this emergency, and now he is missing. He filed the official incident report last night, went home after work, and did not report in this morning. When officers went to his home, they found it unoccupied and completely unfurnished. Did the shock and horror of what McGillicutty saw overwhelm him to the point that he left his job and his new home, or is there something more sinister at work? His fellow officers are investigating, but a source says they have no solid leads. In Plouton, this is Cynthia Coker, channel 7 first news."

I turn the TV off in disgust. Genevieve, however, wears a look of hope and encouragement. "You see?" she says. "It was good news."

I look at her in disbelief. "I'm sorry ... I must've missed the part where it was good news."

"The note. He had written that note a whole week before we got there.

160

Don't you see? You were sent there to save the wife and children. The husband had made his decision, and nothing we could have done would stop him."

"You believe that?"

"I do believe it. You talked to him; you heard how much he was suffering. And you know what he would have done to his family if we hadn't stopped him. No, you couldn't save him. Nobody could. He was dying. He chose his own way out."

"That's colder than I'm used to hearing from you," I tell her.

"It's honest," she replies. "Right now, you're the one who's suffering, and if my assessment of the situation can relieve some of that suffering, then so be it."

"He's disappeared. What a surprise."

"Who? Ephraim?"

"Shep McGillicutty. Lamest fake name ever. They're never going to find him, I can guarantee you that."

"Maybe this time he'll disappear for good," she offers.

"I wish that were true, but I know it's not. He knows more about my own future than I do. He wants me to stop delivering these messages even more than I want to stop delivering them. And the crazy part is, that's all the more reason why I have to keep doing it."

Before she can reply, a sound interrupts—the ringing of my cell phone. It is still in the pocket of my pants from yesterday, so it takes me a few seconds to retrieve it. I bring it back to the living room and look at the caller ID. "It just says Washington, DC," I tell her. "The number is blocked. Benton said that was the pattern when they called him about his medication."

"Are you going to answer it?"

"I think I should." I press the button for the speakerphone. "Hello?"

"Are you alone?" It is a man's voice, unfamiliar to me. It sounds nothing like Ephraim. This voice is guarded, frightened, desperate.

"Yes."

"Are you *sure?* You have to be sure."

"I'm alone. No one else is here, and no one is listening."

"Follow the pills," the voice instructs.

"Who are you? How did you find me?"

"You're on the right track," he continues, artfully dodging my question. "But you can't give up. Benton Tambril was the first. The first of so many."

"Did you have something to do with his death?" I ask.

"The one who sends you will not send you on this errand. You have to go on your own."

"Are you with them?" I ask insistently.

"I can't answer you."

"Who's behind this? Who is SODAR—"

"Stop! Don't say that name. They have people monitoring phone calls, listening for key words. Never say that name on the phone, never use it in a communication. They'll find you, and if they do, they won't let you leave there."

"But if I'm supposed to go to them …"

"It has to be on your terms," he says. "Stay in control. Always stay in control. Never count down. They'll want you to count down."

"Count down to what?" No answer. "You know, no offense or anything, and thank you for the warning, but this would be a hell of a lot easier if you just tell me exactly what I need to know. Names, addresses, the nature of the threat, who's at risk. I like a good mystery as much as the next guy, but if this is as important as you say it is—"

"They've done things to me." His words are delivered through tears of physical and emotional pain. "I know they're going to kill me, but I don't know when. If they knew I was talking to you, I'd be dead already."

"Hang up, then. If you're my only link to this information, you have to stay alive as long as you can."

"Don't know if I can call you again."

"Please try. Find a way to get information to me, but don't endanger yourself."

"It's late …"

"You have to be safe," I tell him.

"They're close …"

"Please, just stay out of danger."

"Follow the pills."

The phone goes silent; the screen indicates that the call has ended. For many agonizing seconds, Genevieve and I stand staring at the phone in my hand, as if looking at it hard enough could will the information to make sense. "Follow the pills?" I ask aloud.

"It has to be the ones Benton was taking. The study he was a part of."

"But how do I follow them?"

"I think there's only one way," she says. "Somehow, you have to sign up to be a part of the study."

"But how do we find these people?"

"We could look them up online. Come on, let's try."

We go to her computer and power it up. After a few minutes, she gets an Internet connection, and we go to a search engine. She enters "cancer research study," and we wait for the results. There are hundreds, even thousands; individuals and groups around the world each with their own particular research or study. Clearly some refinement is needed. "Add some key words," I suggest. "Drug. Washington. Pain."

She types the words and narrows the search. Six results. Two go nowhere, and three lead to medical journal articles. That leaves just one. We click on the link, and it takes us to a simple, text-heavy page headed: CANCER SUFFERERS—JOIN OUR NATIONWIDE STUDY. The paragraphs that follow invite cancer patients to take part in an experimental drug test to relieve the pain associated with their illness.

"This is it," I say to her. "We've found them."

"Why would they make it so open, so available?"

"They need people to find them. To take part in the study."

Reading on, I see that the study is open to patients with any form of cancer. Applicants need to submit a medical history signed by a physician. If accepted, applicants travel to Washington, DC for a brief stay before returning home to continue with the drug treatment.

"Do you think your doctor would help you?" she asks.

"He's honest to a fault. I don't think he'd do it. Which leaves us without a way in."

"Not entirely," she says. "I know someone whose honesty is purchasable. It's not an association I treasure, but he can be of service. It'll cost us, probably five hundred, but he can get you the false medical history. Are you interested?"

I have to think for a bit. It's a dangerous line I'm crossing, but something tells me I have to do this. "Yes. Make it happen."

She makes a phone call, and the details come together. We decide to use my real name and call for a diagnosis of liver cancer. It feels strange, creating this fiction, knowing that we're putting it out into the world. Genevieve arranges a wire transfer of five hundred dollars from my account, and I'm told the falsified medical records will be e-mailed to me within the hour.

My heart is racing at the prospect of what I am about to do. I've taken assignments from unseen forces that have taken me into dangerous situations, but this—this is me, walking blindly into the lions' den, offering myself up as the evening's entrée, and it's more than a little frightening.

"What I said last night," Genevieve says, "I'll say it again. I want to be in this with you. I won't take part in the study, but if you go to Washington, I want to go too. If I didn't, I'd be sick with worry the whole time, knowing you were there alone."

"I would need you to be more careful than you've ever been in your life."

"I can be careful."

"I would need you to trust no one there but me, and I'd need you to trust me completely."

"I already do," she says.

"And I'd need you to put your own safety, your own survival as the number-one priority, ahead of everything else, even my life."

"Can't promise you that one. Have to see what the moment brings."

"Difficult," I say in a tone of playful accusation.

"Count on it."

Forty-eight minutes later, the falsified medical history arrives in my e-mail inbox, stating that I have stage-three liver cancer. I complete the online application, attach the note electronically, and submit it. This is the point of no return. There's no alias, no pretending to be someone else; they'll need identification, so it's Tristan Shays who must step up. My head hurts, not with an assignment, but with old-fashioned muscle tension and anxiety. I'm really doing this.

Once the application is submitted, I pace. Actual moving back and forth in a straight line, alternating directions pacing; the kind of pacing that I thought only appears in movies, but here I am, like the world's most neurotic security guard, tracking a straight line to the computer and away from the computer, to the computer and away from the computer, checking it every minute for an answer.

Fortunately for Genevieve's carpeting, the answer comes in fifteen minutes. I am accepted. Welcome to the study. Attached are directions to the facility and a letter to print out and present to the administrative team upon arrival.

"This is it, then," I utter quietly.

"When do we leave?" she asks.

"Today. As soon as we can. Call whoever you need to call, but don't tell them where we're going. Pack a week's worth of necessities. We'll drive up there. On the way, we'll stop at my house in Maryland and get some things I'll need."

"Tristan, are you sure it's a good idea, not telling anyone where we'll be?"

"No, it's extremely risky. But it's the only way we can keep them safe."

She lets out a big breath. "Okay. Let me get some things. I should be ready to go within the hour."

My name is Tristan Shays, and I am an unpaid employee of the universe. I receive visions of people in imminent peril, and I go to them and warn them, in the hope of saving their lives. Some heed my warnings; others do not. If I show up on your doorstep, please know that I mean you no harm, but something out there does. Listen to what I tell you, and you have a very good chance of surviving it. Disregard what I tell you, and I can't be responsible for what happens. What I say to you might sound like a threat, but you have to understand—it's not my fault, and it's not my choice. So please listen carefully, follow my directions explicitly, and—if it's not too much to ask—please don't kill the messenger.

About the Author

Joel Pierson is the author of numerous award-winning plays for audio and stage, including *French Quarter, The Children's Zoo, The Vigil, Cow Tipping,* and *Mourning Lori.* He also co-authored the novelization of *French Quarter.* How he has time to write is anyone's guess, as he spends his days as editorial manager at the world's largest print-on-demand publishing company. Additionally, he is artistic director of Mind's Ear Audio Productions, the producers of several popular audio theatre titles and the official audio guided tour of Arlington National Cemetery. If that weren't enough, he also writes for the newspaper and a local lifestyles magazine in his hometown of Bloomington, Indiana. He stays grounded and relatively sane with the help of his wife (and frequent co-author) Dana, and his ridiculously loving dogs.

Printed in the United States
by Baker & Taylor Publisher Services